FEVERED FATES

New to the U.S. soccer scene, not to mention the English language, compact yet explosive Chilean soccer legend Rio Vidal is driven to define a role on his new team, Atlanta Skyline. But he must also adapt to a new culture—and accept that he can't do it alone. His beautiful interpreter, Eva, has been his voice, his refuge. But she is becoming so much more. If only he could convince her he isn't like the other men she's worked with, players on—and off—the field.

As a translator for pro athletes, Eva Torres is used to dealing with self-interested super stars. But Rio seems different, and she's blindsided when he locks eyes with her across a church pew. By now, after weeks of close contact with the endearing athlete with whom she shares a language, her thoughts are far from holy. She must remind herself flirtation is probably just his default style. Plus, she's the only one he can really talk to. But when his ambition threatens to derail his career—and their deepening connection—they'll both have to lay their hearts on the center line . . .

Books by Rebecca Crowley

Atlanta Skyline
Crossing Hearts

Published by Kensington Publishing Corporation

Crossing Hearts

An Atlanta Skyline Novel

Rebecca Crowley

LYRICAL PRESS
Kensington Publishing Corp.
www.kensingtonbooks.com

Lyrical Press books are published by
Kensington Publishing Corp. 119 West 40th Street New York, NY 10018

All Kensington titles, imprints, and distributed lines are available at special
quantity discounts for bulk purchases for sales promotion, premiums, fund-
raising, and educational or institutional use.

Special book excerpts or customized printings can also be created to fit
specific needs. For details, write or phone the office of the Kensington
Special Sales Manager:
Kensington Publishing Corp.
119 West 40th Street
New York, NY 10018
Attn. Special Sales Department. Phone: 1-800-221-2647.

Kensington and the K logo Reg. U.S. Pat. & TM Off.
LYRICAL PRESS Reg. U.S. Pat. & TM Off.
Lyrical Press and the L logo are trademarks of Kensington Publishing Corp.

First Electronic Edition: March 2017
eISBN-13: 978-1-5161-0262-4
eISBN-10: 1-5161-0262-2

First Print Edition: March 2017
ISBN-13: 978-1-5161-0263-1
ISBN-10: 1-5161-0263-0

Printed in the United States of America

For Romy Sommer, Rae Rivers and Joss Wood, my Book Sisters, who can always be counted on for words, wisdom and a glass of wine.

Chapter 1

"Rio! Rio! Rio!"

His name was the only word he could decipher as he entered the arrivals area of Hartsfield-Jackson Airport. He was hungry and tired after the overnight trip from Antofagasta and five minutes earlier he'd almost asked a security guard to sneak him out a back door so he could spend the first several hours of his new life in America soundly asleep.

Now, as flashbulbs lit up the already bright airport and a group of reporters thrust a bouquet of microphones toward his face, he thought this might be one of the best moments of his life.

His grin came easily as he surveyed the crowd. Members of the press vied for proximity, a group of fans waved Chilean flags, and a welcoming committee wearing brick-red Skyline jerseys turned in unison to show his name and number printed on their backs: Vidal, 17.

He focused on each photographer in turn, flashing the practiced smile that showcased his expensively straightened teeth. The fans' cheering grew louder, the reporters shouted over them, and by the time Skyline's manager, Roland Carlsson, waded over to him, Rio couldn't make out what the stylish Swede said as he clapped him on the back.

Not that he would've understood the words if he'd heard them.

He blinked up at his new boss, who returned his stare expectantly. He took in Roland's perfect haircut, the touch of grey at his temples, his tailored clothing—he couldn't be more different from the pudgy, tracksuit-wearing manager he'd played for in Chile. After several uncomfortable seconds Roland raised his eyebrows behind his hipster glasses and repeated himself loudly enough for Rio to hear.

"Bzzz Atlanta, Rio. Bzzzbzzzbzzz."

Rio widened his smile, hoping it was an appropriate response as anxiety quickened his breathing. It would be so embarrassing if he turned out to be grinning like an idiot at the man who'd just asked him a question—or fired him.

Roland's friendly expression faltered. Rio's mouth went dry. He quickly inventoried the few English words he could deploy.

Soccer. Bon Jovi. One, two, three...

"*Señor Vidal, buenos dias.*" A woman appeared at his elbow, her Skyline jersey so oversized it nearly met her knees. "*Soy Eva Torres. Su traductor.*"

"Eva the translator, just in time to save my career," he gushed, grateful to be back in the safe waters of his native Spanish. "Please don't say Roland just told me to get on the next plane home to Chile."

Her smile was more magnificent than the flashbulbs sparkling around the room. He took in her small stature, olive complexion, dark hair falling thickly over her shoulders. Her eyes were wide-set, the exact shape of almonds and slightly hooded, as though their black-coffee depths were so accustomed to keeping secrets it had ceased to be a challenge.

From nowhere he thought of his grandmother's obsession with the Virgin of Guadalupe, the paintings and candles and statues that cluttered her curtained-off corner of the tin-roofed shack where he'd grown up. She used to insist the eyes of the Virgin changed, that it was possible to read warnings and reassurances and answered prayers in those heavy-lidded orbs. As a child he'd spent hours nose-to-nose with one of her figurines. Watching. Waiting.

He always blinked first.

But this Eva... He bet the cool eyes she tilted up to him could give that ceramic Virgin a run for her money.

"He welcomed you to Georgia, as does everyone here." She swept an arm to indicate the increasingly frantic crowd. "The plan is for us to make our way to the auditorium for a brief press conference, then you'll be taken home to rest for the evening. I'm sure you're exhausted after your journey."

So polite, so professional. He stole a glance at her ring finger.

Bare.

Encouraging.

"Who could be tired with all this excitement? Lead the way, I'm all yours." He gave her his trademark cheeky grin, which she returned with a slight dip of her chin before ushering him toward a corridor.

He resigned himself to her indifference as she turned her back and walked so briskly he had to quicken his pace to keep up. Evidently his hopelessly romantic side had made it through all those long flights. His celebrity status in Chile certainly hadn't aided his love life, so he was silly to think that would change in the United States. As if the woman of his dreams was going to be the first one he spoke to off the plane—ridiculous.

Signing to one of the best Championship Soccer League teams in America was the biggest leap of his career. He couldn't mess it up, couldn't let it pass him by. Definitely couldn't get distracted by a beautiful woman with secretive eyes.

At that moment Eva glanced over her shoulder, probably checking to make sure he was keeping up. Their gazes locked and in the split second before her expression resettled into cool disinterest, he saw it. Barely a flicker, almost imperceptible, but bright enough to sear onto his memory: the same shimmering, teasing flame of bald lust that began roaring in his gut the instant he'd laid eyes on her.

"This way." She snapped her attention back to the front, walking even more quickly as a door labeled *Auditorium* loomed ahead. The corridor echoed with the shuffling din of onlookers finally being allowed to follow them, and before he could process the sequence of events the heavy door swung open. He was shown to a seat at a table dressed with the Skyline banner on the stage, and the horde that had greeted him just minutes earlier was filing into the room.

Roland dropped into the seat beside him and leaned in, winking conspiratorially. "Bzzzbzzzbzzzbzzz."

Rio glanced around for Eva, who was standing behind the seat on his other side, speaking to a man holding a microphone. Roland seemed to be waiting for a reply, so Rio nodded and smiled. Roland winked again and Rio released an anxious breath, knowing full well that these head-bobbing responses would only suffice for so long.

Eva took her place beside him and he smiled at her for longer than he probably should have, unable to shake the memory of what he'd seen in her face. She gave him a muted nod before turning her attention to the audience, where hands were already raised to ask questions.

Roland spoke first, hushing the onlookers as tiny tape recorders clicked on and pens scratched across notepads. Rio kept his camera-friendly grin fixed firmly in place as Roland buzzed on and on. He caught a few of the manager's words—his own name, the team's name, the name of his fellow midfielder, Nico Silva—but for all he knew Roland could be singing his praises or apologizing to the fans for signing a total unknown from an obscure team in Chile.

When Roland finished Rio glanced at Eva for some clue as to what his boss had said, but there was no time for her to translate as members of the press began firing questions.

"Bzzbzzbzzbzzbzzzzzz?" The reporter barely looked up from his notepad as he spoke in rapid, urgent tones.

"He'd like to know how it feels to join a Championship Soccer League team," Eva murmured.

Rio blinked at the journalist, then at his translator. "Are you serious? That's his question? He sounded so angry, I thought he was accusing me of cheating on my wife."

"But you're not married."

"Exactly."

A suggestion of a smile flickered across Eva's mouth. "That's his question."

"Tell him I'm delighted to be joining Atlanta Skyline. It's the highlight of my career so far. I just hope I can live up to the fans' expectations."

Eva nodded, leaned into the microphone, and buzzed a response to the audience. Approving smiles spread across the room and he sighed with relief. He'd gotten the first answer right, at least.

Another reporter barked a question, extending his tape recorder above the head of the person seated in front of him. Rio looked expectantly at Eva.

"He wants to know whether you've had adequate time to rest after the South American Cup tournament, and if you'll be appearing for Skyline right away."

Roland spoke before Rio could, hunching his big frame over the microphone.

"He's telling them you're fully fit and will start playing immediately," Eva whispered. Rio nodded gratefully, his head beginning to spin with the back-and-forth of translations.

The next question was from a woman who introduced herself in Spanish, explaining she worked for a Spanish-language newspaper. He grinned at her, relieved to be back in control, even if only for a minute.

"I think most of us learned your name for the first time during the South American Cup, from those assists in the early rounds to the goal in the final. You've been playing soccer for twelve years, since you were scouted at the age of fourteen. Why has it taken so long for the world to discover Rio Vidal?"

He exhaled heavily, buying time as he considered his answer. What to tell them? As he looked out over the rows of seats in the dim auditorium he saw his childhood home slouching amidst hundreds of identical shacks on the edge of the desert, the packed dirt in the empty lot where he and his friends played five-a-side, the trail of exhaust from the car his mother borrowed to drive him to youth-league training in Calama, the stomach-dropping lift of the airplane as he took his first-ever flight to Santiago to make his professional debut.

Should he tell them how hard he'd worked to overcome his height, his size, to channel his frenzied energy on the pitch?

Maybe he should tell them it was all thanks to the mining accident that killed his father, the life insurance payout that arrived in the mail, the move to the apartment in the school district where an involved coach made a phone call that changed his life.

Or should he admit that he'd been conflicted about leaving Santiago to join an American team, and that it felt a lot like selling out? Should he remind them of the footage from the Cup final, the famous shot of his eyes welling as he hefted the trophy? Should he explain that nothing he could win at Skyline would compare with the pride and privilege of playing for his country?

He cleared his throat, shifted in his seat. Cameras rolled, pens hovered, and the Spanish-speaking journalist smiled patiently. These would be some of his first words on American soil, his introduction to the fans he was asking to trust him, believe in him, and support him through the season ahead. He wanted to show them his heart. Tell them his story. Share the joy and tumult of his journey to this career-defining moment.

He leaned toward the microphone, summoning every last shred of recollection from the hour he spent half-watching YouTube language lessons.

"I...excite...to play...Skyline."

Laughter and applause warmed the auditorium. The inquiring reporter inclined her head in thanks, blatantly charmed by his broken English. It wasn't his most eloquent statement to the press, but it seemed to have done the job.

Roland interjected in his characteristically thoughtful tone, and Rio sat back in his chair. To think he'd thought the long-haul travel from Chile had been exhausting. Now he knew he was in for the ride of his life.

Chapter 2

Eva led Rio down the carpeted steps to the cinema room, where oversized posters of classic Mafia movies loomed over plush theatre seating. "I don't know if it's exactly to your taste, but hopefully you can deal with it until you find a place of your own."

"Are you kidding?" Rio's jaw slackened as he took it in. "I love it."

Eva bit her lip for the millionth time that day, trying to hide her endeared smile at Rio's enthusiasm. From the middling turnout at the press conference, to her two-door hatchback instead of the limo that had broken down on the highway, and now this ostentatious house, Rio's excitement hadn't waned.

The mansion had been built by former Skyline player Hector González, who'd sold it to the club for a bargain-basement price when he signed a bountiful new contract with a club in his native Spain. He'd been so delighted to get away from Atlanta—and her, by extension—that he probably would've given it away for free if Roland had been more patient.

She hated the seven-bedroom monstrosity in the exclusive Buckhead neighborhood. Every ornate cornice and embellished light fixture reminded her of the two years she'd spent as Hector's interpreter. Two years traipsing behind the most self-centered man on earth, being treated like the semi-human equivalent of a can opener: absolutely essential when you needed it, utterly forgettable when you didn't.

Hector's English was better than Rio's—which wasn't saying much, from the look of things.

Rio would undoubtedly require much more from her, and her contract didn't include overtime, but she didn't mind. Two years with Hector made her hate the job she'd worked so hard to get in a sport she'd loved since childhood. Two hours with Rio had already turned that around.

It didn't hurt that he was easily ten times more attractive than Hector—to her at least.

Hector was classically handsome, and probably spent more time in magazine photo shoots than he did on the pitch. Whenever people found out she was his translator, the first question was always whether she had the inside scoop on his love life. Although she always said no, the answer was yes.

She knew full well how many young, inebriated, dubiously consenting women came and went from his bed. She'd even raised it with Roland, who'd been visibly concerned but said his hands were tied until someone made a complaint. No one ever did, but she still lost sleep over that parade of women and whether she should've—or could've—done more for them.

Every instinct she possessed told her Rio was completely different. For one thing, he was unlikely to grace the cover of a glamorous men's magazine unless it was a special South American issue. At barely five-foot-seven he was short and compact, nowhere near the statuesque, six-foot-two Hector.

And as much as she chastised herself for indulging the stereotype, she liked how Rio looked, well, Latino. She liked his dark-olive skin, his nut-brown eyes, the thick, black hair shaved closely on the sides and coiffed on top. She liked the way he spoke Spanish with a working-class Chilean accent, full of dropped consonants and distinctive vocabulary. She especially liked his smile, its lopsidedness, the way it showed his back teeth, and the frequency with which it appeared. Hell, she even liked his horribly pronounced attempts at English.

Whereas Hector had artificially tanned skin, light eyes, and all the airs and graces of a royal-blooded European, Rio looked and acted authentically, never contradicting exactly who he was: the son of an industrial port city caught between the desert and the sea, where copper mines made people unbelievably wealthy and crushingly poor by turns. The local soccer star who'd caught the world's attention—and hers—with his boundless energy and creativity on the pitch. The new signing trying to make his way in a foreign city, in a foreign language.

Me gustas, Rio. I think we're going to get along just fine.

"Oh my God." Rio pulled open the drawers built into the wall beneath the screen to reveal row after row of DVDs. "I thought I had a big collection but it's nothing compared to this. Why didn't he want to take any of these with him?"

"I don't think American DVDs work in European DVD players." She perched on the edge of one of the leather-upholstered theatre seats, trying and failing to settle her internal debate. She should get going, give Rio space to check out his new house, take a nap, have a shower—she slammed on the mental brakes at that last thought, fighting back an image of the chiseled torso he'd shown millions of viewers when he ripped off his shirt after scoring a goal in the South American Cup final.

She should definitely leave. She'd see him bright and early on Monday morning, and he needed time to decompress after everything that happened today. He was probably jet-lagged, desperate to unpack his essentials, decide which of the seven bedrooms he wanted to sleep in...

He glanced at her over his shoulder. "Are you hungry? Should we order dinner?"

"What? Why? Aren't you tired?"

"Not really, but I am starving. Do you have to be somewhere?"

Say yes.

"No."

Dammit.

One corner of his mouth lifted. "Are you sure? It's Saturday night. I wouldn't ask you to cancel your plans."

He wouldn't? Really? Apparently Rio wasn't just different to Hector, they were total opposites. She doubted it ever occurred to Hector that she had a life outside her employment as his interpreter. If it had, he certainly hadn't let it bother him.

Anyway, why shouldn't she stay for dinner? It would be good for them to get to know each other before he started training with the team on Monday. He'd invited her—why should she feel uncomfortable? Just because he was the hottest man she'd ever been this close to, and she was having intrusive thoughts about touching the bicep tightening the sleeve of his sweater, and she hadn't gotten any action in over a year, well, unless you counted that guy on Halloween, and she totally didn't count him, and—

"So?" Rio's expression suggested she'd overrun the normal-people time limit on accepting or declining in-person dinner invitations. "Do you have plans?"

"I do now," she replied way too perkily, regretting her high-pitched tone as soon as it hit her ears.

Get a grip, Torres. It was going to be a long season if she couldn't pull herself together. Where was the immutable professionalism her professors had raved about during her MA in Translation Studies? Where were the discretion and levelheadedness that had launched her career in sports interpreting? Where was the unflappable ice queen who had sat across the desk from Roland, unshaken by his unyielding, pointed interviewing until he leaned back in his chair and announced, "You're hired"?

Oh right, she was back at the airport, her knees knocking and her heart racing as weeks of Internet image searches in the name of "research" appeared live, three-dimensional, and even sexier than she imagined.

"Eva?" Rio waved a palm to get her attention. "You okay?"

"Yes, sorry, just thinking about dinner." *And your legs. And your chest. And wondering if I should quit now or wait to be fired for sexual harassment.*

"What would you like?"

She shook her head. "It's your first night in Atlanta, so you pick. You can get almost any kind of food here. Chinese, pizza, barbecue—Mexican?"

He rose from his seat on the floor, stretching his arms over his head. Eva tried very, very hard not to notice the way his thin sweater pulled taut against his chest.

"Are you from Mexico?" He shoved his hands in the pockets of his jeans.

"I'm from Texas," she replied stiffly, automatically bristling at the question before considering its context. More gently she added, "My parents are Mexican."

He nodded. "I can tell from your accent."

"I'm not doing a good job, then." She smirked. "I spent a lot of years learning to speak with as little accent as possible."

"I didn't mean it like that. It's nice, the way you talk. Fancy. Not like me."

His playful grin was back. She swallowed hard.

"You speak just fine."

"Not English, though." He began a slow wander around the room, pausing in front of each of the expensively framed posters Hector had left behind. "I tried to learn a bit before I arrived, but I hate studying. I was terrible at school. I skipped class as often as I could. I don't know what I would've done if I wasn't good at soccer." He traced the letters at the bottom of one of the posters. "Been a miner, I guess."

"We'll work on your English at a pace that suits you," she assured him. "I'll teach you differently than you would learn in a class. For a start, we'll focus on the vocabulary you need on the pitch. Then we'll look at conversation as it's relevant to your career, like answering post-match questions from the press. Nothing too technical, at least not until you get the hang of the basics."

He turned back to her with a smile. "That's great. Much better than the ten minutes I spent learning to ask where to board the train."

"Yeah, that's not going to get you too far in Atlanta."

"So, your parents." He was on the move again, continuing his tour of the room's circumference. "Where in Mexico are they from?"

"North," she replied with forced casualness. This was not a topic she liked discussing with anyone, let alone her brand-new client. "In fact, there's a restaurant in town owned by a family from Monterrey. I don't know if they deliver, but—"

"Is that where your parents are from? Monterrey?"

"Juarez," she told him quickly. "I've got the number on my phone, I'll give them a quick call to see if they'll deliver out here. Their beef *empanadas* are absurdly good."

She had scrolled halfway through her contacts when she realized Rio hadn't responded. She looked up to find him studying her from across the room, his high forehead creased in thought.

"What?" The single word carried more annoyance than she'd intended, and she pushed her lips into a smile to soften it.

"I'm just surprised." He propped one shoulder against the wall. "I didn't think I'd ever meet a woman more beautiful than the ones in Chile, yet here you are."

"Rio," she chided, praying the heat climbing her neck wasn't showing on her skin. "Save your smooth lines for the women in the nightclub. They're wasted on me."

"Why?"

"Because I'm your interpreter, and they don't pay me enough to be anything else."

She hoped her joking tone defused the situation without offending him. It worked—he moved back to the front of the room and flopped down on the floor with an exaggerated sigh.

"You break my heart, Eva."

"You'll live." She held up her phone. "Do you want to see the menu?"

He gestured for her to toss him the phone, but she lowered it instead.

"Are you kidding? You play soccer, not baseball. I don't trust those hands."

He hauled himself to his feet with a comical groan and crossed the short space between them. He dropped into the chair beside her and reached across the armrest, but instead of taking the phone, he wrapped his hand around hers where she held it.

"These are the safest hands you'll find," he murmured. He was right beside her now, his face so near she could see the amber flecks in his brown eyes, his body so close she could feel his heat, catch his scent.

Tea tree oil. Saltwater. Asphalt in the sun. She let her lids fall closed as she inhaled, and when she opened them again he was watching her.

He slid his thumb over hers. His skin was warm, dry, slightly rough.

They spent a full minute frozen in this tableau. Her heart raced yet her thoughts had ground to a halt. If Rio had asked her name she probably couldn't have told him. The only word her multilingual mind seemed to retain was yes.

Yes.

He snatched the phone from her hand, shattering the stillness. She dragged air into her lungs as he threw her phone high above their heads and caught it one-handed behind his back.

"See?" He held it up with a wink. "Hands you can trust."

She cleared her throat, tugged at the cuff of her long-sleeve shirt. Hector must have the heating programed on a timer. No way was it this hot when she'd first walked in.

"Beef *empanadas*," she repeated firmly, "With *frijoles negros* for me. Best in town." She grabbed her phone from his hand and started dialing, ignoring the way her fingers trembled.

She raised the phone to her ear. "It's ringing. Last chance to tell me what you want."

He arched a brow.

She ordered without waiting for his answer.

Chapter 3

"Bzzbzzbzzbzzbzz." The trainer flapped the shapeless, Skyline-red garment in one hand and held up what looked like a remote control in the other.

Rio squinted at the man's patient expression, then turned to Eva.

"What the hell is he talking about?"

"Performance monitoring technology," she explained. "The electronic pod has a GPS, heart rate monitor, all kinds of stuff. You put on the vest, tuck the pod into the pouch, and it sends data back to the trainers' computers."

He took the proffered device and, as the trainer disappeared down the hallway, weighed it in his palm. "Heavy."

"You'll get used to it." Eva plucked the pod from his hand and motioned for the trainer to pass over the vest. "We need to hurry up. Roland likes to start on time."

He pulled the tight, mesh garment over his head, realized he had it on backwards, and slid his arms out of the sleeves to twist it into place.

She tucked the pod into the pouch between his shoulder blades and squinted at the final result. "Does that feel okay?"

His training kit was a size too big. He'd already rolled the waistband of his shorts so they wouldn't hang too low between his thighs, but the vest made his shirt tug on his neck and under his arms.

In Santiago he would've changed into an old kit and handed the ill-measured clothes to one of the assistants with instructions to summon the seamstress and have his training gear reissued in the correct size.

Here in Atlanta he didn't want to draw more attention to his size, not to mention get a reputation as one of those players who always complained. He nodded and said, "It's fine."

"It's too big," she pronounced, rolling her eyes. "The brand who produces the uniforms changed manufacturing plants last year and now nothing is ever right. Go on, don't miss the start of training. I'll make a phone call and get you a new set."

"I'll do it," he offered, the impossibility of that statement dawning on him only after he'd voiced it.

"She doesn't speak Spanish," she replied almost apologetically, gesturing toward the door to the gym. "Go, or you'll be late."

Fear shot through his chest as Eva set him adrift, but he did as he was told. Praying no one tried to speak to him before she returned, he pushed through the glass door to the state-of-the-art fitness facility.

The full Skyline squad was already in place, lined up along the padded floor at the far end of the gym. The American striker, Deon Ellis, stood at one end. The wingers and central midfielders came next, then the defensive midfielders, followed by wing-backs and central defenders and the goalkeepers. The interpreter for the two Brazilian player center-backs sat off at an angle, and Rio assumed the empty chair beside him belonged to Eva.

Nerves juddered in his sternum as he jogged to join the team. He didn't know whether there was a hierarchy as far as who stood where. Not to mention Roland was famous for making players fight for their spots on the first team. When he signed, Roland told him he'd be starting for Skyline, but since he was new he wasn't sure whether he was technically only a second-team player. As far as he could tell everyone seemed to be ordered by their place on the pitch and then their seniority, which would put him...

Nico Silva, the Uruguayan winger, called his name and gestured to the gap on his left. "*Aquí.*"

"Thanks," Rio replied, grateful that he and his midfield counterpart had their language in common. He smiled, and his anxiety eased as Nico returned it.

"What am I in for?" Rio asked as Roland entered with the head trainer, Ross Gould. A former center-back for a famous British team, Rio knew him instantly from his build and his expression, although his long Eighties-style hair had given way to total baldness.

"You'll be fine." Nico waved a dismissive hand. "Mondays we do two rounds of isometrics, then hit the field. Nothing insane."

Rio was on the verge of asking for more detail when Roland concluded his chat with Ross and left the room.

The trainer advanced on the group, tucking his clipboard under his arm and squaring his stance.

"Bzzzbzzzbzzz! One, two, three! One, two, three!" he barked.

Rio remained standing as his teammates dropped to the floor, rolling from a left-side to center to right-side plank. He joined them as soon as he figured out the sequence, but the sweat breaking out on his forehead had nothing to do with the intensity of the exercise.

What if Ross tells me how to correct my form and I don't understand?

Rio fretted as they repeated the movement, his stomach in knots. His logical mind insisted that players weren't kicked off teams for failing to understand a few minutes of instructions during training. The less rational and much louder part of his brain reminded him this was his introduction to his new team, and while messing up may not end his contract, it wasn't the best way to start off, either. They might think he was incompetent, unprofessional, or—worst of all—lazy and complacent.

I'm in way over my head, here. Where the hell is Eva?

As if on cue, the gym door swung open and Eva hurried across the long room. He watched her take the chair beside the Portuguese interpreter, so relieved his arms nearly buckled beneath him.

She shot him a quick, reassuring smile. It took everything he had not to dart across the room and sweep her into his arms.

"Bzzz ten. Ten, nine—"

He glanced at Eva, who murmured, "Hold for ten seconds."

He grinned at the floor beneath him. He'd hold for a hundred if she asked.

By the time the team's session in the gym finished an hour later, Rio wasn't sure which had gotten a tougher workout: his body or his ego. Training with Skyline was far more structured and technical than he was used to back home, and although he had no problem keeping up physically, it was a stark reminder of the giant leap he'd taken when he boarded that plane to the United States.

He'd spent twelve years involuntarily building his reputation in Chile, signing with a professional club when he was still a teenager, earning respect for his drive and commitment, and eventually claiming national-hero status with his performance in the South American Cup. It was only in the last couple of years that he'd become a truly household name, but he hadn't worried about his status amongst his teammates for just under a decade. Everyone knew how hard he worked, how devoted he was to club and country. He was well-liked, valued, and deeply trusted.

His Skyline teammates weren't rude, but they weren't warm either. One or two seemed mildly curious, most appeared indifferent, and one—the young, American midfielder, Brian Scholtz—was openly hostile.

"So you're from Chile," Brian stated in simple Spanish, having caught up to Rio as they made their way out to the pitch.

"Yes. You speak Spanish?"

"A little. I am from America."

Rio nodded. Eva walked a few feet behind them, watching their exchange.

"I have played for Skyline for a long time. Since I was small."

The team was barely twenty years old, but maybe Brian didn't know the word for young. Rio nodded again, unsure how else to respond.

"This year, I was going to play your position. Then you came."

Rio raised his hands, trying to frame his response in a way Brian would understand. He wasn't offended by Brian's statement; in fact he sympathized. It was a big blow to a young player to be replaced by an international signing. He doubted Brian's Spanish extended to the story about his replacement by a Colombian shortly after he made his professional debut, but maybe if he—

"You're so short," Brian added with palpable disgust.

Tell me how you really feel, Brian. Don't hold back.

Rio grinned automatically. "Short and expensive."

Brian muttered something under his breath and jogged away.

"And I can't even speak English," Rio called after him, but if the younger player heard or understood he gave no indication.

"Don't worry about him. He's having a difficult season. His contract expires at the end of the year, and Roland warned him last week that he has three months to improve or he'll ride it out on the bench." Eva came level with him as they crossed the threshold onto the immaculately manicured pitch outside the fitness center.

"He's young." Rio shrugged.

Whether she agreed or disagreed, thought he was being magnanimous or naïve, he had no idea. After those few fleeting glimpses of genuine emotion he'd seen on Saturday, Eva had crawled back behind her shuttered expression and stubbornly remained there. Her manner was so determinedly neutral that he wondered whether he wasn't making it all up. The hunger that flashed in her eyes, the lingering touch in the theatre room—maybe they were all tricks of his jet-lagged imagination.

This morning had already shown him his learning curve at Skyline was going to be a lot steeper than he expected. Maybe he was equally deluded about Eva, and his assumption that a sophisticated woman like her could be attracted to an uneducated footballer like him was just as misguided.

"I can't help you much while you're on the pitch," she was explaining when he tuned back in. "During matches I'll sit behind Roland and call out to you when he asks me to, but for the most part you're on your own. Let's see how you manage today, and from there we'll figure out which words and phrases you need to learn first."

"Perfect," he lied, and then jogged out to join his teammates in the center of the pitch. How on earth was he going to make this work without Eva to help him communicate?

As soon as they were all gathered and shivering in the early-March chill, Roland launched into a long explanation of something, occasionally punctuated by equally incomprehensible hand gestures. Rio concentrated harder than he had during a single lesson in school, but only came away with "pass" and "ball."

The group began to spread out and Nico waved Rio over. "How much of that did you get?"

"Nothing," he admitted.

Nico's grin was so free of judgment that it soothed Rio's bruised ego. "Roland's nickname is the Philosopher, because sometimes he uses way too many words to express simple plans. We're going to run an assisting exercise. Deon will stay by the goal, and the idea is to negotiate the ball past the defenders and cross to him for an assist. Got it?"

"Got it."

Central midfielder Laurent Perrin was up first. Rio watched carefully as the tall Frenchman barged through the four defenders only to lose control of the ball on the other side. Roland stopped him, pointed here and there as he spoke, and then signaled for him to try again.

Again Laurent lost control, and again Roland made a series of gestures. Bewilderment was written all over Laurent's face until Deon shouted something from his position outside the box. Comprehension lit up the midfielder's expression and he started the exercise once more, this time completing his cross and assisting the goal.

"Communication," Nico muttered to Rio as Roland turned their way. "Deon and Roland both told Laurent to communicate through the assist, to listen for Deon's instructions and keep an eye on his position."

"Rio," Roland called from his place on the sideline. The manager pointed to the pitch.

His turn.

Rio felt the rapt attention of his teammates as he made his way out to the starting point. If this exercise was really all about communication, he was screwed.

He took his position behind the ball and looked up at the two nearest defenders, poised for him to begin. One was a five-foot-eleven Swede he'd played an international against a couple of years ago, who made up for in speed and creativity what he lacked in sheer size. The other was a Togolese player barely out of his teens, whose stacked physique belied his impressive agility. Behind them were the two Brazilian center backs, both over six feet tall, both sizing him up with hardened expressions.

On the other hand, he considered with a smirk, if this exercise was about getting the ball into the net, he'd be just fine.

He ran up to the ball and feinted right, sending the two men in front curving in that direction while he raced left. They quickly recovered and pivoted in his direction as the two Brazilians—Paulo and Guedes—charged forward. Behind them Deon had darted right, then left, trying to position himself to receive the ball.

Rio stopped. He looked past the four big men to the empty space beside Deon. There was no way he could dribble through all four men, but that didn't matter. There were other ways to get the ball in the goal.

He drew back his right foot and booted the ball high over the defenders' heads. Its long descent gave Deon plenty of time to get under it, and he shot it squarely into the net.

Rio smiled at his handiwork. It wasn't the most elegant solution, but it worked. He'd barely taken five steps from where he'd started.

For a split second no one made a sound. The defenders stared helplessly over their shoulders. Roland's eyes were wide with excitement. And Brian—standing on the sideline with the other second-team players—had dropped his jaw so far Rio hoped none of his teeth fell out.

Deon broke the silence with vigorous applause, and the rest of the team joined in, whistling and cheering their approval.

Roland jogged onto the pitch and slapped him on the back, buzzing his exuberance. Rio couldn't understand a word he said, but he didn't need to. Soccer was a language all its own, and he was fluent.

* * * *

"Hey, Eva, can you come through to the locker room? Roland wants to talk to Rio."

Sure thing." She shoved her phone in her purse and followed Ross, Skyline's British trainer, down the hall.

"Why Roland always insists on having these conversations immediately after training, I don't know." Ross shook his head. "Half the time the guys are so exhausted they don't absorb a word he says."

She shrugged. "You know how he is. Why do something in five minutes' time when you can do it now?"

"And why say it in ten words when you can say it in fifty." Ross sighed as he held open the door to the locker room, allowing Eva to precede him inside. The echoing din of chatter and the distinctive post-training smell hit her instantly, but she adjusted quickly. Roland's impatience meant she'd had plenty of locker-room interpretation sessions over the last couple of years, so she was immune to the sights and sounds of twenty-odd men in various states of undress. The players were so used to her presence they'd abandoned all efforts at modesty, and by this point she doubted there was anything she could see that would shock her.

Until Rio grinned at her from across the room, wearing nothing but black compression shorts and a telltale bulge.

It turned out the phrase "to stop dead in her tracks" was based on a real phenomenon, because for several seconds she totally lost the power of forward motion. Ross was three feet ahead of her by the time she recovered control of her legs, and it took all of her remaining strength to keep her chin from hitting the floor.

Photos on the Internet were one thing, but seeing Rio's bare body in three glorious dimensions was quite another. The wrought-iron arms, the countable six-pack, the ledges of muscle over his hips…

Roland waved her over. She gritted her teeth, pasted on what she hoped was a detached smile, and looked anywhere but below Rio's neck.

The manager launched into one of his characteristically long-winded summaries of the training session. Eva translated for Rio whenever Roland took a breath, so she didn't have to remember and relay everything at once.

"According to the computers," Roland continued, and Eva worked to capture the manager's nuances as he explained the data that resulted from the session and how he wanted Rio to respond to it.

Hector would've already interrupted Roland several times to argue or object, but Rio just nodded.

"Do you understand?" she asked in one of Roland's pauses.

"Perfectly," Rio replied. "Keep going."

She did, but after another few minutes of interpreting Roland's intricate ideas she felt Rio's gaze intensify. She chanced a look at him and realized he was staring at her, not with the attentiveness of someone absorbing information, but with the thinly restrained anticipation of a thirsty man watching someone pour a cold glass of water.

She faltered, momentarily tuning Roland out. Rio smiled and she knew he was being deliberate. He could've pulled on a shirt for this meeting, not to mention a pair of shorts. Or he could've stayed in his training gear and not gotten undressed at all. Regardless of his wardrobe choice—or lack thereof—she was damn sure he didn't have to stand so close to her, close enough to tell that he hadn't shaved that morning, to count the beads of sweat still clinging between his eyes.

When Skyline's player services manager told her she'd be working for a Chilean, Eva had emailed one of her graduate-school classmates who, though American by birth, had spent a year in Chile with the Peace Corps. She'd asked for advice on the cultural and linguistic nuances a translator should take into account.

The stereotype is that most Chilean men are super old-school and unreconstructed, her friend wrote, *which can be good or bad. Watch out for* piropos, *supposedly harmless, flirtatious compliments that can feel an awful lot like sexual harassment. On the other hand, you might get a gentlemanly* caballero, *who will hold the door and refill your glass and charm you off your feet!*

Eva narrowed her eyes at Rio, trying to read between the lines of his confident posture and keen expression. For all her skill with language, the strings of old, unanswered calls and text-message disagreements clogging up her SIM card bore testament to her profound inability to understand the difference between what men said and what they meant. She always seemed to be on the wrong side of whether sex was for fun or implied commitment, and had spent so long nursing devastation after being left that she'd more or less given up entirely. She had other things to focus on: her career, her goals, a future still very much taking shape.

Last month she celebrated her thirtieth birthday party at a favorite downtown dive bar. At some point during the evening she'd looked around her crowd of friends and realized she was the only single one left. Rather than face the realization head-on, she ordered another double tequila and promptly hit on a college student playing pool.

She woke up to her second day of thirty-hood in a bed in a fraternity house, her head pounding, a twenty-one-year-old asleep by her side, her designer bra missing in action.

In the taxi home she promised herself this would be "The Year She Got Serious About Men." No more casual hook-ups. No more second dates with guys who were hot but unemployed. No more acting like she had unlimited tomorrows and endless time to find "The One", and no more assuming he'd fall into her lap. She was getting too old, too lonely, and too tired of living her romantic life entirely on the surface—physical fulfillment but never emotional or intellectual.

This was the year all of that would change. Her eyes were on the horizon, not three feet ahead of her, and she was determined not to waste any more time.

This situation with Rio should've been simple. All signs shouted at her to steer clear. He was too young, too famous, too smooth, and as her client he was off-limits anyway.

So why couldn't she look at him without wondering how he'd feel on top of her?

"Did you catch all that?"

She nodded automatically to Roland, mentally chiding herself for losing her train of thought. She translated as much as she could for Rio, whose grin stretched even wider.

"You didn't get half of that last part, did you?" he teased.

"I'm sorry, do you want me to ask him to repeat himself?"

He shook his head. "I absorbed as much as I'm going to today. Tell him thanks, and I'll try to pick up on his suggestions tomorrow."

She passed on Rio's message to Roland, who had already half-turned to deliver a similar analysis to one of the other players. As the manager strode across the locker room Rio crossed his arms over his chest.

Don't look at his arms, don't look at his arms—oh God, free ticket to the gun show and the weapons are locked and loaded...

"I'm thinking of buying a car this afternoon. Want to come?"

She blinked. "Well, I can if you need me to. Which I guess you do."

He frowned, his rock-solid self-assurance cracking for barely a second. "Oh. Yeah. But I meant, you know, I'd like you to come." His lopsided grin returned, stronger than ever. "It'll be fun."

"I don't know much about cars, but if you need help negotiating I'm happy to—"

"Vidal, are you buying a car? What are you going to get?" Nico approached on her left with one towel wrapped around his waist and another draped across his neck.

"I don't know yet. I thought I'd have a look, maybe test drive some options."

"Awesome, I know the best place. My guy will take care of you, no problem. I've bought, like, five cars from him."

She'd always gotten along well with the intelligent, multilingual Uruguayan, and when he shot her a subtle wink she knew he thought he was doing her a favor by relieving her of car-shopping duty.

And he was. Wasn't he?

"I'll leave you boys to it. I'll see you tomorrow morning, Rio."

Rio glanced between her and Nico. "Wait, tomorrow? Are you sure you don't want to come with us this afternoon? Or maybe afterward, we—"

"Don't let him spend his whole salary," she joked to Nico, who crossed his heart with his index finger.

She turned her back to her client and took calm, measured steps out of the locker room. Finally she'd regained the upper hand in this situation. Now she had to hang onto it for dear life.

Chapter 4

"Hold on two seconds, I'll just go get him."

"Take your time, Miss Torres. Only an idiot wouldn't wait for a woman looking as beautiful as you do tonight." The driver smiled at her through the open window, then cut the engine on the sleek, luxury sedan.

He's paid to be flattering, she reminded herself as she made her way across the flagstones to Rio's front door, yet the memory of the driver's approving smile as he'd picked her up from her condo put an extra spring in her step. Skyline had used the same charter car company for years and this particular driver had taken her to and from at least a dozen team-related events.

He'd never been quite so complimentary about her appearance before, though, and not in a creepy way. He seemed sincere, maybe even impressed.

They've probably introduced a compliment quota system. Tell the passenger she looks nice at least twice or your pay will be docked.

Then again, she considered as she caught sight of her reflection in one of the tall glass windows bordering the door, she did look pretty damn hot. She'd splurged on a blowout and a manicure, justifying them as special new-client, new-season expenses. She'd also finally found time to take a clearance-rack cocktail dress to the seamstress for alterations, and its newly bespoke fit accentuated all the right places. Her boobs looked bigger, her waist looked narrower, and her unapologetic Latina booty was wrapped up tight in a brand-new, racecar-red thong.

Not that it mattered. This was the third time she'd attended the pre-opening match dinner at Roland's house, and not because she was an invited guest. It was work, plain and simple. If Skyline didn't have a player requiring her translation services she'd be on the couch with pizza delivery and the home improvement channel.

She rang the bell, rolling her eyes at Hector's customized chime of a popular R&B bassline. What an asshole.

Within seconds Rio flung open the door, and her breath caught at the sight of him in a slim-fitting, tailored black suit. He grinned and opened the door wider, revealing a bottle of wine and two glasses on the table in the entryway.

"Chilean red," he explained, and she shivered deliciously at the way he rolled the *"r."* "Can I pour for you?"

She shook her head. "We have to go. Dinner is served promptly at eight, and it's sit-down. No room to be fashionably late, I'm afraid. Anyway, should you be drinking the night before a match?"

"I thought I'd make an exception." His expression was only mildly disappointed as he shut the door and followed her to the car.

He hadn't put up much of a fight—did that mean he expected her to decline? Or did he not really care one way or the other? Maybe he was just a flirt. Maybe he'd finally gotten the message that she wasn't interested.

Because she definitely wasn't.

Right?

No, she scolded herself as he held open the car door. He was as out of bounds as it got. No matter how good he looked—so, so good—or how nice he smelled as he slid into the seat beside her—like fresh sea air on a breezy morning—there could be nothing between them as long as Skyline paid her to be his translator.

Although if she quit...

The driver pulled away from the big house and Rio turned to her. "Do you have a boyfriend?"

"I'm not sure that's any of your business," she replied primly, ignoring her traitorous heart turning cartwheels in her chest.

"I don't have a girlfriend," he offered.

"I'm sure you'll have no trouble finding one."

"Is that a proposal?"

"Absolutely not."

He sat back in his seat with a playful smile. "Eva Torres, woman of many mysteries. What would you be doing tonight if you weren't in this car with me? Hitting the town with your boyfriend? Is he a big guy? Should I be worried?"

"I'd be doing what I do whenever I'm not working. Sleeping and studying."

"Studying for another degree, or for fun?"

"Neither, really." She hesitated. She hated telling people about her plans, in case they didn't work out. "It's for admission to law school."

He whistled, impressed. "You want to be a lawyer? Interpreting for footballers must be worse than I thought."

"I love my job," she told him earnestly. "I spent years working to get it and I'm not in a hurry to leave. The law school idea is more of a side interest. Something I'm still considering."

"Fair enough. What kind of lawyer would you become?"

"Immigration," she replied shortly. "This is Roland's house, just here."

The brief drive came to a well-timed end as the car pulled up in front of Roland's sprawling house. He'd upgraded last year when Skyline reached the league semifinal, and Eva was interested to see how he'd put to use the additional million dollars the papers reported he'd spent.

The driver eased the car around the circular driveway and stopped in front of the double-door entrance. Before she could move Rio darted out to open her door, extending his hand to help her out of her seat.

She didn't need to, but she took it. His palm was smooth and warm, and when she tried to pull her hand away he caught it and tucked it into the crook of his elbow.

"Rio," she scolded gently, disentangling her hand.

"Right, I forgot." She could just make out his knowing wink in the early-evening darkness. "Your boyfriend."

She said nothing as they made their way inside. The warmth and noise of the party absorbed them as soon as they crossed the threshold and joined the full complement of the Skyline squad, staff, and attendant wives and girlfriends.

Despite the event's size the mood was subdued—a far cry from the last time they'd all been together at the boozy Christmas bash. The waiter who greeted them at the door had glasses of champagne or sparkling water on his tray; Rio took the latter. Normally sociable players were distracted, fiddling with their cuffs, tugging on their ties. They were guided into a high-ceilinged great room where Skyline-themed decorations felt more threatening than celebratory. Tomorrow's season opener hung like a cloud over the room, ominous and preoccupying.

If the atmosphere affected Rio, he didn't show it. He moved through the room like a pro, shaking hands and smiling as if he understood every word that was said to him. Meanwhile she slid into professional mode, becoming a conduit for conversation rather than a participant. She spoke quickly and without hesitation, almost closeting her consciousness as her brain acted as a vessel. Content flowed in, content flowed out, but she didn't engage with it.

Rio mingled for thirty-five exhausting yet energizing minutes before their circuit paused and she got a break. All she wanted to do was stare at a wall in silence while she recharged, but it was obvious from Rio's expression that he had other plans.

"I have an idea. I want you to help me—"

"Eva! So good to see you!"

They turned toward the approach of Deon and his fiancée, Olivia.

Eva's smile came easily. If she hadn't known that Olivia Shields was a medical student who'd grown up with Deon in Baltimore, she probably would've guessed she was a runway model scouted in a remote African village. Dark-skinned and statuesque, Olivia smiled warmly as she greeted them.

"Oh my God, you're so tan," Eva gushed as they exchanged hugs. "I guess the weather in Cape Town was pretty good."

"Life tip: if you want to get engaged on New Year's Eve, do it in the southern hemisphere."

"I hope you're not missing Hector too badly," Deon joked. "I'm sure I've still got his number if you need it."

"Oh, I'm pretty sure we said all we had to say to each other before he left," Eva replied.

Olivia extended her hand to Rio, who shook it politely. "Rio, so nice to finally meet you. I was glued to the screen during that penalty shoot-out in the South American Cup, so it's a privilege to see you in the flesh."

Eva relayed Olivia's words to Rio, who smiled broadly as he asked, "Can you get rid of them?"

Eva did a double-take. "Can I what?"

"Make an excuse. We'll be sitting down for dinner in a few minutes and I need to talk to you."

"Deon's your striker, I really don't think you should—"

"I just need five minutes. I'll catch up with them later."

She turned back to Deon and Olivia, racking her brain for a viable exit. "Yes, he's sorry he hasn't had a chance to get to know you yet. Would you excuse us? He just wants to—uh—wash his hands before dinner."

"Of course. We'll talk later." If Olivia suspected anything, she gave no sign. Then again, she was exactly the type who noticed everything and revealed little. Eva shoved aside that disquieting thought as she led Rio back to the entryway.

"They think you're going to the bathroom, so we need to figure out where that is."

He shook his head. "This won't take long. Remember earlier, when Nico said lots of players give toasts at this dinner? I want you to help me write one."

"Rio, I don't think we can..." She trailed off at the sight of his keen expression. It must be so frustrating to try to develop relationships with your new teammates when you can't speak their language. Who was she to tell him no? If he wanted to give a toast in his painfully broken, heavily accented English, she'd just have to cringe through it.

"Okay," she agreed. "Let's ask one of these waiters if there's an office or something."

A few minutes later they were seated behind a huge desk in Roland's ultra-modern office, complete with black leather-upholstered chairs and stainless-steel accents. Thankfully the desk was immaculately clean—as the waiter ushered them inside she had paranoid fantasies about having to try to ignore papers full of proprietary salary information or unannounced transfer plans.

Instead Rio had pulled out her chair before pulling up another one beside her, and they bent over a piece of scrap paper as she wrote out phonetic translations for what he wanted to say.

"And Deon, put something in there thanking him for his leadership."

She nodded, carefully spelling out each word in the clearest handwriting she could manage.

Rio leaned in more closely, flattening his hand on the top of the page as he angled it for re-reading. She was suddenly acutely conscious of everything in the moment: the squeak of leather as he moved on the chair, the fine black hair on his wrist where it emerged from his sleeve, the more intimate scents of shampoo and soap she could pick up beneath his cologne. He had the slow breathing of a professional athlete with a low resting heart rate, and she thought of the speed he'd shown on the pitch that week, the height he'd obtained during jump training.

Her nipples tightened inside her bra. She swallowed hard, praying he wouldn't notice.

"Looks good. I just want to add one more thing."

She cleared her throat and picked up the pen. "Go for it."

"I want to thank you for helping me communicate with everyone."

Her cheeks were on fire. "That's kind of you, but not necessary. It's my job."

"And you're very good at it, so you deserve recognition."

"Not in front of the whole team."

"Why not?"

"I hate being the center of attention."

Without warning he lifted a lock of hair from her shoulder and rubbed it between his thumb and forefinger. She froze, afraid to move—afraid she wouldn't able to control her reaction if she did.

He let her hair drop, smoothing it against her back. Then he traced a lazy line over her shoulder, down her arm, finally covering her hand with his.

He brought his mouth close to her ear. "Do you really have a boyfriend?"

"No." The single syllable scraped out of her throat, harsh and primal.

Rio didn't move. His peculiarly slow breaths lightly stirred her hair as she filled her lungs with his scent and heat.

Kiss me. I won't stop you.

A sharp rap on the door echoed around the room, and they jolted apart less than a second before a waiter leaned in.

"Sorry to interrupt," he said mildly. "Dinner is served."

Nerves plagued her through dinner as she worried about Rio's speech, ruining her appetite for the exquisite meal. She wasn't sure what had her so anxious. She'd only worked with Rio for a little over a week so it was hardly a reflection on her if his English wasn't immaculate.

And yet she wanted nothing more than for him to deliver his brief speech smoothly, impressing his teammates and trainers and cementing his place at Skyline.

He smiled at her as Deon opened the round of speeches, no shortage of confidence in his expression. She forced herself to smile back, crossing her fingers under the table.

"And finally a warm welcome to our newest player, who we're hoping will grow an inch or two under Roland's expert guidance." Deon smiled and raised his glass. "To Rio Vidal."

Upon hearing his name Rio started to stand up. Eva caught his arm halfway and tugged him back into his seat as Deon finished speaking.

"Now is it my turn?" he whispered.

She shook her head. "After Nico."

"What did Deon say about me?"

"He made a joke about your height," she told him cautiously. "He said they're hoping Roland can help you grow an inch or two."

He grinned. "That's funny."

They sat through three more speeches, and Eva translated enough to give Rio the gist without disrupting the room with constant whispering.

Finally it was Rio's turn. A sea of heads turned toward her expectantly, and before she fixed her gaze on the tablecloth she saw at least one player frown in confusion as Rio stood and she remained seated.

He unfolded the piece of paper and cleared his throat. She held her breath, digging her freshly painted nails into her palms.

"*Hola*, Skyline," he began, his grin as charming as ever. "I want say *gracias* to Roland for bring me from Chile, Deon for lead the team, *y* Eva for help to speak. *Gracias*."

Okay, it was atrociously pronounced Spanglish and he'd only read out a third of her meticulously handwritten phonetics, but she didn't care. She was so proud, her cheeks ached from beaming.

The applause was thunderous to the point it bordered on patronizing, but if Rio noticed he clearly didn't care. He inclined his head in thanks before resuming his seat, and as left-back Oz Terim rose to give the first of the defenders' speeches, he turned to her, eyes bright with excitement.

"I know I skipped most of what we wrote down. I thought it would be better to get a short speech right than a long one wrong. How did I do? Did I pronounce everything okay?"

"You did great," she assured him, and meant every word.

Chapter 5

Rio shifted his weight from his left foot to his right foot and back again as the players lined up in the tunnel. The announcer's voice rang over the noise of the packed stadium and echoed off the concrete walls, distorting so it sounded like the tunnel was under water.

He rolled the waistband of his shorts, then unrolled it, then rolled it again. Nico stood in front of him, the number on the back of his shirt looming in his vision.

Eleven. He looked down at the number on the left leg of his shorts. *Seventeen.*

His number on the Chilean national team was seven. Seventeen was seven plus ten. Was that a good omen or a bad one?

The line began to move forward. The stadium erupted in cheering.

This was it. His Championship League debut.

The noise of the crowd was an indecipherable wall of sound as he followed Nico out of the tunnel. His heart raced and he forced himself to focus, to be calm, to shut out everything but the task ahead.

He made the sign of the cross as he stepped onto the grass. He joined his team's procession to shake hands with the opposition, then took his place on the right wing as Deon moved to the center of the pitch for the coin toss.

Every seat in the stadium was full, an undulating ocean of Skyline red. He squinted at the fans, as unknown to him as he was to them. He had to earn their respect, show them he was money well spent. Today he would give them a goal.

He rolled his shoulders, flexed his ankles, breathed out.

He was ready.

The whistle blew and the match was underway.

Suddenly his world was only as long and wide as the pitch beneath his feet. His rational brain stepped aside, letting his instinct and muscle memory take over. His senses became a jumble of angles and motion, responding to every tiny adjustment of the passage of a white ball through space.

The opposing team, Pittsburgh Steel, was aggressive but clumsy. Rio jogged behind the action as Steel's forwards pushed into Skyline's half, where for ten nerve-wracking minutes the defenders in red fought them off.

Guedes finally broke free and charged toward Steel's half. Instinctively Rio shouted at him in Spanish, and despite the language barrier he got the message across. Just as two Steel defenders rounded on him, the Brazilian shot the ball to Rio.

With a burst of speed Rio danced the ball toward the goal, pivoting and spinning to avoid Steel's defenders. He saw his chance, and popped the ball toward the top-right corner of the net. Steel's goalkeeper caught it in two hands and booted it back to the center line, but the elevated volume of the crowd assured Rio it had been a good chance.

Close, but not close enough. He shoved aside his disappointment and flung himself back into the game.

After a few minutes Nico pried the ball away from Steel and slipped it down the pitch to Deon, but the offside flag went up just as the striker took his shot. It flew inches wide of the right-hand post.

Rio followed the ball back down the center, glancing at the clock. Twenty-five minutes—already on their way out of the first half. Steel were tough but Skyline's players were smarter, more sophisticated, he considered. They should've scored by now.

He caught up to one of the center midfielders, Laurent.

"Their center backs are dawdling," he called over the din. "If we can keep possession we can run them down, go straight through the middle."

Laurent squinted at him.

Rio sighed, exasperated. "Down the middle," he repeated. "Follow me, I'll—"

Laurent shook his head and jogged away. Rio stared after him for several bewildered seconds before realizing his teammate couldn't understand a word he said.

And vice versa.

His pace was slower as he rejoined the action, doubt creeping into his thoughts. He normally tried to tune out the constant shouting during the match, but now he listened in, testing how much he understood.

Nothing.

Panic swelled in his throat. Were his teammates trying to call to him and he couldn't understand? Was he missing out on changes in tactics? The opposing players could say whatever they wanted and he'd have no idea.

The Brazilians can't speak English either, he reminded himself. Well, they knew more than he did, but in most matches a name and a hand gesture usually sufficed.

Still, he couldn't shake the crack in his confidence or recover the intensity of his focus. Suddenly the Steel players seemed bigger and faster than they had earlier, and he became acutely aware of his size in a way he hadn't for years. A quick glance up and down confirmed his fear.

He was the smallest player in the match.

The situation wasn't new—he'd been one of the smallest players in the league in Chile—but his sharp drop in confidence was. His speed, agility, and selfless teamwork used to mean his size made no difference. Now he was an outsider, playing alongside strangers whom he couldn't speak to and who couldn't talk to him in turn.

The whistle signaled the end of the first half. The scoreboard was goalless. Rio trudged off the pitch, buried deep in his thoughts.

"I have no idea what he just said."

"Sorry." Eva's expression was sympathetic. "Sometimes no amount of translation can bring clarity to Roland's halftime talks."

Rio dropped onto the bench in front of his locker. "Thanks for trying. I'll see you in the second half."

She turned to leave, paused, turned back. "Are you all right? Need anything?"

He shook his head, managing a weak smile. "I'm fine."

"Okay." She smiled encouragingly. "*Viva Chile.*"

"Thanks," he replied quietly, watching her depart the locker room. Then he stood and stared into his open locker—and the Chilean flag hanging inside.

Pull it together, Vidal. You scored the winning goal for your country in an international tournament. This is just a run-of-the-mill league match, one team playing another. Get over yourself and win, dammit.

His nerves had settled by the time he exited the tunnel to start the second half. He prayed, crossed himself, took his place.

Make it happen. No more excuses. Viva Chile.

Both teams were unchanged as the whistle blew to start the second forty-five minutes. No substitutions, no injuries. No reason not to be able to predict exactly how each member of the opposition would play.

Rio made an early move for possession, maneuvering through two Steel forwards to retrieve the ball. He pivoted toward the goal and the next thing he knew he was facedown in the grass, his nose pressed into the earth.

He rolled onto his back and sat up, legs spread ahead of him, as his Skyline teammates pointed angrily at the Steel forward who'd tackled him. He watched the exchange, understanding nothing but his own name, as Deon pointed accusingly and the Steel player held up his hands in innocence.

"Are you okay?" Nico came to his side and extended his hand. Rio took it and hoisted himself up.

"All good."

The referee produced a yellow card. The Steel players shouted and shook their heads, but the match continued.

Rio took the free kick, passing to Laurent who ran down the left-hand channel toward the goal. He clipped the ball to Deon, who snapped a shot at the goal. It was deflected by a clump of Steel defenders, but Rio smiled. They were beginning to press Pittsburgh, now. They were getting somewhere.

Skyline spent the next fifteen minutes in Steel's half, consolidating, pushing, running them until they were breathless. Deon made a good but unsuccessful attempt to score, and the goalkeeper hurled the ball back into a cluster of Steel players.

Rio was nearest the forward who took possession—the same one who'd fouled him earlier. He sprinted to the bigger man, nicked the ball out from between his legs with a neat tackle and darted away, taking several seconds to realize the forward had hurled himself to the ground.

"Oh, for God's sake," Rio muttered. The six-foot-plus Californian clutched his shin, rolling back and forth on the grass.

The ref jogged over and Rio held up his palms. "Come on, he's twice my size. There's no way I could've—"

Of course. He sighed as the ref blinked at him and looked away. *He has no idea what I just said.*

Steel players crowded around the ref as Skyline players also joined the conversation. Rio stood to one side, feeling increasingly superfluous as voices rose, fingers pointed, and the referee raised his arms to encourage everyone to calm down.

The Californian pointed to his calf, then indicated the studs on his shoes, implying that Rio had deliberately spiked his leg—an offence punishable with an automatic sending-off and a three-match ban.

He rolled the waistband of his shorts, unrolled it, rolled it again. His stomach tightened as what he thought should've been an obvious overruling seemed to take much longer. The ref looked angry, the Steel forward even angrier, and players from both sides gestured and shouted and squared up to each other.

On the plus side, he wouldn't need an interpreter if the ref sent him off with a red card. Too bad he'd probably never start for Skyline again if he got booked for violent conduct in his first appearance.

"Rio!"

Her voice sliced through the cacophony like the first drops of rain arcing through a hot, dusty afternoon.

Eva stood beside Roland on the sideline, waving for his attention. When he made eye contact she cupped her hands around her mouth.

"Roland says that guy always dives. Keep up the pace, don't let him put you off."

He knew they were Roland's sentiments, but hearing them from Eva's mouth somehow made them much more important. Then she smiled, and he knew nothing would stop him from putting that ball in the net.

When play resumed—with no cards given—he was calm, calmer than he'd been since he boarded the plane to the United States. He saw everything, missed nothing, read the opposition's moves long before they made them. He was in his element, doing what he loved, never doubting he was one of the best players on the pitch.

One of the Steel players faltered near the midline and Laurent captured the ball, steaming it into Steel's half. Nico powered into the area to receive the pass and was upended by a Steel forward. Nico slid across the grass and Rio saw his opportunity.

He dropped his shoulder and booted the ball into the goal. It slammed into the top-right corner, the net shaking and shimmying from the impact.

Rio fell to his knees as the stadium exploded into cheers and his teammates piled on top of him, hugging him around the neck and slapping his back and mussing his hair. He couldn't understand what they said, but he didn't need to. There were times when action meant more than words, and this was one of them.

He'd proven himself.

For now.

He grabbed his teammates' arms and pulled himself to his feet. The clock was still ticking—the game was far from over. He waved his thanks to the crowd. Then he kept running.

Chapter 6

Eva nodded to her fellow parishioners as she slid down the pew to take her usual seat at Sunday-morning Mass. Third row, far right-hand side. Terrible view of the altar, but within touching distance of a six-foot-high statue of Our Lady of Guadalupe.

Most of the time Eva made a concerted effort to listen to the Spanish-language sermon. She liked Father Diego and she respected the way he engaged with the mostly Mexican, mostly undocumented parish community. He was smart and progressive, and she usually left his Masses with interesting food for thought.

But some Sundays—like this one—she stared at the Virgin's serene expression until her eyes lost focus and she sank deeply into her thoughts, wading through fears, anxieties and dreams.

Today she'd checked out of Father Diego's sermon before she'd passed through the doors of the church. There was so much on her mind to parse through she didn't know where to begin. Rio, yesterday's match, her career, her mother—always her mother.

At least the hour-long Mass gave her space to think. Sixty minutes to reflect, to analyze, to figure out how she felt about the events of the last week and what she intended to do about them.

She smiled, mentally humming the tune she couldn't shake after yesterday's match. In the seconds after Rio scored what turned out to be a game-winning goal the crowd had burst into song: "Rio" by Duran Duran. Despite a lifetime as a soccer fan she'd never quite understood how thousands of spectators knew what to sing and when, especially for a brand-new player like Rio. Was there an online message board where these things were debated and decided? Was there an email newsletter? How had these things been agreed in the days before the Internet?

She was still puzzling when she became aware of a hushed commotion at the back of the church. Whispers spread in waves across the pews, and the high-ceilinged building echoed with the rustling of turned heads and shifting bodies. Everyone was trying to get a glimpse of something, or someone, and she glanced over her shoulder to see what the fuss was about.

Oh, just Skyline's latest import from Chile.

Rio caught sight of her before she could swivel back toward the front. He flashed his trademark lopsided grin and soon every set of eyes in the church was following his path straight to her. She hunched her shoulders and stared intently at the base of the statue, cheeks burning.

The whispers crept closer and grew louder, and then a familiar pair of legs appeared in her line of vision. She followed the slim-cut dark slacks up to a gray button-down shirt, finally meeting Rio's brown eyes.

He nodded to the stone Virgin. "Friend of yours?"

"We go back a long way." She slid down the pew to make space. "Looking for somewhere to sit?"

"Not anymore."

He squeezed into the end of the row, and Eva had to force herself to keep breathing as her shoulders pressed against the hard muscle of his bicep.

"What brings you out to Chamblee?" she murmured as he settled into the tight space. "I'm sure they have Catholic churches in Buckhead."

"I know a lot of people would say the sermon is secondary to the socializing, but I have this thing about being able to understand what the priest says. José, the gardener, suggested I come here."

She was about to ask another question when the priest entered from the side of the altar. The parishioners quieted as the service began.

Father Diego was a soft-spoken man in his mid-forties. His parents had come to America from Oaxaca and he'd spent his childhood barely a stone's throw from the El Paso neighborhood where she'd grown up. He opened his sermon with a recollection of a candy store in El Paso, and although she listened intently, she had absolutely no idea what he was talking about.

Because no matter how hard she tried, she couldn't find room in her brain for anything other than the man wedged in beside her.

Despite what ended up being a winning performance, yesterday had been hard for Rio—and for her. When he was confident on the pitch, he was a thing of beauty. He never stopped moving, running at a blistering pace until he seemed to be everywhere at once. His energy was unflagging, almost chaotic at times, yet he made cleverly weighted passes and took clear-headed shots that belied his constant, frenetic motion.

She wasn't sure why he lost focus at the end of the first half, but it was obvious when he did. He slowed, hesitated, wore his self-doubt so prominently that she knew the opposing team could read it as clearly as she could.

The Rio she saw at halftime bore no resemblance to the charming, self-assured flirt who'd found every excuse to meet her eyes during the team dinner on Friday night. His face was drawn, his forehead creased, and she'd wanted nothing more than to fling her arms around his neck and tell him to stop worrying, he was one of the most beautiful players she'd ever seen, and that he belonged in the Championship Soccer League.

Instead she'd given him the space he seemed to need. She'd paused in the hallway outside the dressing room, where the walls were lined with photographs of the players in action. This was Rio's first appearance for Skyline so the only photo of him was from the press conference when he signed his contract, smiling as he held up his new Skyline jersey.

She stared at her feet beside the kneeler, her cheeks reddening as she recalled that moment in the corridor. Checking both directions to make sure no one saw her, she'd quickly put her fingertips on the number seventeen in the picture, shut her eyes, and said a quick prayer. *Blessed Virgin, I'm sure you have much more pressing issues to deal with, but if you found a way for Rio to regain his confidence and help win this match, I would be super grateful. Amen.*

She'd crossed herself and instantly felt foolish. Did she really just waste the time of a Catholic deity—a deity she wasn't even sure she believed in—praying for the outcome of a soccer match? Ridiculous!

Now, as Father Diego's voice droned at the back of her consciousness, she snuck a suspicious glance at the stone Virgin.

No way. Despite her regular attendance at Sunday Mass, she was a pretty terrible Catholic. She doubted she was on the top of any saints' lists for answered prayers, soccer-related or otherwise.

Then again, maybe Rio was the good Catholic? He shifted at her side and she resisted the urge to look over. Was he listening to the sermon? Staring blankly into space? Or was he like her foster mother, Juana, craning his neck to look at the other parishioners and assess their outfits?

She slapped a hand over her mouth just in time to smother a hysterical giggle at the image of Rio squinting down his nose at the underdressed worshippers. She faked a cough before she put her hand back in her lap but Rio didn't buy it. She could feel the weight of curiosity in his gaze, although she refused to meet it.

What if he turned out to be a super-serious Catholic? Maybe she was destroying her credibility, sitting here blatantly not listening to the sermon. Maybe he thought she was disrespectful and rude. Maybe he was so religious that despite appearances he was actually a virgin.

Heat roared up her neck. That was the dirtiest thought she'd ever had in church.

Plus she was almost certain it wasn't true. The Chilean tabloids were full of stories of Rio's supposed conquests—most of whom were models several inches taller than him—and in the months before his arrival in Georgia they'd detailed what had apparently been his acrimonious break-up with his blond, beauty-queen girlfriend. If the articles were to be believed she'd become too clingy, too sexually demanding, and he needed to focus on his newly international career, and—

She shook her head sharply to shut down that train of thought. It was stupid tabloid gossip, and unfair of her to give it any air time. Rio would show himself to her in due course.

Which part he chose to show her, well…

She cast a sidelong glance at the Virgin's disapproving face, and mouthed "I'm sorry" as Father Diego led the congregation in the Our Father.

* * * *

Rio stretched as the service ended and the parishioners rose from their seats in the pews. It had been years since he'd regularly attended Mass, but after spending a couple of weeks before flying to the States with his twice-a-week-attendee mother, he thought he'd try to get back in the habit.

If his performance on the pitch yesterday was any indication, he'd take all the help he could get.

Eva looked up at him, her expression as unreadable as ever as she nodded to the crowd lingering outside the door. "You'll have a few requests for autographs, I imagine. Hope you weren't planning on a quick escape."

"People asking for my autograph has never gotten old. I should've brought a pen."

"I've got a spare in my purse."

He followed her down the side aisle. He'd been having sinful thoughts ever since he caught sight of her in her modest yet fitted gray dress, hair gathered in a clip at her nape, exposing the long line where her shoulder met her neck. He'd spent the priest's entire sermon in vivid awareness of her scent, her proximity, each minute motion of her body.

This Sunday morning had turned downright unholy.

Just as Eva predicted, when they reached the entrance he was besieged by autograph seekers. With the exception of one openly flirtatious young woman—whose smile he didn't dare acknowledge in case she had brothers watching—the fans were mostly children and teenage boys who'd watched him in the South American Cup.

It only took ten minutes to pose for selfies and sign everything in sight, but it was refreshing to chat in his own language for a while. The priest—who by comparison had relatively few parishioners vying for his attention—shot Rio a not unkind half-smile, which Rio interpreted as tacit approval. As the last fan departed, proudly tweeting his selfie, Rio thought he just might find his place in Atlanta.

He met Eva's ever-watchful gaze. "Can I take you out to lunch? We haven't celebrated my first goal for Skyline."

She shook her head, checking the time on her phone. "I run a drop-in center after Mass. In fact I'm late to open it up, but since you just signed an autograph for the son of my first appointment, I'm not sure she'll mind."

"Drop-in center?"

"Behind the church." She thumbed in the direction of a double-wide, prefabricated trailer at the end of the parking lot. "On Sundays we run an open-door session where people can come for advice. The rest of the week we try to offer appointments, depending on how many volunteers we have."

"What sort of advice?"

She shrugged. "Legal stuff, mainly. Questions about eviction notices, debt programs, employment." She lowered her voice. "Most of the people who come in are undocumented, so they're afraid to ask for help through normal channels."

"Got it." He looked at the rundown trailer, where a line was already forming at the door. As soon as he'd seen Eva in the church he'd decided he would invite her out to lunch, and he'd spent a significant portion of the Mass deciding where to go and what to order. His racehorse metabolism meant he could always find an appetite, and after an extra gym session this morning he was starving. He'd already done pretty much all he could do for the parishioners at this church—sign scraps of paper and pose for photos they could post on social media. He was tired and stiff and his stomach was growling. He wanted a steak, and he wanted it ten minutes ago.

He also wanted to spend time with Eva, however he could get it.

He grinned. "I'll help you."

"Help me with what?"

"As you said." He gestured toward the trailer. "Advice."

She blinked several times, clearly taken aback and unsure how to dissuade him. "It's boring. People bring legal and financial documents in English and I read them out in Spanish."

"Good. I need to practice my technical English."

She laughed, rare and musical. "You need to work on your basic English first."

"Come on," he goaded, walking backward toward the trailer. "What if someone has a specific question about being a Chilean in America? I'm your man."

"I can't remember ever having a Chilean drop in," she countered, but started toward the trailer. "Here's an idea. I let you sit in on my sessions today, and you agree to pose for some photos we can pitch to a couple of local newspapers to generate some publicity for the center. Deal?"

That was easier than a penalty kick against a third-team goalkeeper. "Deal."

"Follow me."

He smiled inwardly as she led him to the trailer, ignoring his protesting stomach. He had to satisfy his curiosity about this woman, figure out why she intrigued him so relentlessly. His appetite could wait.

Two hours later his stomach was the last thing on his mind as he listened to yet another parishioner seeking help to stop a deportation.

"My husband was an emergency-room doctor in Tegucigalpa," Virginia, a fifty-something Honduran, explained in crisp, well-educated Spanish. "One night he saved the life of a young woman who'd been stabbed and left on the side of the road. The following night someone shot a machine gun through our front window, because it turned out she was a witness against one of the local gangs. The next morning we applied for tourist visas for the United States, and we moved around different hotels each night until they were issued, so we didn't put any of our friends or family at risk. We hoped the violence would die down by the time our visas expired, but when that day came my husband was still a known target in Tegucigalpa. So we overstayed." She threw up her hands with an apologetic sigh.

"My husband took odd construction jobs and I found work as a cleaner. For two years we thought we might just survive, then last year one of the sites where my husband worked was raided and he was arrested. He was deported, and a week after he arrived in Honduras he was shot on a local bus."

Rio swore under his breath. Eva cast him a sharp-eyed glance before turning back to Virginia. "I'm so sorry."

She waved a dismissive hand, her face stony and unemotional. "The issue now is my son. He turned eighteen in the fall and is in his last year of high school. Over the Christmas break he was in a car with some friends and they were in traffic accident. It should've been nothing—just a stupid fender bender—but the other driver was an off-duty police officer and he reported my son to the immigration service. Now we've gotten notice that removal proceedings have been initiated against my son, which is how my husband's deportation began." She scrubbed a hand over her eyes. "We spent all our savings and most of our extended family's savings on my husband's case, and now I don't know where else to turn."

"They can't send him back." Rio turned his outrage toward Eva, disbelief and fury vying for dominance in his chest. "Not after what happened to his father. It's inhumane."

Virginia looked at him as though seeing him for the first time, her eyes dragging into focus. "Oh, yes, are you the soccer player? You took a photo with my son after Mass. Thank you for that, he was so excited."

"We keep in touch with a network of lawyers willing to take immigration cases *pro bono*," Eva explained, ignoring his outburst as she pulled a sheet of paper out of a manila envelope. "I know these three are no longer accepting cases"—she scratched off three names before sliding the page across the table—"but one of the others should be willing to help. In addition, here at the drop-in center we offer a complementary service if you're struggling to get face-time with your lawyer. Some of them may only be able to offer to appear in court for you, in which case we can help review and prepare all the documentation you'll need for the proceedings."

"So I phone one of these lawyers, but I can still come back here?"

Eva nodded. "I'm in regular contact with each of them. They all speak Spanish, and after you've made the initial call, they'll be in touch with me to let me know how much or how little we'll need to support you here at the center." She reached into one of the dented metal desk's rickety drawers and produced a crookedly printed pamphlet. "We also have a weekly women's group here at the church, on Tuesday evenings. It's very friendly and informal. Quite a few of our members have been where you are, and it's a great place to get advice and support."

Virginia took the pamphlet gingerly, as though it might crumble between her fingers. She unfolded it, refolded it, and burst into tears.

Rio shot to his feet but Eva beat him, rounding the desk at lightning speed to draw the taller woman into a hug.

"You don't have to go through this alone," Eva murmured. "I'll be here for you whenever you need me."

Virginia stepped back, visibly embarrassed by her burst of emotion. Rio snatched up a tissue from the box on the desk and handed it to her, unable to stop himself from putting a comforting arm around the woman's shoulders. She was painfully thin.

Eva produced her business card, which bore the Skyline logo. "My cell number is on the bottom. Give me a call as soon as you've spoken to the lawyers on the list and we'll take it from there."

Virginia rose from her seat, her chin held high as she patted Rio's hand. "Thank you both. I really am grateful."

"We'll speak again soon," Eva assured her. Virginia left the trailer with the straight back of someone who refused to be cowed, no matter what life threw at her.

"That was a tough one," Eva muttered as she resumed her seat.

Rio dropped into the chair Virginia had just vacated. "They can't really deport her son, can they? He's only eighteen."

She shrugged. "He's in the country illegally. She's going to have a difficult time making a case for him to be allowed to stay."

"But he'll be killed if he goes back to Honduras."

"Probably."

He threw up his hands in exasperation. "Then how can they send him?"

Eva's small smile was her most enigmatic yet. "Exactly."

He exhaled heavily, leaning back in the creaking metal chair. "I guess I didn't realize how insulated I've been from all this stuff. I mean, back home you occasionally hear about people leaving to try to cross the border, but life in Chile is completely different to Honduras, El Salvador, those kinds of places." He shook his head. "Then again, maybe my upbringing was more sheltered than I thought."

She narrowed her eyes. "Sheltered?"

He nodded. "I'm very lucky."

She paused, as if choosing her words carefully. "Maybe the press gets it wrong, but what I read of your background didn't sound particularly sheltered."

"What did you read?"

"That your father died in a mining accident."

"True. And the settlement money was enough for us to move out of our tiny house in the village and into a really nice apartment in Antofagasta. We didn't even have an indoor toilet in the village, but in town we got a TV, a microwave, lots of stuff."

She studied her thumbnail. "So the story about your cleats, is that true?"

He inclined his head, absorbing the realization that she'd read up on him. He knew exactly which article she meant, but he asked, "Which story?"

"I read something about you not having enough money to buy soccer cleats, and the village clubbing together to buy them for your youth league tryout." She avoided his gaze, taking an intense interest in her manicure.

He shook his head, endeared by her shyness. His life had been an open book for so long, he couldn't remember the last time anyone cared about his privacy. "These tabloids get it all wrong. Our neighbors in the apartment block got together to buy the cleats. We were long gone from the village by then."

"Okay, but—"

"I'm serious. The people who came to see you today have real problems. Yeah, maybe we were poor when I was very young, but I signed my first professional contract when I was seventeen and never thought about money again." He propped his elbows on the table and leaned forward. "I just watched you solve major issues. People losing their jobs, declaring bankruptcy, trying to keep their family members in the country. You changed people's lives this morning. It was incredible."

She gathered up the papers and brochures scattered across the desk and shuffled them into a manila folder. "That's nice of you to say, but all I do is put people in touch with the people who can really help them."

"Is that why you want to become a lawyer, so you can be that person?"

"Yes." She paused, then continued tidying the edges of the papers without looking up. "My mom was deported when I was twelve."

Rio watched the brisk movement of her fingers, her swift, efficient motion as she needlessly reshuffled the pages.

"I'm sorry," he said quietly.

"It's fine," she replied with the kind of certainty that implied it was anything but.

He pried the folder from her fingers and set it on a corner of the desk. She hesitated, and then met his gaze for the first time in ten minutes.

"She came over from Juarez with my dad," she explained, crossing her wrists in front of her. "I was born in El Paso about eighteen months later. They were never married, and my dad split when I was still a baby. Other than that, life was pretty normal. We lived in an apartment, my mom worked as a cleaner in a hotel, I went to school. I didn't even know my mom was undocumented until the day she was arrested."

He shoved his hands in his pockets. "What happened?"

"Similar story to Virginia's husband. The immigration service raided the hotel where she worked. She was taken into detention and eventually deported." She shrugged. "One morning she left for work and I never saw her again."

"You didn't even get to see her before they sent her away?'

She shook her head. "If I know my mom, she probably lied and told them she had no children. One of our neighbors took me in, and in retrospect the seamlessness of it suggested she knew that day might come and had a backup plan in place."

He exhaled, noting the calm efficiency with which she delivered this traumatic story. This woman wasn't only beautiful, intelligent, and compassionate. She was tough.

"That's rough, Eva. Are you in touch with her now?"

"At first I got a few letters, but after a couple of years they trailed off." She brightened. "But last year I got the money together to hire a private investigator who specializes in tracking down people who've been deported. A couple of months ago he said he'd gotten a promising lead, so I'm hopeful."

"Good." He managed a smile, although his mind spun with Eva's revelation. He couldn't imagine losing his mother so suddenly, not to mention spending the rest of his life wondering where she was and whether she was all right.

His chest tightened as he tried to understand what Eva had been through. He thought of his five-foot-nothing mother, her endless patience with his awful academic performance, her unwavering support when he was first scouted. He was her complicated, difficult, demanding middle child, who'd always lacked the steadiness of his older brother and the intellectual firepower of his younger sister. Who would he have become if she hadn't been there, encouraging him, understanding him, believing in him when no one else did?

He'd be a miner. Working hard, drinking harder, barely scraping by.

"That's it for today." Eva shoved the files in a drawer and shut it. "I'll lock up and we're done."

Rio waited at the bottom of the church steps while she secured the trailer door and dropped off the keys with Father Diego. He squinted at the watery, early-spring sun as he processed everything he'd seen and heard that morning.

He thought he'd be dropping into Mass to ease his conscience. Instead he had a whole new perspective on his good fortune—and on the woman who formed an increasingly large part of it.

Eva reappeared and joined him on the front walkway.

"So." She looked away, looked back, crossed her arms in front of her. "Did you say something about lunch?"

"Yes. Wait, what time is it?"

She glanced at her phone. "Almost two o'clock. That took longer than I expected. You must be starving."

He was, but there was something even more pressing on his mind than his stomach. "I told Nico I'd meet him at two-thirty to train."

Was that a flash of disappointment in her eyes? "Oh. I'll see you tomorrow, then."

"I'll reschedule." He took out his phone and was halfway through his contacts list when she pushed down his hand. It was a fleeting touch, but it ignited his senses with such heat that he tugged on his collar to get some air against his skin.

Eva fascinated him like no other women he'd met. It was unsettling, yet so exhilarating.

"Don't cancel with Nico on my account. I need to run some errands this afternoon, anyway. Although…" She smiled. "What'll you give me to not tell Roland you're training on your rest day?"

He took a step toward her, pocketing his phone. "Name your price."

"I'm expensive."

"I'm rich."

The look she gave him was pure heat, molten desire swirling in the depths of her dark eyes.

He suppressed a shudder as he took another step to narrow the space between them. He had no shortage of experience with women—appearing on Chilean sports pages from the age of seventeen had done more for his sex appeal than anything he'd ever worn or said—yet everything about Eva caught him off-guard. If she'd coolly assessed him in a nightclub, or shyly approached him in a store, or called his name as she leaned over the barriers outside the stadium he would've known exactly how to handle her.

Instead she showed perfect restraint, occasionally pierced by flashes of attraction so scalding he was left looking for scars.

He wanted her. But he had no idea how to win her.

He was a risk-taker by nature—probably so were all professional soccer players—but his success was rooted in knowing when to take the safe option, too. When to pass instead of shoot, when to kick it out instead of fight to play on. He needed to know Eva better before he made his move, make sure the step he took was the right one. Because when he won her, he intended to keep her.

"But nowhere near rich enough to pay what you're worth," he added. Eva glanced away and the moment was gone, but he couldn't bring himself to move back. He savored their closeness, the faint scent of her perfume. It might be awhile before he gave himself permission to be this near to her again.

She made the first move, turning toward her car. There were only a handful of vehicles remaining in the parking lot, and her hatchback was at the opposite side to his high-end convertible.

He noticed her looking at it. Did she think it was an ostentatious waste of money? Or did she think it was cool? Probably the former, he concluded grimly, but that was only because she hadn't taken a ride in it yet.

One of these days he'd take her out, find an empty back road and show her what that high-performance engine was capable of. He'd leave the top down for the ride, then put it up for the lovemaking that followed.

"Tell Nico not to work you too hard."

He'd been grinning, thinking about Eva's hair tangling from the wind, but her brisk tone snapped him out of his fantasy and back to the realization that he had a lot of work to do before he could even touch that hair.

Eva was smart, sophisticated, sexy. Fame and fortune wouldn't be enough to woo her, not even close. He'd have to prove himself, show her how hard he worked, how seriously he treated his profession, convince her he was more than just another showboat athlete.

First he'd show her the man. Then he'd show her his heart.

He raised his hand in farewell as she started toward her car. "Thanks for letting me tag along this afternoon."

"I'm here every Sunday. You're always welcome to join."

"See you tomorrow."

"Bye, Rio."

She climbed into the driver's seat, started the car, and pulled out of the parking lot without a second glance in his direction. He stood on the asphalt for a long time afterward, contemplating the challenge ahead.

It would be harder than any international cup final he'd played, but this was a match he couldn't afford to lose. He'd win her. It would take time, and effort, but he'd do it, and it would be the sweetest victory of his life.

Chapter 7

"Stop fetching the ball like a Goddamn terrier! Stay in your area! For God's sake, Rio, you're all over the pitch like a rash!"

Rio slowed as he jogged past, looking at Roland and then Eva.

She smiled encouragingly, mentally editing the manager's colorful language. "Roland likes your speed, but he wants you to keep to your area just a bit more."

Rio grinned. "Tell him I can't help it, I love to run."

As Rio rejoined the second-half action Roland turned to her, then held up his palm. "Let me guess. He likes running?"

"It's what he always says. Maybe it's true."

"I'm sure it is. No one can be that hyperactive unless they're getting something out of it."

She moved to step out of the manager's sideline box when he touched her arm to stop her. When she turned Roland wore a stony expression, concern plain in his features.

"He's going to burn himself out if he doesn't slow down. His style—this constant motion, sprinting all over the pitch like he's the only player on the field—it's not efficient and it's not sustainable. I've told him this over and over again, but he doesn't listen."

"I think he worries that he'll lose his spot on the team if he doesn't work hard," she ventured carefully.

"There's working hard, and there's running yourself ragged." Roland returned his attention to the pitch, signaling that this conversation was nearly over. "I need you to make sure he observes his rest days. No more of these secret training sessions on Sunday."

Her cheeks reddened. How had he found out about those? "I'm only his interpreter, how can I stop him?"

Roland glanced at her over his shoulder, his gaze heavy with meaning. "You watch him every second of every day, that's how."

With a troubled sigh, Eva slunk back to her seat on the sideline. She never imagined it would be the case, but more time with Rio was, in fact, the last thing she needed.

Today marked exactly a month since his arrival, and three weeks since that deeply unholy moment when they'd stood in the church parking lot and she'd had to muster every ounce of self-control to keep from dragging his head down to hers and kissing him until she couldn't breathe.

That afternoon she'd been sure she read matching attraction in Rio's expression, but the days passed and the weeks piled up and he gave no indication that they were anything more than translator and client. He lived up to his Chilean-tabloid reputation for being affable and outgoing, and although his English hadn't perceptibly improved since the day he arrived he was a willing student. But that was it. No more stolen touches, no more heavy glances.

Just yesterday she gave herself a stern self-talk on the drive to a pre-match press event, deciding once and for all that Rio's flirtatious charm was his trademark, and in no way deployed specially for her. Even if it was, it couldn't mean anything. This was her year to stare down her fear of commitment and start on the path to permanency. Rio was a sweet guy but imagining he could be marriage material wasn't realistic. He was rich, handsome, and had his pick of women. Sure, he'd probably be up for a fling with her, but the chances he'd be willing to convert that into something serious? Zero.

It was for the best, she reminded herself as she watched the Portuguese translator leap out of his seat to communicate instructions to one of the Brazilian players. She regularly compromised her professionalism by softening Roland's criticisms in some ridiculous attempt to shield Rio, and what good did that do anyone? Roland was sending a message, his player wasn't receiving it, and it was her fault.

"Buck up," she chided herself under her breath, watching Rio spring up from a tackle that'd sent him sprawling on the grass. He didn't need protection, and she was in no position to offer it.

Roland cursed in what she assumed was Swedish as the clock ticked down to nothing and three minutes of injury time were added onto the end of the match. The scoreboard was goalless, which was a disappointing result—by all accounts Skyline was the stronger team in this home-turf showdown with Cleveland Thunder.

But Cleveland had a new striker in Costa Rican Gonzalo Rubio, who was perhaps best known for taking down Rio in a studs-up tackle that earned him a red-card sendoff in the South American Cup's quarter-finals. The way he'd played this match suggested he was looking for revenge, and he had repeatedly gone after Rio with force that was truly excessive considering his six-inch, fifty-pound advantage.

Gonzalo was big but slow, and that was even more evident now the match had gone into injury time. Gonzalo was sluggish on the pitch, his movements heavy with fatigue, while Rio flitted back and forth in tight diagonals that would make a hummingbird dizzy.

Skyline had led possession in the second half and as the clocked ticked down the visitors' goal was crowded with red jerseys. One of the Steel players booted a long ball down the pitch, and while much of Skyline ran after it Rio lingered near the area, jogging at angles to avoid coverage from Steel's defenders.

There was a fight for possession and suddenly Deon broke free, dribbling the ball down the right-hand side. As all four of Steel's defenders closed in on him Rio called his name.

Deon fired the ball toward Rio but overshot, sending it to the empty space in front of the goal. Rio and the goalkeeper lunged for it simultaneously. The noise in the stadium tripled as fans shouted their suspense. Rio ran so fast his feet barely seemed to touch the ground but the goalkeeper was right there, throwing himself at the ball, arms outstretched, fingertips nearly touching it…

Rio's toe connected. The ball soared over the goalkeeper's head, hitting the top of the net before smacking against the grass.

Rio punched the air. The crowd sang his name. The referee blew the whistle, and the final score was one-nil to Skyline.

Eva filed off the sideline and into the tunnel alongside the rest of the staff. The mood was buoyant, but she couldn't celebrate just yet. Normally they only spoke to the captains and managers, but as the lone goal scorer the press would expect post-match interviews with Rio.

He hadn't done any before, and she supposed he was overdue. Plus he had plenty of media training from his career in Chile so he was hardly an amateur. All she had to do was what she did best—translate. There was no reason to be nervous.

So why was her stomach turning somersaults?

The noise level in the tunnel tripled as the players streamed in, shouting and laughing and celebrating their win. Rio appeared last, and as soon as he saw her he rushed over and swept her off her feet, swinging her in a circle before putting her back down.

She laughed his name, but her playful scolding caught in her throat as he looked at her lips, angled his head, and lowered his face toward hers.

Oh my God, he's going to kiss me.

Except he didn't. He stopped half an inch short, released his hold on her upper arms and stepped back.

"Sorry. I need a shower."

Her thoughts spun as she processed what just happened. The heat of his body as he lifted her, the iron-hard muscles she'd clutched for stability. He was soaked in sweat yet she could smell his skin when he'd leaned in, count the fine lines on his forehead, catch the amber sparkles in his brown eyes.

"You're fine," she assured him breathlessly. Her heart beat so fast she could barely spare the oxygen to speak. She cleared her throat. "I hope you're ready for some post-match interviews."

"As long as you're with me, I'm ready."

"I'm not going anywhere."

They stood in silent accord, each holding the other's gaze in a way that made the moment tantalizingly intimate despite the very public setting. Eva knew she should look away and break whatever boundary-crossing spell Rio always managed to cast on her, but she didn't want to. Instead she indulged her desire as the seconds ticked by, losing herself in his attention, his presence.

A member of the grounds crew accidentally bumped into Rio as he passed, jolting them back to the cacophonic present.

"We should go." She nodded in the direction of the press room.

He gestured for her to lead the way, his grin showing all of his teeth. "After you."

* * * *

"Bzzzbzzz bzzz bzzz bzzzbzzzbzzzz?"

"You had plenty of offers after the South American Cup," Eva translated. "What made you choose Atlanta Skyline?"

Jesus, can't they come up with a new question? Rio's whole body felt heavy with fatigue and his knee twanged every time he put weight on it, but he forced another smile for the journalist. She was the last one, probably just as ready to leave as he was, and it never paid to be rude to the press.

"I saw Skyline as a team on the rise with a gap for an attacking midfielder. I've always wanted to play in the CSL and Skyline's offer was an opportunity not only to join the league but potentially to win it as well."

Eva relayed his statement, the journalist scribbled. He wondered if it was possible to sleep standing up.

With a smile the journalist buzzed again, and Eva asked, "Does that mean you think Skyline can win the title this year?"

"Now that I'm here, anything's possible." He winked, the journalist blushed, and the interview was over. He shook her hand and waited for her to turn around before he let the smile dissolve from his face.

"I'm not sure which I want first: a steak, a shower or a nap."

"You can have all three in whatever order you'd like." Eva glanced over at the PR manager, who nodded to confirm they were done, then guided him out of the press room with her hand at the small of his back.

The instant she touched him he was reminded of his reckless loss of control in the tunnel. He didn't know what he'd been thinking, sweeping her up like that. Only that he hadn't been thinking at all.

He'd never worked so hard to endear himself to someone as he had these last three weeks. He studied his English lessons late into the night, ensured he was charm personified in every interaction with Eva, and nearly killed himself in training whenever he knew she was watching. He wanted so badly for her to see him as responsible, committed—worthy.

But if she did, she gave absolutely no sign.

When he saw her in the tunnel he'd acted on pure instinct. He was high on adrenaline, lightheaded with excitement after his match-winning goal, and his rational brain was nowhere to be found as he scooped her up and swung her.

Thank God he'd regained some shred of awareness before he kissed her. He'd been seconds away from doing exactly that—seconds away from ruining his chance with the hottest woman he'd ever encountered.

She looked up at him as they walked down the corridor, wearing her default-encouraging expression. "I can't believe I haven't congratulated you on that goal yet. I thought we were headed for—"

"Rio Vidal." It was more of a statement than a greeting, and when Rio noted the source he understood why.

"Gonzalo," he inclined his head to the Costa Rican, who had showered and changed and was probably on his way to the Cleveland Thunder bus.

"Sorry for kicking the shit out of you in the Cup," he said in Spanish, his tone suggesting he wasn't sorry at all.

"No problem, it's the end result that matters, right?" Rio grinned.

Gonzalo shrugged. "Looks like both our performances got us to the Championship League."

"Exactly." Rio stuck out his hand. "Nice to see you again."

The big Costa Rican ignored his proffered handshake, sliding his gaze to Eva and back again. "I've been wondering. Why do you keep speaking in a woman's voice?"

He dropped his hand back to his side. "Excuse me?"

Gonzalo nodded toward Eva. "My interpreter's a man. Couldn't they find one for you?"

Fury squalled in Rio's chest. He grabbed fistfuls of his shorts and pressed his clenched hands against his thighs, reminding himself that Gonzalo was a third-rate player and a fifth-rate human being. He couldn't let himself be baited. It wouldn't serve either of them to get into a stupid feud.

Rio managed a smile. "Come on, Gonzalo. Don't be jealous that my interpreter's hotter than yours."

Gonzalo snorted. "Please. Whenever those rumors about closeted gay players start spinning, we all know who they're talking about."

He heard Eva's sharp intake of breath but didn't acknowledge it. "If I was gay I wouldn't hide it. I'd be proud. This is where you go wrong, my friend—you think you can shame people, when no one actually cares what you think. What was that word you used to describe the referee who sent you off in the Cup? I can't quite remember, but I think it had something to do with him being black."

The striker's eyes narrowed. Rio continued, "Anyway, it's good to know I can call you for advice if I ever have to make a public apology. Which would be delivered in this fine woman's voice, of course."

He slung his arm around Eva and dragged her toward the Costa Rican, whose hand he pried away from his side to shake.

"Seriously, it's good to see you, man." Rio slapped Gonzalo on the back. "Guys like us, we have to stick together on this side of the border."

"See you in Cleveland, little worm," Gonzalo sneered. Rio didn't look over his shoulder as he led Eva toward the dressing room, and soon he heard the Costa Rican's footsteps retreating down the hall.

Eva ducked out of his grip and he was once again self-conscious. Was he too sweaty? Was she angry that he'd picked her up? Did she just not want him to touch her?

She stopped their progress, putting her hands on her hips. "Little worm?"

He laughed, unable to help himself. If that was the worst thing she came away with, maybe he hadn't done too badly.

"That's what he called me in the quarter-final match when he got sent off for a late tackle that could've broken my leg. No idea where he got it from, not for a big guy like me."

He winked, and he nearly collapsed with relief when she returned his smile.

"I like the way you handled that," she remarked.

He waved his hand dismissively, secretly thrilled at her compliment. "I've known Gonzalo for years. He's a stupid, racist bully. What he lacks in skill he tries to make up for in intimidation. It's never worked with me and he hates that."

She looked up and down the hallway, and waited for one of the PR assistants to slip into the press room before she spoke again.

"Do you really think I'm hotter than his interpreter?"

His face lit up as hope swelled in his stomach. He'd had weeks of cool professionalism and immaculate restraint from Eva. The odd flash of friendliness, and that was it.

But unless he was hallucinating from exhaustion, he was pretty sure she just flirted with him.

"No question. Hottest in the league, in fact. You're the World Cup final. Everyone else is scrabbling around in the second division."

She rolled her eyes but her smile didn't wane. "Have you even seen any other female translators?"

"Sure," he fibbed.

"Yeah? Who?"

"They were all so unremarkable that I can't remember."

"Of course." She reached across the short space between them and fixed the hem of his jersey, freeing a spot where the material had caught on itself.

She stepped back, clearing her throat. "Thanks for sticking up for me. I know what Gonzalo was saying wasn't really about me, but—" She shrugged. "I liked hearing it anyway."

"I meant every word."

She smiled up at him, then ducked her head shyly. "I'll let you get your shower. Or did you decide the steak should come first?"

He pulled the front of his sodden jersey away from his chest. "Definitely shower. But maybe I'll see you for steak afterward? A bunch of the players are going out for dinner for Deon's birthday."

"Would you like me to join you?"

"It's last-minute, so if you have other plans…"

"You know my contract includes team social events. Would you like me to join you?"

He paused, trying to read between the lines. Did she want him to ask her out? Or were they back in client-translator territory?

"I would," he replied carefully. "But only if it suits your schedule. Your *personal* schedule."

"Then I'll see you there," she informed him chirpily. She pivoted and made a brisk exit down the hallway, leaving him to watch her depart.

He may not have been the smartest kid in class, but he was pretty sure he knew an invitation when he got one.

He grinned as he headed toward the changing room. Enough proving himself. Time to make the first move.

* * * *

Olivia had reserved the wine cellar of a steakhouse for Deon's birthday dinner, and Eva felt underdressed as she descended the narrow stairs into the elegantly decorated space. The long table was laid with fresh flowers and bottles of wine, players' wives and girlfriends circulated in chic cocktail dresses, and low lighting gave the bottle-lined walls an intimate ambience.

"I should've gone home to change," she fretted aloud, glancing down at her too-big Skyline polo and dark-wash jeans. Rio looked flawless in all black, and she looked like what she was.

Staff.

"You look great," he assured her, already flashing his grin as Deon's fiancée approached them.

"*Buenas noches,* Rio," Olivia attempted, then laughed self-effacingly. "That's about all I know, I'm sorry."

"Don't worry, that's what I'm here for," Eva replied, suddenly fighting an urge to burst into tears.

She spent several minutes translating pleasantries for Olivia, and then Deon, and then a number of other players and their partners. Outwardly she was polite and professional, but inside she felt like her heart was bleeding from a thousand stinging paper cuts.

After all her self-talk about guarding her emotions and convincing herself Rio wasn't right for her at this point in her life, she'd gone and done exactly the opposite. All he had to do was say one flattering thing to her and she melted like a popsicle in August. She'd hung around the stadium waiting for him to shower, accepted a ride to dinner in his super-fast convertible, and happily chatted on the journey, all the while thinking he wanted her to attend as more than his paid interpreter.

Some stupid, foolish part of her had decided he actually *liked* her, and that on some level this was a date. She knew that's what she wanted in the short term, but never gave a second's consideration to whether that's what she needed in the long term.

And now he'd made the decision for her. The more they mingled, the clearer it became that he'd invited her in a professional—not personal—capacity. He barely looked at her, certainly didn't draw her into any of his conversations, and she felt more like an accessory with every passing minute.

Moron. She cursed herself silently as she offered a smiling translation to yet another of Rio's teammates. Brian was clearly trying to make amends for being rude on Rio's first day, but all Eva could think about was the way Brian's girlfriend kept looking Rio up and down like she hoped there was more than just steak on the menu tonight.

"That was very grown-up of him," Rio remarked as the couple moved away.

"His girlfriend's certainly a fan of yours," she muttered.

He looked at her in surprise, but Laurent approached them and he said nothing more.

The cocktail hour seemed to drag on forever, and by the time they were seated toward one end of the long table Eva was exhausted. She smiled through Olivia's opening toast to Deon's birthday, translated a brief conversation between Rio and Laurent on his right, then opened the menu.

"So," she began, readying herself to talk Rio through the options. "Starting from the upper left-hand corner we've got—"

"It's okay." He held up a hand to interrupt her. "I think I can figure most of it out. I've been practicing, remember?"

His smile was hopeful, so eager for her approval, but she just couldn't give it to him. She leaned over the menu, blinking furiously against the tears threatening at the corners of her eyes.

Great. Soon he won't need me at all.

"Hey." His hand found her arm, and she pried her face out of the leather-bound menu.

"Need help?"

"Did I say something wrong?"

"No, why?" she asked, too brightly.

His expression was unconvinced. He leaned back in his chair and signaled to one of the two private waiters standing at either end of the room. "What are you drinking?"

"Nothing. I'm on the clock."

"Not anymore." The waiter arrived and, in terrible English requiring extensive gestures, Rio ordered water for himself and a glass of champagne for her.

"That's not fair," she protested as the waiter departed.

"I'm in training, and I'm driving." He grinned. "But if you insist, after dinner we can go back to my place and I'll teach you how to drink pisco."

Her brief flash of happiness as he'd ordered her drink fizzled and died. How much more mixed could his signals get? One minute he flirted, then they were professional, and now he was flirting again. It could only mean what she'd always suspected. He was charming to everyone—it wasn't sincere and it didn't make her special.

She sighed her resignation as her drink arrived and she took a hearty gulp. This was all part of her great romantic restructure, she reminded herself. It wouldn't only be a matter of willpower and foregoing instant gratification. Sometimes she'd be on the receiving end of rejection, too. Rio wasn't a plausible relationship candidate anyway, so this was her chance to toughen up in case she ever got the same response from someone who was.

Dinner proceeded more or less as she expected. Except for a few snatches of conversation between the two of them, she spent most of the appetizer and main course translating for Rio as players and their partners shuffled around the table. She chased the glass of champagne with two generous glasses of red wine from the wildly expensive bottles on the table, and although it took a hell of a lot more for her to be drunk, by the time the sparkler-heavy birthday cake was cut she felt warm and relaxed.

Most of the women in the room waved away their portions of cake, and as it had between every course, the room began to fill with diners standing up from their seats to talk or look at the cellar wines or pop out to the bathroom. Soon she and Rio were virtually alone at their end of the table, with only a few other diners seated in the nearby vicinity.

"Are you going to eat that?" Rio pointed his fork at her slice of red-velvet cake.

"Hell yes."

"Damn." He looked at his own empty plate, then back at hers. "All of it?"

"Make me an offer."

He drummed his fingers on the table while he thought. "Half of your slice for an extra hour of English-language lessons."

She laughed. "Are you crazy? I lose half of my cake *and* I have to listen to your crazy pronunciation for an extra hour? No way."

As soon as it left her mouth she felt bad, and searched his face for any sign that she'd offended him. She found none.

"Okay, that was a bad trade." He reconsidered. "Half of your cake and I'll play you a song on the piano upstairs in the restaurant."

She shook her head. "Way too embarrassing."

"Half of your cake and I'll specifically thank you for sharing it with me in my next press interview."

"Even worse. I'm the one who'd have to translate that."

"Half of your cake, and…"

"Forget it, Rio." She cut into the moist slice. "You have nothing I want."

"Really, nothing," he replied, his tone unexpectedly serious. "That's disappointing."

She cast him a sidelong glance but said nothing. She was done falling for his *piropos*.

"Any news on your mother?"

She looked up sharply, alert for any hint of mocking or insincerity. Instead his expression was earnest and attentive. He put down his fork and threaded his fingers, offering her his full attention.

"No," she answered. "Not yet."

"And you've hired a private investigator? You're not going through a charity or something?"

"Private investigator," she confirmed. "And he's not cheap."

Damn, another sentence she wished she could rescind as soon as she'd spoken it. She narrowed her eyes at her wineglass. *Looks like you and I are done for the night.*

"This lady who took you in, where is she? Does she know anything about where your mom might have gone?"

She shook her head. "She was another single mom, living in the apartment above ours with her two kids. She and my mom were good friends. She worked in the restaurant of the hotel where my mom was a cleaner, and because they often had opposite shifts, they used to shuttle us kids between the two apartments for babysitting."

"Do you still keep in touch with her?"

"Oh, God, yeah." Eva smiled as she thought of her surrogate mother. "Juana raised me from the age of twelve, got me through high school and into college. She's still in El Paso. I call her once a week. She's kind of like my stepmom, only there's no dad in the picture."

"And her kids?"

"Lulu is a year younger than me, and we see each other twice a year or so. She lives in California. She's got a physical therapy practice in Sacramento. Eriberto is another story." She bit her lower lip. "He got mixed up with the wrong crowd in high school, started dealing drugs, that kind of thing. He's in jail right now, awaiting trial for assault."

"Not good," Rio commented.

"Not good at all." She licked some of the cream cheese frosting off her fork. "And your siblings? What do they do?"

"My brother works for a shipping company. I'm not sure exactly what he does for them—he wears a tie and types on a computer." He shrugged. "My sister finished university last year and joined a big oil company. She's doing some round-the-world thing where they send you off to different countries and then figure out where you should work. She's in Australia now, and after that she's going to Singapore."

"That's pretty cool. Will you go visit her?"

"When I have time, definitely." He grinned. "She teases me about ruining her chance to be the most successful sibling, but really I think she loves being able to point to her brother on TV."

"You must miss them."

He gestured dismissively. "I'll fly them all out here at some point, and I'll see them when I go back for internationals. You're the one who must miss people. I've been thinking about it since you told me, and I can't imagine what you went through when your mom was sent away."

She eyed him skeptically, watchful for ulterior motives.

His brow was furrowed, and he flattened his hands on the table. "I've never been great with words, but I hope you know what I mean when I say that's horrible, what happened to you."

She paused, pushing the remaining cake around on her plate as she considered her response. He certainly sounded sincere.

Her instinct told her to believe him.

Her brain told her to be very, very careful.

"Thank you," she ventured. "I appreciate that."

They sat in silence for a few moments, inhabiting a hushed world of their own within the increasingly noisy wine cellar. She processed what he'd said and how he'd said it.

Then she put down her fork and pushed her plate of half-eaten cake in front of Rio.

She waited for him to say something, but when she finally looked over he was solemn.

"I don't want your cake," he murmured.

He shifted in his seat. Then his hand found hers under the table.

His touch was confident but not arrogant, his big palm spreading over her hand where it rested above her knee.

She stopped breathing as his fingers moved on top of hers, warming them, threading through them until he could tighten his fist around hers.

He cleared his throat, inched his chair closer. She sucked in oxygen with such urgency that for a second she was lightheaded, her vision tilting and reeling before it righted again. She closed her eyes, indulging in the momentary bliss of the weight of his touch, the specialness it bestowed on her.

Then she slid her hand out from under his.

"Rio, you know we can't—"

"Why?"

"It's unprofessional."

"We don't have to tell anyone."

"That's not the point, it's—"

"Don't you like me?" His grin had lost some of its wattage.

"Of course I like you, but…"

But I can't like you so much I can't hold you at arm's length.

But it's been so long since I let anyone get close I'm not sure I remember how.

But I can't believe you won't move on as soon as you get your bearings in your new country and realize you can have any woman you want.

"But I think we both know I'm not really your type," she fibbed, trying to make a joke out of the situation with a teasing smile.

He sat back, looking mildly offended. "What do you know about my type?"

"Nothing," she backpedaled. "I'm sorry, it was a bad attempt at humor."

"Are you talking about Mercedes?" he asked, referring to the Peruvian pageant queen the Chilean press had linked him with over the last year.

"It doesn't matter. Forget I said anything."

"Mercedes has a degree in political science," he said pointedly. "And no matter what the tabloids said, we broke up because she was moving to Paris for graduate school."

"I didn't mean—"

"Just because I didn't finish school doesn't mean I can't appreciate smart women."

"Rio, I just—"

"And it's possible to be smart *and* beautiful. You of all people should know that."

Her cheeks heated at his compliment but she stuck to her resolve. "You have a lot going on right now. New team, new city, new country, new language. Give yourself a chance to get settled. Then start thinking about what you want in the relationship department."

His expression could've melted a stick of butter from a hundred paces. "I know exactly what I want. And I'm not going to change my mind."

"We'll see." She resumed her professional smile as one of the player's wives approached.

"Yes, we will," Rio promised.

Chapter 8

Rio drummed his heels, clicking his cleats against the concrete beneath his feet. After sixty minutes Skyline was a goal down in their away match against Tucson United and he was sitting on the Goddamn bench.

He tugged at his mesh sub's vest, rolled his shorts high on his thighs, rolled them back down. Then he twisted in his seat to speak to Eva, sitting in the row behind.

"I should be out there," he informed her for the thousandth time.

"Roland wants you to rest," she replied calmly.

He turned his attention back to the pitch. "No point in being rested to play for a losing team."

Eva said nothing and he drummed his feet even faster. He hated watching his teammates run while he sat, hated that he kept seeing goal-scoring opportunities he couldn't take, hated watching them look around for someone to receive a pass and not being there to do it.

Most of all, he hated that it wasn't even an injury that put him on the bench. It was his manager's *fear* of an injury.

Two afternoons earlier he'd insisted to Roland—via Eva, of course—that he'd always trained harder and longer than his teammates and never gotten an injury. They'd gone back and forth for nearly an hour, but in the end the manager's word was law. The manager had consulted with the team physician and the training staff, all of whom shared his concern that Rio would burn himself out, particularly given his abbreviated pre-season rest period after the South American Cup. For the next week Rio was limited to one training session per day, and he wouldn't start with his teammates when they played away in Tucson.

He'd bottled his anger until they turned the corner into the lobby of the training facility. Life-size cardboard cutouts of all the Skyline players stood in a bunch in one corner, presumably awaiting transport to a press event. His was bang in the front, and it was at least three inches shorter than all the others.

He hardly ever lost his temper, but that diminutive cardboard replica pushed him over the edge. He marched across the room and picked it up, fully intent on ripping it in half when he heard his name.

A crowd of kids from Skyline's youth academy stood in the entrance, watching him with wide eyes.

He'd made a joke out of it, pretending he was trying to stretch the cutout to make it taller, then put it down behind all the others so it couldn't be seen. The kids laughed and took out their phones, and ten minutes later he left a delighted group of students comparing selfies as unreleased frustration still simmered in his chest.

That same frustration flared again as Rio swore under his breath, watching Laurent lose possession to Tucson. He started to turn to vent his annoyance to Eva, then changed his mind. His beautiful, enigmatic interpreter was proving to be almost as problematic as his stubborn manager.

His approach to soccer had always been almost childishly single-minded. He cared less about intricate maneuvers and complicated formations than he did simply having the ball. When someone took the ball away from him, he couldn't think about anything other than getting it back.

Eva was proving to be the human equivalent of a soccer ball.

If she were any other woman he would've accepted her polite brush-off at Deon's birthday party and left it there. And he'd tried—he'd really tried. But he couldn't get her out of his thoughts, and he wasn't ready to give up.

He'd replayed their exchange in his mind a hundred times, usually at two o'clock in the morning after waking from a tantalizingly erotic dream about her. He still didn't fully understand why she'd turned him down. She'd mentioned something about her job, and about other women he'd dated, but neither of those rang quite true.

Okay, her job was a legit reason. But surely not completely insurmountable if both parties were willing? He'd once met an interpreter who'd worked for a very famous British player when he joined a Spanish team, and if her stories were to be believed...

He exhaled hotly. This was ridiculous. He was Rio Vidal, dammit. In Chile the press called him *el Príncipe*—the Prince. Tens of thousands of people chanted his name in stadiums and women gave him their phone numbers in the middle of the street. Once he'd handed up his cleats to a schoolboy fan and the kid had kissed them. Literally kissed his boots!

And now he was sweating his balls off in Tucson, sitting on the bench, while the woman he wanted to impress more than anyone tapped her foot and checked her phone.

The clock above the pitch ticked up to seventy minutes. Deon stuck his hand in the air to show he was open. Brian attempted a pass to him. Intercepted.

Rio shot to his feet with a string of curses, glowered at Eva, and thumbed toward Roland. "Go tell that clown to put me on if he wants to win this match."

She blinked at him, still holding her phone. "I beg your pardon?"

"Sorry." He cleared his throat. "Please, Eva, when it's convenient for you, would you ask Roland to put me on? I've had seventy minutes of rest and I really think my presence in the team will be critical to winning this match." He grinned to his back teeth.

She rolled her eyes but got to her feet. "I'll phrase that somewhere between the first and second versions."

He sat down and watched anxiously as she crossed the short distance to the manager's box. At first he waved her away distractedly, but she said something and pointed to Rio. Roland looked at her, then past her at him, and then back to her. Then he looked at the scoreboard.

He made a "come here" gesture with his fingers, signaling to Rio to start warming up.

Rio leapt onto the sideline like he had springs in his heels. He started his routine, trying not to rush it as his heart raced with excitement.

Sidestep to the left, one, two, three, four… *You've asked for this, that means you can't fuck it up. You have to go out there and perform. Prove your worth.*

Sidestep to the right, one, two, three, four… *Everyone's watching you now, relying on you to turn this around. You cannot fail.*

Jump up, one, two, three, four… *Do you want to crawl back to Santiago at the end of your contract after two years as prince of the bench? Hell no.*

Kick right, kick left, kick right, kick left… *Come on, Vidal. Show your manager you know what you're doing. Show the team you deserve your spot. Show Eva you're so much more than she thinks.*

"Substitution," boomed the announcer. The digital scoreboard showed Scholtz, number thirty-seven, subbed out for Vidal, number seventeen.

The small section of away fans cheered politely, a far cry from the hysteria Rio was used to when the crowd saw him warming up to join the match. He shook Brian's hand as they passed at the halfway line, then jogged out to take his place in the midfield.

Immediately he sensed his teammates' fatigue. The afternoon was unseasonably warm, particularly in comparison to the cool spring they were having in Atlanta. Brian's poor support meant the midfield had worked harder than usual, and Tucson United's inelegant, bullying style of play was exhausting Skyline's defense.

Meanwhile Rio brimmed with unspent energy. He caught sight of the ball and practically salivated.

He exploded into motion, spending his first several minutes on the pitch hunting down the ball, nimbly negotiating Tucson's players, putting his speed and agility into full effect. The clock was ticking and he knew he'd only get one, maybe two chances to change the number on the scoreboard.

He danced around the edges of play, trying to avoid coverage by the other team, looking for his opportunity. And when he saw it, he didn't hesitate.

He knew the second the Tucson midfielder raised his boot that his pass wasn't going to hit its mark. Rio dove into the ball's trajectory and stole it, pivoting to drive it toward Tucson's goal as quickly as he could. Deon drove on ahead, and he glanced between his teammate and the defenders bearing down on him as he angled left, then right, then left again, executing a series of step-overs to throw off Tucson's coverage.

His striker was in position, but so were Tucson's two biggest defenders. The duo bore down on him, one a Colombian he'd played in internationals, the other a Nigerian he'd only seen on television. They were both over six feet tall and, it seemed to Rio, nearly just as wide. He got a last glimpse of Deon before the defenders shouldered him backward, and he saw his opportunity as clearly as he knew he had to take it.

He turned his back on the two defenders, practically trembling from the adrenaline pouring through his veins. He flicked the ball into the air with his toe, then booted it over his head in a high-angled volley.

He didn't need to turn around to see the result. The noise from the away stands assured him that Deon had knocked his cross soundly into the net. He spun on his heel and ran into the waiting arms of his striker, clutching Deon in celebration as Laurent and Nico piled in with them.

Elation lightened his steps as they broke apart and the cheering died down. A quick glance at Roland found the manager applauding in delight and encouragement. Rio looked away quickly—he didn't want Roland to think he was gloating. He wasn't, and wouldn't. He was just grateful to be on the pitch.

Play continued at pace, with both teams trying to shake Skyline's equalizing goal to pull out in front, so Rio didn't have time to celebrate. He didn't mind, though. One glimpse of Eva's approving smile gave him more fuel than any electrolyte drink or protein bar.

Tonight, he decided, hurling himself after the ball. Tonight he would talk to her, tell her how he felt, lay it all on the line and ask her to decide. If she turned him down, he wouldn't ask again. If she said yes, he'd be the happiest man in Arizona. And if she said she needed more time, well…

He intercepted a pass and sped toward Tucson's goal, powered by adrenaline, excitement and hope.

* * * *

"*¿Hablas español?*"

Eva flushed with embarrassment as Rio leaned into the window and asked the taxi driver if he spoke Spanish. Evidently they needed to have a discussion about racial assumptions in America, and whether or not—

"*Sí, señor. ¿Eres Rio Vidal?*"

"All day, every day." Rio grinned as he held open the door to the backseat and motioned for her and Nico to get in. "And this is Nico Silva and Eva Torres."

"It's an honor." The driver shook Rio's hand as he settled into the front seat. "I can't wait to tell my family in Mexico that I've just shaken hands with the man who knocked us out of the South American Cup."

Rio put his hand on the door latch. "Should I get out now?" he joked. "You're not going to kidnap me?"

"Only if you promise to join Cruz Azul when your Skyline contract expires."

"I'll speak to my agent." Rio grinned.

Nico relayed the directions to the salsa club where the Skyline players were meeting and the driver pulled into traffic. Eva watched the lights of Tucson glancing across the window, as nervous as she was excited to be along for the ride.

Rio had behaved impeccably since their difficult conversation at Deon's birthday dinner. Occasionally he shot her a perceptibly longing look, which she ignored, although her heart leapt every single time.

And on her side? She'd never been so confused. Not that she should be—it was easy to tick off reasons not to give a fling with Rio more than a second's thought. First and most obvious, it wasn't part of her plan. Second and related, she could lose her job and the salary she relied on. Third and much more complicated, she was afraid.

Her fear was the toughest to tackle because it was the least familiar. By nature she was not a fearful woman. On the contrary, she'd always been strong-willed and confident.

She'd been a bold child, never hesitating to stand up against bullies despite always being one of the smallest in the class. When her mother disappeared she barely cried, firm in the belief that her mother would return as soon as she could and that she could take care of herself in the meantime. Then she'd stormed into adulthood, won scholarships for college, graduated with high honors, gained admission to a top grad program, and landed the coveted sports translation job she'd always wanted. Along the way she'd dated, lost her virginity, gotten drunk, made mistakes, gotten back on her feet, and hit her thirtieth birthday largely unscathed.

Or so she thought.

Over the last week, every time she looked at Rio she realized there was one big, glaring experience missing from her repertoire.

She'd never been in love.

Not that she was in love with Rio—far from it. Sure, he was charming and sexy, but at times his boyishness reminded her of the four-year age gap between them. He was a dreamer, an idealist, insisting he could train to exhaustion and avoid injury, assuming the best in everyone he met, facing every obstacle with buoyant optimism. He probably even believed in true love.

His eyes were on the stars, her feet were firmly on the ground.

So why did just the thought of kissing him fill her with terror?

Because he's the first man I've met that I could love. And the one least likely to love me in return.

"Turn it up, I love this song," Rio told the driver before twisting around in his seat. "Eva, can you tell me what this guy is saying? I can sing along to the whole song but I've never known what it means."

And now she had to translate a mid-nineties power ballad about love. Perfect.

"The chorus is 'always', and he's saying he'll be in love with this girl—or guy, I guess—forever."

"And this part?" He nodded toward the radio.

"I'll be there 'til the stars don't shine, 'til the heavens burst, and the words don't rhyme."

"Amazing. I knew this was a great song, I just didn't know how great."

She exchanged bemused looks with Nico as Rio sang along to the English lyrics. His pitch was surprisingly good, although his pronunciation left something to be desired.

"Forget this cheesy stuff, man." The driver switched stations and turned up the reggaeton track that blasted through the speakers. "This is how we roll in Tucson."

Eva startled as Nico let out an excited whoop beside her and joined Rio in shout-singing the Spanish lyrics. Soon all three men were punching the air in time to the high-octane beat and she found herself bouncing along, gripping the edge of her seat as the taxi careened around the city streets.

"We destroy this song in Montevideo," Nico called over the music, prompting an agreeing hoot from the driver.

"Not like we do in Santiago," Rio countered, leaning around his seat. But instead of looking at his teammate his gaze locked with hers, and for a split second she felt all his excitement, his energy, the relentless positivity that made him such a joy to be near.

Then he swiveled back to the front and she exhaled. They were only blocks away from the club. Time to leave Rio to his fantasy and rediscover the limits of her professional role.

The salsa club was cavernous and the line leading up to the velvet-roped door snaked down the block. Clearly word had gotten around that the visiting Skyline players had booked the private room, because many of the waiting clubbers had their cell phones at the ready as soon as the taxi pulled up. Eva wanted nothing more than to dive onto the floor of the car and order the driver back to the hotel, but when Rio came around to open her door and offered his hand to help her up, she had no choice but to take it.

She tried to hang back, hiding behind the two soccer players flashing trained smiles at the crowd. Rio had perfected the casual-cool look in dark jeans and a black T-shirt with a deep V-neck, and Nico looked every inch the dapper athlete in a slim-cut blazer. She knew she looked good in her tight-fitting red dress, but that didn't mean she wanted her picture to be on all these different cell phones. She loitered near the taxi until Rio tucked her hand into the crook of his elbow and tugged her into his side.

"*Esta es Eva, mi traductor hermosa,*" he called to the crowd.

My beautiful translator. She didn't know whether to blush or cringe at Rio's over-the-top effusiveness. Maybe he was used to this level of attention, but she wasn't.

She tried her best to smile at the fans and prayed the Internet wasn't filling with constipated-looking photos of her. She could just imagine tomorrow's gossip-page headline: *The language of love? Chilean soccer star Rio Vidal steps out to a salsa club with his interpreter—but will she make all the right moves on him?*

"I will never live this down," she muttered as they crossed the threshold into the darkly lit club and traded screaming onlookers for a sensual salsa beat.

"You need to lighten up," Nico remarked unhelpfully.

"You were fine," Rio added, his white-toothed grin luminous against the low lighting.

She slipped her hand off his arm and pointed to the back wall. "The bouncer said the private room is this way."

They weaved through the raucous crowds lining the dance floor, which was packed with what looked to her novice eyes to be salsa experts. She could smell mojitos and licked her lips, trying and failing to resist the infectious party atmosphere.

Technically she was here to work and translate for Rio as long as he required. But that didn't preclude a cocktail or two, did it?

They reached the private room, the bouncer opened the door, and her swelling sense of enthusiasm popped like a balloon.

The Skyline players' party was dead.

Maybe it was the lower volume of the music inside, or the relative lack of wives and girlfriends who'd traveled to this away game, or overwhelming exhaustion among the players after a tough match in hot weather. Whatever it was, it was not a celebratory vibe.

Rio's disappointment was palpable as they found seats along a row of short, velvet-upholstered stools. Nico crossed the room to speak to Laurent and Rio turned to her.

"I'd promised myself a drink tonight if I got an assist," he said glumly. "Hardly seems worth it now."

"Everyone's tired," she told him apologetically.

He raised a shoulder. "I know. I only played fifteen minutes, so."

She bit her lower lip, hating to see him so unhappy. She'd also been looking forward to a little more excitement, especially after their bass-heavy taxi ride and beat-pumping walk through the club. Though not a big clubber she loved going out with friends and drinking until the edges blurred.

Fuck it. I've made so many mistakes with Rio—what's one more?

She nudged his shoulder. "Go on, I'll have a drink with you."

His eyes lit up. "You're sure?"

"Just this once."

He was on his feet, crossing the room in three quick strides to speak to the waitress. After a second she realized he might need help to speak to her, but by the time she was halfway off her seat he was making his way back.

"Luckily there are some words that are the same in Spanish and English."

She arched a brow. "Such as?"

"Tequila."

She slapped her hand over her eyes. "Can't we just have a beer?"

"If I'm going to cheat and have one alcoholic drink, I need to make it count. Why, don't you like tequila?"

"I love tequila."

He grinned. "So what's the problem?"

"Like I said, I *love* tequila."

His grin broadened. "We'll sip, not shoot. Like we're in Mexico."

When the tequila arrived it was one-hundred-percent blue agave, three-years-aged, and breathtakingly expensive. There was something sinfully attractive about the way Rio counted high-worth bills out of the wad he'd taken from his pocket, and she indulged a frisson of desire as they clinked their glasses together.

"To victory," she offered.

"To beauty," he countered.

They sipped, their gazes locked over the rims of their glasses.

The tequila slid down her throat like liquid gold and she lowered her glass, determined to savor it.

"I may be small, but out of all my friends, I hold my liquor the best." Her comment was pointed, intended to put paid to any notions he might have about plying her with alcohol.

"You can probably drink me under the table, then. Twelve years of full-time training means my tolerance is practically nonexistent."

"I'm surprised you're such a teetotaler," she replied. "Hector drank a lot."

"Hector is a lot slower than I am."

"True." She took another sip of tequila, nodding her head in time to the tune playing over the sound system. "Is salsa music popular in Chile?"

"Reasonably popular, I guess. Most of the nightclubs would play reggaeton, though."

She inclined her head. "Is there a type of music native to Chile? Like salsa is from Cuba, and mariachis are from Mexico?"

"We have *cueca*. It sucks."

She laughed, which prompted an answering smile from Rio. "Never heard of it."

"Trust me, it's not cool."

She drew breath to ask him another question but Brian arrived with his girlfriend on his arm, and she was brought back down to earth with an unpleasant thud.

As usual, Brian began his conversation with Rio in simplistic, broken Spanish, then depleted his limited vocabulary and switched to English. Dutifully she switched into interpreter mode, ignoring Brian's girlfriend's wandering eyes and ensuring the tone of her translations concealed her skepticism at Brian's sudden friendliness toward his midfield rival.

"And I realized that if I'm going to be subbed out of a game, I want it to be so you can come on," he asserted with such excessive sincerity Eva struggled not to roll her eyes.

She translated his statement for Rio, who smiled warmly at his teammate as he said, "He's so full of shit."

She did a double-take. "I can't tell him that."

"Tell him whatever you want. It's the truth."

"Rio's glad he could, uh, contribute to the team. You know, with an assist. So Skyline drew with Tucson."

Brian nodded sagely. "You tell Rio we're glad to have him, not just at Skyline but in America."

Brian stuck out his hand and shook Rio's, adding a fist bump and a fraternal nod.

Brian's girlfriend—whose name Eva didn't even know, she realized—smiled broadly at Rio and then turned to her.

"Tell Rio I also think he did a really, really good job today."

Eva relayed her sentiment as neutrally as she could, and Rio flashed his trademark grin at both of them.

"Thank you very much," he said in English, which came out sounding like *sank you ferry mush.*

Brian's girlfriend clapped her hands together in delight while Brian raised his palm for a high five.

"Awesome," he lauded his teammate. "You'll be fluent in no time."

The couple lingered a bit longer, then Nico motioned Rio over. Eva started to follow him but he held up his palm to stop her.

"Nico can help me for a while. Why don't you go talk to some of the other women? You shouldn't have to feel like you're stuck beside me all night."

"Oh, okay." Her heart dropped into her toes as she watched Rio walk away, already laughing with Nico.

Had she just been brushed off?

She stood still for a moment, digesting the situation, paralyzed by indecision.

If Rio didn't need her here to translate, she should probably leave. Strictly speaking she was contracted by Skyline to provide translation services where needed, and hanging around while the players socialized seemed sort of inappropriate.

On the other hand, British trainer Ross and the team's medic, Tony, often popped up at social events with their respective other halves in tow. They'd both worked for Skyline about the same length of time she had so it wasn't a question of seniority.

And, she supposed, when she worked for Hector there were times she couldn't wait for his rude dismissal so she could get as far away from him as possible.

"Eva!" Olivia—looking picture-perfect in a black cocktail dress, with her hair in a chignon—gestured her over from across the room. That settled her dilemma, at least for the next few minutes.

"I didn't see you come in," Olivia said too brightly, rising to meet Eva a few feet ahead of the table. Eva didn't know the two women seated behind her. The third was Brian's girlfriend.

"I hate this wives-and-girlfriends crap," the medical student muttered for Eva's ears only. "I need to speak to someone with a brain before I kill myself."

"Sorry, I didn't even realize you'd made the trip out here or I would've tried to rescue you sooner."

"I have cousins in Tucson so I thought I'd tag along. Now I remember why I avoid long trips for away games."

"I can't remember Brian's girlfriend's name," Eva confided. "And who are those other two?"

"A couple of randoms some of the second-team players picked up in the club. I'm keeping an eye on them to make sure they aren't working for one of the newspapers or gossip sites." Her smile returned as she led Eva to the table and raised the volume of her voice. "And of course you already know Leah, Brian's girlfriend."

"Of course," Eva echoed, taking a seat.

"Where's Rio?" Leah asked.

"Over there, with Nico." Eva nodded toward the two midfielders.

"Is he single?" Blond Random peered over Eva's head.

Olivia shot her a sharp glance, but she knew better than to give a straight answer. "I'm not sure, we haven't discussed it. You could ask him, I suppose. Do you speak Spanish?"

"I speak French," Brunette Random offered. Eva lifted one shoulder in an oh-well gesture.

"Cool." Olivia turned decisively toward Eva. "Deon and I have to get you and Rio around for dinner one of these days."

"Definitely," Eva replied, assuming she meant they would invite Rio for dinner and she would be there as a necessary accessory.

"You're Rio's interpreter, right?" Blond Random clarified.

Eva nodded, and Brunette Random added, "So you basically get paid to hang out with a super-hot professional athlete all day. That is amazing."

"It has its ups and downs."

Blond Random sat up straighter. "Oh my God, I need to have your job. Maybe I'll learn Portuguese. There are a lot of Brazilian players, right?"

"It's a little more complicated than just knowing the language," Eva offered almost apologetically, trying not to sound arrogant. "You have to know a lot about the sport itself and what its technical terms are called in each language. It's also good to get a grounding in the athlete's home culture so you can help them adapt to different nuances and ways of doing things."

"Like what?" Leah asked.

Eva considered her response. "Different eating habits would be one, I guess. I learned that in Chile, lunch is the main meal of the day and people only have a small dinner after eight o'clock." She smiled. "But Rio eats constantly so that doesn't really apply."

"I guess you knew a lot about soccer before you arrived at Skyline," Olivia remarked. "I grew up with Deon so I understood the basics, but it seems like a lot of people have to learn everything from scratch."

"I've always loved soccer. I wanted to play myself until I realized I had zero coordination."

Brunette Random tilted her head thoughtfully. "I like soccer players more than I like soccer, I think. But I like both more than I like football."

Olivia widened her eyes at Eva over the rim of her wineglass. It should've been conspiratorial, but it made Eva uncomfortable. She and Olivia weren't equals, not really. Olivia was the star striker's fiancée, for all intents and purposes the queen of the Skyline hive. Eva was just a humble worker bee, buzzing a busy orbit around Hector or Rio or whoever needed her next.

She looked at the tequila left in her glass and made a long-overdue decision to leave. She was out of place here, useless and inappropriate without Rio, like the spare part for her old vacuum she found two days after selling it online.

One last sip. She pushed aside her maudlin mood as she finished off the tequila. She loved her job, and she was lucky to have it, and she had no excuse not to be content. She'd go back to the hotel, read a book and be refreshed for tomorrow's early-morning flight back to Atlanta. Meanwhile

Rio would get the space he needed to develop his friendships, and hopefully pick up a bit of motivation to work harder on his English and loosen his reliance on her.

"I think I'm going to call it a night." She placed her glass decisively on the table and stood up. "It was a pleasure meeting—"

"*¿Adónde vas?*" Rio appeared behind her, his timing uncanny.

"I'm tired," she lied. "I was going to head out. Unless you need me?"

"I don't need you to stay, but I would like you to."

That begging-puppy look of his had to be practiced. No human face could inadvertently be so endearing.

"I'm exhausted."

"Can I walk you out?"

"Sure." She waved goodbye to the four women, hyperaware of the two randoms' watchful gazes as she followed Rio out of the private room.

She was hit with a wave of music as soon as they stepped into the main part of the club, where the dance floor was even busier than when they arrived. She had a pang of envy, wishing she could be so carefree and full of joy, losing herself in a salsa beat on a Saturday night.

Maybe she'd go wild back at the hotel and order an Irish coffee and an ice-cream sundae from room service. She could really live on the edge and charge it on expenses.

Rio leaned in and spoke to her, but she couldn't hear him over the music. She gestured for him to repeat himself, and he slipped his arm around her waist and brought his lips close to her ear.

"You're not leaving until you dance with me."

She shot him an incredulous look, shaking her head. "I've never danced to salsa before, I wouldn't know where to begin."

"It's easy." He slipped his hand into hers and tugged her toward the dance floor. "Follow my lead."

"Rio, I literally have no idea how to—" But her words were lost in the music and his smile and her resistance died a well-deserved death. She let him pull her onto the dance floor, let him raise her arms and angle them so they made the right frame, and then she let him guide her into the sensual rhythm of the song.

"I don't know what to do with my feet," she called. "Do I try to step where you're—"

He shook his head to silence her, and within seconds she realized just how well his nimble-footed certainty on the pitch translated to dance. She'd heard that salsa was all about leading and following, but she had no idea how easy being led could be. He pivoted her, turned her, spun her and dipped her, until she lost all self-consciousness about her movements and gave herself over to the experience.

The tequila burned low in her belly and she matched Rio's grin, relaxing into his grip and adding her own embellishments to his patterns. He nodded encouragingly and soon she forgot all about her job, her mother, the money she owed the private investigator, the end of her vehicle service plan, all of it. There was only the music, and the movement, and Rio's hands, strong and safe and steady. Each press of his fingers told her he knew how to hold a woman, and a hot, sinful shiver shimmied from her shoulders to her toes.

She noticed one of the other dancers raising her arms and crossing her wrists and copied her. Rio gripped her waist and pulled her close, and when she lowered her arms again her fingertips almost touched behind his neck.

Their thighs bumped and their hips met and their proximity made dancing much harder and far better. Serious intention replaced Rio's boyish grin as all traces of humor disappeared from his eyes, leaving only hunger behind.

She knew she should pull away, jerk out of his grasp, and make the exit she'd decided on fifteen minutes earlier. She should laugh off this brief interlude on the dance floor, take a taxi back to the hotel, and flip through the channels until she fell asleep. She should ensure this brief lapse of judgment had no consequences, because she had walked away in the nick of time.

But he smelled so good, salty sea air and tea tree oil. His body was so warm, so hard, his arms like steel cables beneath her hands. She slid her fingers up the back of his neck, into his close-cropped hair, thick and short and soft. He tightened his arm across her lower back and she felt his arousal, saw the way his eyes changed when she pressed against it, sensed the force of his self-restraint as he gave her plenty of time to stop him, to move away, to say no.

Instead she met his gaze, telling him yes.

The music swelled. The dancers surged and spun around them, a sea of color and motion. Rio stilled, raising one hand to her cheek.

He kissed her.

* * * *

The ringing in Rio's ears drowned out the thumping salsa beat, and his pounding heart competed with its vibrations pulsing under his feet. His awareness shrunk to the space around the five-foot-one woman beneath his hands and little else, until what shreds of consciousness flared in his brain consisted only of her scent, the soft tendrils of her hair sliding over his hand, the taste of tequila warming her mouth.

Damn, she felt so right. Her body fit snugly against his, every dip and curve lined up perfectly. He pulled her closer and she pressed into him, her nipples hard points in the softness of her breasts. He dared the hand on her waist lower, tracing the swell of her hip, following the delicious line of her backside.

He suppressed a shudder as he toured the contours of her figure. Full breasts, softly rounded stomach, and a rear end that could fill both his palms. He wanted to see her skin, discover whether her nipples were the same lush, dusky pink as her lips, trace the valley of her lower back with his tongue. He hardened with each thought, knew she could feel his arousal against her abdomen, and hoped he excited her as much as she excited him.

As if in answer to his quandary she parted her lips and widened her jaw, granting him access. He responded almost too eagerly, holding himself back after the initial thrust of his tongue, forcing himself to slow his movement and follow her cues.

Slow down, he cautioned himself. Don't rush. She felt too right to hurry, tasted too good—tequila and high hopes and sweet, seductive temptation.

He hadn't struggled with his self-control this badly since he was an awkward teenager with a bad haircut and crooked teeth. His confidence had grown with his fame, and now it should be at its peak—so why this sudden reversion to his jittery adolescent self?

Because Eva intimidated him, that's why, and it had been at least ten years since any woman had.

He'd dated women who were smart. He'd dated women who were beautiful. He'd dated women who didn't fall for him right away, whose interest he had to work for. He'd dated women who were all of the above. None of them made his hands shake and his heart race like Eva.

He broke the kiss in an attempt to steady himself, to draw some air, calm his nerves and start over. He smiled at her, trying to communicate the charm and self-assurance he was working to pull together, enjoying the way her lids rolled open sleepily above her pouted lips.

Then one of the other dancers bumped into her, and ice-cold clarity shone in her wide eyes.

"Oh my God." She jerked away from him, frantically glancing around. "What if someone saw us?"

Well, that didn't help his ego. "What if they did?"

"Olivia was worried that these two girls were… We have to go."

She turned to leave but he caught her hand and pulled her back. "Eva, it's okay. We're two single adults. We didn't do anything wrong."

"Let's go," she reiterated through clenched teeth, snatching her hand out of his so she could use it to grab his shirtsleeve and tug him toward the exit.

"You're overreacting," he called, but his words were lost in the music as he allowed her to drag him out of the club.

Paparazzi cameras started flashing the instant they hit the doorway—clearly word of the team's night out had made it to the local press. He was unfazed, and took a moment to stand still and pose for their pictures, having learned that the best way to deal with the press was to give them what they want and keep them from wanting more.

By the time the paps had shot their fill and were checking the digital screens on the cameras to see what they'd gotten, Eva was gesturing impatiently for him to join her in the taxi parked against the curb. He slid into the backseat beside her and shut the door.

She slapped her hands over her eyes and leaned back as the car pulled into traffic. "I cannot believe we did that. I am older than old enough to know better."

"It's really not a big deal," he muttered, feeling more bruised with every word out of her mouth.

"Easy for you to say," she replied bitterly. "No one's going to fire you for—"

"Hey," the taxi driver interrupted in Spanish, glancing at them in the rearview mirror. "Aren't you Rio Vidal?"

He and Eva exchanged knowing glances, and after a few pleasantries with the driver they fell into careful silence.

Rio stared out the window, but instead of the cityscape he saw Eva sitting with Olivia and Leah in the back room, how seamlessly she seemed to fit in with them. No one would've guessed she wasn't a player's girlfriend—she was certainly pretty enough, and had all the poise and charm of the stereotypical soccer spouse.

When he encouraged her to join the conversation with the other women he'd been trying to give her a break, to show that he wasn't totally dependent on her and give her a chance to be a real part of the social side of life at Skyline, not just his paid hanger-on.

At first he was disappointed that she wanted to leave, wondering if his plan had backfired, but then she'd joined him on the dance floor and, oh, God, had he seen a new side to this already complex woman.

What she lacked in instruction she made up for in unbelievably sexy instinct. Eva always seemed so cautious, so considered, and he always had the sense that she was only saying about ten percent of what she was thinking. But every one of her barriers disintegrated as she danced with

Rebecca Crowley

him. She moved, reacted, became totally unencumbered, and it was one of the most erotic experiences of his life.

He looked at her across the space between them. She stared out the window, brow furrowed. He wanted to hold her hand. He wanted to tell her she could trust him.

"You said it was a mistake," he ventured, aware of the driver's listening ears. "Did you mean that personally or professionally?"

She frowned at him, shaking her head to show she didn't understand.

He cleared his throat. "Is it your job, or is it me?"

"Rio," she murmured, her eyes softening. "It's not you. If circumstances were different... You know what I mean."

"That makes it worse." He managed a tight smile.

"I know. I'm sorry."

He exhaled, glanced through the windscreen at a long line of red stoplights, then turned back to her. "Is it actually in your contract? That you can't?"

"Not in writing, no. But ethically..." She shrugged.

"Because Nico was telling me that Roland met his wife when she was in the marketing department at—"

"I know. But that's different."

"How?"

"It just is."

"How?" he repeated.

"Because that's them and this is us."

"Don't speak in riddles."

She nodded toward the driver.

He rolled his eyes. "Not good enough."

"What do you want me to tell you?"

"The real reason."

She stared at him, a series of fleeting, ambiguous emotions shaping her features.

He held her gaze, waiting for an answer.

"Here we are," the driver announced, pulling into the hotel's semi-circular driveway.

She said nothing as Rio paid the fare and posed for a selfie with the driver. They crossed the lobby in silence that followed them into the elevator. Eva offered no opinion when he didn't press the number for his floor and got off with her, walking beside her as she crossed the quiet, carpeted hallway to her room.

"This is me," she told him finally, stopping in front of a door. She crossed her arms, which he took as an unsurprising signal that he wasn't invited inside.

"You haven't answered my question."

"Which is?"

"Why you keep running from what's happening between us."

She raised her chin defiantly. "I'm not running."

"You are. You're hiding behind your job when you know it isn't the problem."

"Not everyone is a million-dollar athlete, Rio. For some of us, work is the difference between eating and—"

He silenced her with a finger on her lips. "Believe me, I know. I also know that as long as my performance on the pitch doesn't decline, Roland doesn't give a shit who I sleep with. If anything, being with me makes you indispensable."

She blinked. Had that genuinely not occurred to her, or was she surprised he'd put it together?

"Tell me why." He smoothed his thumb over her lips, moved his hand to cradle her hip.

Her gaze lingered on his mouth before rising to meet his eyes. In the quiet hallway he could hear her short, sharp breaths. He pressed closer, hardening as the rapid rise and fall of her breasts brushed his chest.

He leaned in, bringing his lips to her temple. "Remember we talked about the *cueca*?"

"The dance?" Her voice was husky, like the words were rushing out of her throat.

"Did I tell you want kind of dance it is?"

She shook her head.

He closed his eyes, breathing in the scent of her hair.

"It's a courting dance. And I know every step."

Her hands flew to his arms, just above his elbows, and she squeezed his biceps as she pressed her face into his sternum. He felt her eyelashes fluttering against the skin at the base of his throat and he raised his hand to cup her cheek but just as quickly as she grabbed him she let go.

"Goodnight, Rio," she told him firmly, spinning out of his grip and shoving the magnetic card into the lock.

The door slammed in his face.

"Goodnight, Eva," he told the indifferent wood. Then he headed back to the elevator, more confused—and more besotted—than ever.

Chapter 9

"I have bad news and worse news." Eva dumped the laundry basket full of soccer balls beside Rio's already massive pile. "One of the publicity assistants found these in the storeroom. They all need to be signed as well."

He capped the black marker pen and shook out his right hand. "What's the worse news?"

"There are two more baskets after this one."

Rio groaned as he shifted his position on the floor, tugging the basket of unsigned balls to his left side, with the heap of signed ones on his right.

She took a seat on the floor beside him and looked around the gym, where the members of Skyline's first team had developed a circuit-style solution to signing fifty soccer balls for tomorrow's event. Each player signed a pile of balls until they were done, then moved on to the pile their teammate had just finished.

It seemed like a sensible approach, but then it turned out someone on the events team had accidentally confirmed almost three times as many kids for the Junior Skyline rally. Accusations were hurled, additional balls were purchased, and at eight o'clock on a Thursday night the eleven players were only halfway through their signing frenzy.

"Someone's going to get fired over this," she murmured to Rio, noting the players' scowls and the terse conversations happening in the hallway outside.

"These things happen," he replied distractedly. His genial dismissal belied the dark shadows beneath his eyes. He was exhausted, and it showed in every line of his body.

She pulled up her knees and propped her chin on her hand. She was worried about him. He hadn't been himself since they got back from

Tucson on Sunday, and she knew it was at least partially her fault. What she didn't know was how to fix it.

They hadn't talked about what happened on Saturday night. They hadn't talked about much of anything, in fact. Despite Roland's admonitions Rio trained harder than ever, swearing her to secrecy about the early-morning runs around Buckhead and late-night sessions in his home gym. She wanted to chide him, but felt she'd lost that privilege after her behavior in Tucson.

She'd lost everything, actually.

The change in Rio was undeniable even though it had only been a few days. He was as polite and affable as ever, but his withdrawal from her was palpable. He was slow to smile, quick to look away. He answered her small-talk questions but didn't ask any in return. And when their gazes met she saw only distance and detachment—none of the simmering hunger she'd grown used to catching in his brown eyes.

He was such a good, sincere man, and she'd wounded him. Pulled him in and then pushed him away, like the worst kind of manipulator.

Except manipulators knew what they were doing, she thought gloomily, whereas she'd gone from confident and in-control to not knowing how she'd feel from one hour to the next.

"Can you believe it?" Laurent called out, stretching his arms over his head. "Over a hundred balls and they couldn't find any bigger than mine."

The tension in the room eased as the players chuckled at Laurent's joke.

"I'm handling so many balls, it's like a day in the life of Laurent's mom," Nico countered, and the laughter grew louder.

Eva watched Rio smile softly, glancing between his teammates, aware they were joking with each other but unable to join in.

Her heart clenched. She hated to see his isolation.

"Why don't you try to put some of your English lessons to use?" she suggested gently. "Ask the guys what they did last night, and you can tell them about the movie you watched, the one you mentioned this morning."

He wrinkled his nose, not looking up from the ball in his lap. "Maybe another time."

She linked her hands in front of her shins and leaned back, studying him as he took a ball from the pile to his left, scrawled three letters on it, and placed it in the pile on his right.

What was it about him that pulled and pushed her simultaneously, that made her lose her mind and become one of those mixed-signal-senders she swore she'd never be?

Yes, he was super hot and exactly her type, aesthetically. He was also kind and funny. But so were a lot of men.

He was rich? No, that didn't interest her.

He stretched his legs in front of him. She looked at the black Converse on his million-dollar feet and sighed.

The truth was all these whys didn't matter. Maybe her rebuff had wounded him this week, but soon he'd be fine. He was twenty-six, freshly signed to an international contract, excelling on the pitch, and sexy as hell. His English would improve, he'd get to know the Atlanta nightlife, and within a couple of months he'd forget all about his brief, misguided interest in his interpreter.

But her? She wouldn't recover so quickly or completely. At thirty her priorities were different. After so many years running from permanency and commitment, she was ready to embrace them. She still wanted stability. She wanted marriage and family. There'd been a time when she would've happily slept with him and not expected anything more, but those days were gone. Even more attractive to her than an expensive car and aged tequila were predictability, reliability, the freedom to be fully herself without worrying he would leave once he saw her ugly qualities as clearly as her good ones.

In a way she guessed she owed Rio her thanks. She hadn't been sure she could stick to her love-life resolution until he came along. The odd one-night stand or friends-with-benefits scenario might've been tempting enough to test her willpower with anyone else, but the intensity of her attraction to him had prompted her to examine what she really needed, and commit to holding out for the long-term relationship she wanted.

Too bad he wasn't the right one to seek that with, but at least she had clarity.

Anyway, she decided as he added another signed ball to the pile, even if she only wanted sex, it wouldn't be right to take advantage of his loneliness and inability to communicate. On the contrary, she should be helping him integrate. She'd definitely been letting him down on that front, and that was an issue she had to rectify sooner rather than later.

He glanced at her over his shoulder, giving her the barest glimpse of a smile before plucking another ball from the laundry basket.

Pushing him to speak English would definitely help, she concluded. The less he depended on her, the greater the distance between them would get. And then it wouldn't hurt so much when they inevitably split apart.

"Game, set, match, Laurent Perrin!"

Laurent raised his ping-pong paddle in triumph while Rio spread his palms in defeat. Eva joined the applause of a hundred and fifty children as Laurent and Rio returned to their seats on the stage.

Although all of the players had grumbled as they'd finally finished signing balls at nine o'clock the previous evening, they were on good form at that morning's Junior Skyline event. The children had been bused to the indoor arena where Skyline trained from all over the state, and the faces filling the stands were rapt with delight. A small platform had been set up in the center of the pitch, facing the kids. Rio's seat was on one end and Eva smiled at him from her chair beside the platform as he returned to take his place.

"There goes your second career as a ping-pong pro," she joked. He showed her the same subdued smile he'd shown her all week.

She brushed off the pang of disappointment his politeness inspired and refocused her attention on the proceedings. They'd had a kicking demonstration, a keep-up competition, and a silly ping-pong tournament. Now they'd have a question and answer session, and then the players would be dismissed while the kids had lunch and collected their merchandise.

One of the assistant publicists was emceeing the event, and he stepped out into the center of the platform to take questions.

Inevitably the first few were for Deon, and every few minutes Rio glanced over at her for a translation. She gave him quick summaries of the discussion, just enough to keep him in the flow without relaying every sentence.

After Deon finished there were some questions for the goalkeeper, whose role on the pitch was evidently very interesting to eight- and nine-year-olds, and then a few questions for Kojo Agassa, the Togolese right-back.

"And how about you in the third row, boy in the green shirt." The emcee gestured for the kid to stand up.

Someone passed him the microphone and the boy said, "This question is for Rio Vidal. Rio, was it exciting to win the South American Cup?"

Recognizing his name, Rio looked to her for help. She explained the question, Rio gave her an answer, and she turned to the young fan.

"He says it was one of the best moments of his life. He loves playing for Chile and was proud to win for his country."

The kid sat down, satisfied, and the emcee indicated a girl two rows behind him.

She stood up. "What do you miss most about living in Chile?"

Again Eva translated, and again he gave her the reply. "He most misses the ocean, because he grew up right on the coast. But he's heard there are a few beaches not too far from here, which he intends to check out when the weather gets warmer."

"Thank you," the girl whispered into the microphone, eyes like dinner plates.

"Okay, who's next? How about you, blue shirt in the sixth row."

A boy, younger than most of the other children, stood as the emcee identified him and gingerly accepted the microphone.

"Hi, Rio," he began, voice trembling. "I just have one question. What do you like about America so far?"

Rio turned to her, and she decided she wasn't going to speak for him on this question. He'd been at Skyline going on six weeks—it was time he found his voice.

"He wants to know what you like about America thus far."

"Lots of things. I've always wanted to live—"

She shook her head. "You tell him."

He frowned, incredulous. "I can't."

"You can. We practiced exactly this kind of conversation on Tuesday. Answer him in English."

He glanced at the audience, then back at her. "Next time. I haven't prepared what I want to say, and I—"

"Answer him in English," she repeated more firmly. "I know you can do it."

The kids were watching them intently, perhaps wondering why it was taking so long for Rio to answer the question. He straightened on his chair, visibly gathering himself as he considered his reply.

"America is… very good. I like, uh, these movies…and…the Bon Jovi."

For several seconds the entire arena was silent, processing that Rio had just spoken in reasonably coherent—if heavily accented—English.

Then the kids burst into unanimous applause, shouting "Go, Rio!" in encouragement.

Rio ducked his head and smiled, but Eva could see he was more embarrassed than triumphant. Instantly she regretted putting him on the spot, and as the emcee moved on to a series of questions for Nico her stomach churned with regret.

What on earth was she thinking? She hated that she'd pushed him, hated that he'd let her, hated that all anyone heard was his thick accent and comical pronunciation and none of them had any idea how charming and clever he truly was.

She reached across the short space between them and brushed her fingers over his hand where it rested on his thigh.

He glanced at her, his fleeting smile barely a shadow of that back-teeth grin she'd grown used to.

She pulled in her hand and stared unseeingly at the audience.

What had she done?

Within half an hour the question-and-answer session was over. The kids filed out of the stadium after a dutiful chorus of thank-you and the players wasted no time crossing the indoor pitch to the exit, each one of them eager to take advantage of their free afternoon before tomorrow's home game.

She walked alongside Rio, who said nothing as they made their way down the hallway.

"What are your plans for the afternoon?" she asked finally, slowing as they reached the lobby.

"I'll head home for lunch, then maybe come back here this afternoon and run some drills." He shrugged.

"You know you're not supposed to—" She stopped herself mid-sentence. Rio was an adult. He knew what he was and wasn't supposed to do. She would do well to remember that.

The rest of the players had filed out the door, but she lowered her voice as she spoke. "Look, I want to apologize for putting you on the spot to speak English in front of all those kids today. It wasn't fair."

He frowned. "I don't understand. You're right, I need to get more comfortable speaking English and practice is the best way to do that. What's the problem?"

"Nothing," she assured him, not wanting to knock his confidence. "You did really well. I just meant that next time we'll prepare something together, so you know what you're saying ahead of time."

"That'd be good. Then I can think of something more interesting to talk about than Bon Jovi."

His grin hinted at his cheeky self, and she returned it as broadly as she could. He held open the door for her to walk through, and as she stepped out into the spring sunshine she wondered whether she should suggest an extra English lesson that afternoon. If she could convince him they needed to prepare a statement for his post-match interview tomorrow, maybe she could occupy him long enough that he didn't have time to train on his rest day, and—

"Mr. Vidal! Mr. Vidal, please!"

"Sorry about this, sir." A security guard held the woman back, but she pushed against his arm as she repeatedly called Rio's name. Behind her stood a blond boy, around seven years old, eyes round with concern.

"Please," the woman repeated, her gaze darting desperately from Eva to Rio and back again. "I promised my son he could meet Rio Vidal for his birthday, only I didn't know the tickets were so expensive. We drove all the way down from Spartanburg, and I know I should've checked the prices, but we were using our neighbor's Wi-Fi and he moved out and my phone was out of data, and then I had to leave straight after my shift to get here in time, and—"

"That's enough, ma'am." The security guard bundled her backward. "You need to leave now."

"*Espere*," Rio told the security guard, raising his palm as he turned to Eva. "What's going on?"

"She drove a long way with her son to attend today's event, but when she got here, they couldn't afford the ticket." She didn't tell him that the woman's accent was pure Appalachia, or that the kid's shoes were obviously secondhand, or that the beat-up sedan at one end of the parking lot probably didn't have airbags, probably needed new brakes, and was probably what they'd arrived in.

"Okay ma'am, time for you to go." The security guard took her by the elbow and turned her around.

"No, it's fine," Rio protested, nodding to Eva. "Tell him it's fine. I'll sign something for the kid, I don't mind."

Eva communicated Rio's decision to the security guard, who hesitated, then reluctantly let the woman go. He took a few steps backward but hovered around the arena entrance, keeping a watchful eye on the situation.

The woman was so grateful she was on the verge of tears. She grabbed her son by his bony shoulders and thrust him toward Rio, the words gushing from her mouth so quickly Eva could barely catch them all, so she knew Rio must have no clue.

"Oh my God, thank you so much, you have no idea how much this means to us. He watches you every week, he even pretends to be you when he plays soccer with his friends, on account of he's not the tallest— no offense—but he tries super hard. When I heard you were doing this event for the kids, and it was on his birthday, well, we just had to come down." She smiled nervously. "Anyway, our neighbors are Puerto Rican and they taught him a little Spanish to say to you. Go on, Jackson, show him what you learned."

The little boy looked up at his idol and said, barely above a whisper, "*Hola. ¿Cómo estás?*"

Rio's grin could've lit up a cloudy day as he knelt down to Jackson's level and shook his hand. "*Estoy bien, ¿y tu?*"

Eva suppressed a smile at Rio's rapid-fire accent, which turned the first word into "*e'toy*" and sped through the rest. No wonder Jackson's stare was wide-eyed and unblinking.

"Did you bring something for Rio to sign?" she asked Jackson's mom, who quickly rummaged through her purse to produce a red Skyline T-shirt. Eva cringed when she realized it was a knockoff, not official merchandise, but if Rio noticed—actually, of course he noticed—he said nothing.

He had a marker pen in his pocket from the event, which he used to sign the shirt, then he posed for several photos with a shell-shocked Jackson. He shook the boy's hand again and inclined his head at the mother's next round of thank-yous.

"Okay," he told her in English. "Very good."

Eva waited with Rio while Jackson and his mom walked back to their car, the boy visibly shaking as he climbed inside. They waved at the beat-up vehicle as it left the parking lot, then Eva thanked the security guard for his vigilance.

"Poor woman," Rio remarked as they walked toward their own cars, now two of the only ones left in the lot. "Why didn't she realize she didn't have tickets before she came all this way?"

"It's not that she couldn't get them, it's that when she arrived they were a lot more expensive than she expected."

"How much were the tickets?"

"I'm not sure."

He paused beside his driver-side door. "You must have some idea."

"About a hundred dollars, I think."

"For the parent and the kid?"

"Just for the kid."

He gaped, then swore under his breath. "A hundred dollars to watch me lose at ping-pong. That's insane."

"Plenty of people want to pay it. Remember all those soccer balls last night?"

"These events should be open to any kid who's interested in the game, not just the ones with rich parents. If match tickets had been that expensive when I was a kid…" He shook his head, his expression somewhere between horror and dismay. "My life would be very different."

He looked back at the arena, his expression thoughtful. "I'm going to speak to some of the publicity guys, see if we can't arrange something for kids who can't afford these big events." He smiled sheepishly. "By which I mean I'll ask you to speak to them, of course."

"Or we can squeeze in a couple extra hours of instruction this afternoon and you can ask them yourself."

He shrugged. "Maybe."

She hesitated, glancing up at the clear sky before posing her next question. She wasn't a hundred percent sure she had cause to ask it, but she wanted the answer regardless. And anyway, how much more awkward could things get between them?

"Did you really not know how expensive the tickets were?"

"No, why?"

"And that kid, you just wanted to be nice to him, I guess."

"What's your point?"

She inhaled, counted to three, exhaled. "Did you do that to impress me?"

He stared at her, his forehead creased. She gritted her teeth, wondering if she'd just made the biggest mistake of her life.

Then he burst into one of the broadest, brightest grins she'd ever seen.

"Are you saying you liked that? You were impressed?"

"No, no." She held up her palms. "I'm asking if you did it for my benefit, or if you—"

"I can't remember the last time I did anything that wasn't from my heart. I don't perform—it's not in me to be anyone but myself. But for you..." He leaned toward her, his gaze sweeping her face, his lips quirked in a charming smile. "I'd sign ten thousand autographs if you asked."

Goddammit, her traitorous heart was skipping beats again. What happened to all that self-aware resolve she'd gathered? Where was her clarity around long-term commitment and serious relationships and not falling for a Chilean soccer player whose grin lit up her world every time she saw it?

He shifted his weight. "You said something about a couple of extra hours of English lessons this afternoon?"

"I did, didn't I?" she agreed glumly. She couldn't renege on it now, plus there was the added component of restricting his time to over-train. She supposed she owed him, oblivious as he was to her inner turmoil. After all her mixed signals, the least she could do was save him from himself for a couple of hours.

"Need a lift?" He pressed the remote-start button on his keychain and the engine hummed to life beside them.

She rolled her eyes playfully. "That is ridiculous. And you're ridiculous for buying such a ridiculous car."

"Was that a yes or a no?" He jangled his keys.

"No. I'll follow you." *And spend every minute of the drive to Buckhead trying to figure out what the hell is happening to me.*

Chapter 10

"I am. You are."

"I am, you are." Rio rushed through the repetition, less than half-listening to Eva's lesson. He raised the barbell one, two, three times, blowing out hard and racking it back onto the bench press with a clatter. He swiped the back of his hand across his eyes, breathing heavily.

"He is. They are."

"He is." His vision was starting to swim but he needed seven more repetitions to complete the set. He heaved the barbell off the rack and brought it down toward his chest. "They are."

"She is. We are."

Four. Tomorrow's match was against the Memphis Bluffs and their midfielders were huge. In the footage he'd watched they looked like a bunch of refrigerators jogging up and down the center of the pitch.

Five. Weight training had never been his strong suit, but he had to bulk up if he was going to make his mark in the Championship League. Thank God Hector had built this gym in the basement. In Chile he'd lifted weights to resist dirty tackles. In America, he needed extra muscle mass just to stay on his feet.

"Rio?"

"Sorry. She are, we are."

"She *is.*"

Six. "She is, we are." There was a lot riding on tomorrow's game. There was a lot riding on every game these days. No more snoozing against bottom-of-the-league clubs, no more showboating and walking off the pitch five goals to the good. The skill level in the CSL was higher than he ever imagined.

"I was. You were."

Seven. His arms trembled with exertion. His lungs burned, his chest ached. He'd had a nagging pain in his calf since Monday and his knee hadn't felt quite right since Phoenix, but he hadn't told anyone. He didn't want to give Roland any reason to sit him out tomorrow.

Eight. Would the Bluffs play their new defender, the young guy from Ghana? They'd only just begun to pluck him from the subs' bench, but he'd made a good showing against Pittsburgh last week. Maybe they'd start him tomorrow. If they did, Skyline was in trouble. Deon was powerful up front but he was carrying all the goal-scoring expectations, and if—

"Rio," Eva snapped, slapping her papers onto the floor beside her. "You're not listening to a word I say."

Nine. "Sorry. I were?"

She huffed exasperatedly. "Not even close."

Ten. He used all his remaining strength to rack the bar, then pulled himself into a sitting position on the bench, blinking away a wave of dizziness as he grabbed a bottle of water. "Okay. I'm paying attention."

"What you're doing is wasting my time."

"I told you, I'm listening."

"You shouldn't be training anyway, and you know it," she grumbled, shuffling the papers. "If Roland knew I was sitting here watching you lift weights, I'd probably get fired."

"Then quit," he shot back, storming to his feet. He'd had it. He got plenty of aggravation from his manager, he didn't need it from her too.

Her eyes widened. "Excuse me?"

"You heard me. Quit or let him fire you, because I'm sick of you holding your job over my head and making it my responsibility."

"How do I make it your responsibility?" she demanded, scrambling up from her place on the floor.

"You know how," he muttered, snatching up his towel and heading toward the door.

She ducked in front of him, barring his exit. "No, I don't. Tell me."

"You're too smart to play dumb, Eva. Are you going to pretend you don't remember what happened on Saturday night?"

Her stare hardened, and his groin twitched unhelpfully. He'd always had a thing for fierce women, and she'd worn that extra-sexy dress for the Junior Skyline event...

Head in the game, Vidal. She rejected you, remember?

"First I can't ask you out because you'd lose your job. Now I can't train because you'll lose your job. Fuck your job," he seethed. "My job keeps us both employed, and if I don't train, we're screwed."

She blinked, and he couldn't tell whether she was shocked or hurt or both. His resolve faltered. He hardly ever lost his temper, and when he did it usually only took a couple minutes for him to feel sheepish at overreacting. His posture softened, and the apology was forming on his tongue when she crossed her arms and narrowed her eyes.

"I don't think Roland will fire you if I tell him you're training on your rest day. He'll just stick you on the bench for two weeks and give Brian his shot on the wing." She tilted her head to one side. "Shall we call him and find out?"

"You wouldn't dare," he scoffed, shoving past her and slamming into the laundry room. He tugged his shirt over his head and flung it in the washing machine, then banged through the door to the home theatre to take a shortcut to the stairs.

"Tell that to your manager. Call him right now and tell him you want someone else." She followed him into the theatre, her eyes so bright with challenge they were practically glowing despite the ambient lighting. "Oh, wait. You keep blowing off my English lessons, so you can't tell him shit."

He came to an abrupt halt in front of the screen, clenching his hands as he absorbed her words. His back was turned but he heard her stop behind him, heard her short, angry breaths.

He loosened his fists, pulling his temper under control. "That was low."

For what felt like several minutes they stood there in silence, neither one moving, neither one speaking. He stared at the plush, cream-colored carpet beneath his bare feet and wondered how everything had gone so wrong.

"I'm sorry." Her voice was soft and contrite. "You're right, that was uncalled for."

"It's okay. We're both frustrated." He turned, and his heart skipped when he caught sight of her under the dim lights. The filtered bulbs found a multitude of new shades in her dark hair, and her heavy-lidded eyes wouldn't have been out of place in a stained-glass window.

He swallowed hard as he approached her. He knew his loose gym shorts didn't conceal his burgeoning erection. He didn't care.

He brushed her hair over her shoulder. "Tell me why you don't want me."

"Rio, it's not—"

"Tell me." He stepped closer, crowding her backward.

"It's not a question of what I want. You know that."

"No, I don't."

She met the wall, flattening her palms against it.

"I'm an adult, I can handle it." He raised one hand to her waist. She put hers over it, her thumb smoothing his knuckles.

He angled his face toward her, fixating on her slightly-parted lips. "I just want to know why."

"I do want you, Rio," she murmured, tilting up her chin. "But only if you really want me, too."

He frowned. "Of course I do. Why else would I go to all this trouble?"

"Trouble?" She smiled coyly. "Who're you calling trouble?"

Her words lingered in his mind, unsettling him, but as soon as he saw that sly curve of her lips he had to act. He shoved his unease to the back of his thoughts and kissed her like he'd wanted to for days.

* * * *

Eva didn't bother fretting over the situation, worrying about her job, her promises to herself, or second-guessing Rio's motives. She was tired of thinking and analyzing and questioning everything she said or did around him. She wanted to put her brain on hold and let her libido take the reins for a while.

Not to mention the last hour spent watching him lift weights had ground her self-control into dust.

She luxuriated in his kiss, cracking her jaw to let his tongue find hers, savoring the taste of salt on his lips, inhaling the scents of sweat and aftershave and unadulterated male.

She'd never been one for the pretty-boy celebrities and pop stars filling the pages of women's magazines. She liked muscles defined by purpose, men whose good looks were secondary to their abilities to run and kick and win. As she raised her hands to Rio's arms and traced the definition in his triceps her heart thudded, and air stalled in her lungs when his rock-hard thighs knocked against hers.

These legs were the quickest on the pitch, these arms chiseled to resist tackles. It had only been a minute since he first touched her but already her panties were soaked. She had a flash of embarrassment as she hoped he didn't notice—then a flash of arousal as she hoped he did.

He reduced the space between them, tightening one arm around her waist as his other hand slipped into the hair at her nape. Her nipples pressed against the unyielding plane of his chest, and she moaned inadvertently, prompting him to break the kiss and look down at her.

His smile was bemused. "Good?"

She nodded. "Very good."

He trailed his tongue along her lower lip, then resumed his exploration of her mouth. Her eyes drifted shut as she gave over to sensation, to the smooth skin of his chest, the thick hair at the back of his head, the erection threatening to rip a hole in his shorts.

He'd asked why she didn't want him and she hadn't known what to say. She'd never wanted anyone so badly, or had to fight so hard to keep herself in check in his presence. There had been times during his English lesson she'd had to literally bite her tongue to quell the urge to throw herself across the room and drag it over his six-pack.

She found those abs now, running the heel of her hand over his taut muscles. A sound of approval rumbled deep inside his chest and she slid her hand lower, following the southbound trail of hair beneath his belly button, peeking her fingertips below the elastic waistband of his shorts.

He swore in his delicious, street-roughened dialect, and then in a series of movements so quick she barely registered them he shoved her into one of the leather-upholstered cinema chairs and dragged her leg over the armrest, splaying her thighs wide.

She opened her mouth to protest, then wondered why on earth she would ever stop what was about to happen.

With visibly trembling fingers Rio flung her skirt up over her waist, yanked her sodden thong down to her knees and put his mouth between her legs.

Eva didn't have time to worry about how long it had been since her last wax, whether she'd shaved her legs thoroughly that morning, or if a month from now Rio would still be this enthusiastic about her. Her rational mind took a long-term hiatus as she closed her eyes, clutched the armrests on either side, and sank into the moment.

The man was a pro. His creativity on the pitch barely touched the sides of the rhythms and patterns he weaved with his tongue.

She abandoned all self-awareness, losing track of time, of place—at some point she wasn't even sure she was still human. She moaned and bucked and begged in two languages, but she couldn't escape the insistent ministrations of Rio's tongue, and then his lips, and then his fingers, until she thought she might sob with delight.

He moved one hand to grasp her hip, and as soon as his fingers closed around the joint she knew she was finished. The possessiveness in his grip, the certainty and self-assurance—whatever shreds remained of her consciousness dissolved. Her ears hummed, her back arched, and she fell hard beneath a crushing wave of ecstasy.

Just like when she'd been knocked down by a wave at the beach, it took some time for her to right herself. She had to find her balance on the sandy bottom, figure out which way was up, break the surface of the water and trudge back out of the ocean.

When she did Rio was lounging in the seat beside hers, grin stretching from ear to ear.

He propped his head on his hand, his elbow against the back of the seat. "Are you all right?"

"No, but I will be. Maybe. Someday. Ask me again in ten years."

"Is that a promise that I'll still know you in ten years?"

She shook her head, nowhere near stabilized enough to face that particular angle on reality. She wanted to stay in this hazy, sexy, sensation-blurred world just a bit longer before returning to the real one. She clambered onto the floor and positioned herself between his knees.

His eyes widened with excitement but he put a stalling hand on her shoulder. "Are you sure, because—"

"Hush," she instructed, yanking down his shorts and the boxers he wore beneath in one fluid motion.

Her breathing, so recently returned to something resembling normal, became tight and frantic. On the pitch surrounded by six-foot-tall giants Rio didn't look like a large man, but he was, in fact, plenty big where it mattered.

She murmured in blasphemous Spanish as she stroked his thighs, licking her lips. She rarely deemed men worthy of her much-complimented oral talents, but Rio had earned it. And, frankly, she might enjoy this more than he did.

She started at the tip, relishing the soft, uncircumcised flesh. Then she slowly worked her way down, leading with her hands, stroking him firmly while her mouth followed suit.

She closed her eyes and enjoyed the clean taste of his skin, the way his erection throbbed against her tongue, the raw, strangled moan that was doubly erotic in its contrast to his normally smooth manner.

How many women would kill to trade places with her right now? Rio was Chile's favorite son, tabloid darling, and national sex symbol. A quick Internet search pulled up hundreds of photos of him posing with model ex-girlfriends, being mobbed at airports, standing in the middle of stadiums with his hands raised in victory as ten thousand fans chanted his name.

But today he'd chosen her. He could have almost anyone, and she was the one he wanted.

She increased the pace, rewarding his decision, validating his choice. She would show him he was right, no one suited him better, out of all those screaming fans she was the best woman for him.

And all he had to do was stay.

He shifted restlessly beneath her, signaling the nearness of the end. He fidgeted and groaned and muttered filthy things in the working-class accent that never failed to turn her on. She sucked him harder, moved her hands faster, savored her power over him and pushed away the intrusive thought that they may never be this intimate again.

He jerked forward, shouting her name as he tried to push her back, but she held fast. His release spilled into her mouth and she swallowed it deftly, tenderly holding him through the aftershocks. Finally he sagged against the chair and she released him, and flopped onto her back on the floor.

She exhaled, staring at the ceiling. "Wow."

"Yeah," he agreed.

She pulled herself into a sitting position. Rio reclined languidly in the chair, a fine sheen of sweat covering his bare chest, which rose and fell rapidly with his panting breaths. His legs were splayed wide, his shorts bunched above his knees, and his still semi-erect manhood lay across one of his muscular thighs.

He was the sexiest thing she'd ever laid eyes on.

He smiled lazily. "Where were we? I am, you are, they was?"

"They were," she corrected. She tried to return his grin, but a sobering rush of reality was seeping into her bones like a cold draught on a damp winter evening. She had to look away, clearing her throat as she took stock of her disheveled appearance.

Some of the confidence drained from his face as he watched her tug her thong back into place, then rearrange her skirt over her thighs.

He yanked his shorts up over his narrow hips. "That was an unexpected turn of events. Do I owe you an apology?"

She frowned up at him, shaking her head. "Of course not. Why would you ask me that?"

"I didn't rush you into…whatever that was? I know we were still talking about—"

"You were fine," she interrupted, skirting around a flicker of anxiety as he raised their still undefined relationship. "Great, actually."

His smile held palpable relief, yet she still sensed his hesitation. He rocked forward to prop his elbows on his knees.

"I know you're a grown woman and you know what you're doing, but I just wanted to make it clear that…" He glanced down at his clasped hands, then back at her. "I don't expect anything. Now. Because of that."

"You're right. I do know what I'm doing." *Most of the time. With everyone except you.* "And I know I'm not ready to have sex with you."

He nodded vigorously. "Yes, that's what I meant, you don't have to—"

"I mean, I may not ever be ready." She drew a deep breath. The happy, sensual fog had definitely dissipated and the promise she'd made to herself throbbed heavy and insistent at the front of her mind.

Might as well get this out there.

"I can't do the casual sex thing, not anymore. I want a relationship. And unless I know you want that too, this—we—can't work."

She hadn't thought about his reaction before she said it, but now that her words hung between them, loud and irreversible, she realized how badly she wanted him to say yes.

Yes, of course I want us to have a relationship, he'd tell her with that charming smile. Didn't you realize that's what I meant all along?

Or his expression would turn serious and he'd say, yes, I'm in exactly the same place and casual sex holds no appeal for me. Let's get serious. When can you move in?

No—he'd drop to one knee. Take her hand in his. Yes, Eva, I want to be with you, and only you. Will you marry me?

Instead he said nothing, and stared at the carpet between his feet.

She examined her thumbnail, her hope depleting with each passing second. The usually-dominant realist in her figured he would balk, but her oft-silenced inner optimist had been in charge for the last hour, and had filled her brain with the belief that an encounter that hot couldn't be possible without a real, underlying, mutual connection.

As Rio's silence stretched on, she felt like smothering her inner optimist with a pillow and dumping her into a river.

When he finally looked up at her his smile was apologetic. Her heart sank faster than a lead weight.

"My head's all over the place today, with the event this morning, the match tomorrow, not to mention…" He gestured between the two of them. "Let me think about it, okay?"

"Of course," she insisted way too cheerfully. "I didn't mean to give you an ultimatum or anything. I just wanted you to know where I am."

"I appreciate that. I'm not saying I'm not—I mean, you know I wanted us to—I just need time."

"Totally get it," she replied brightly, even though she totally didn't. He'd pursued her to this point and now he was backing off? Maybe it really was all a front for getting her into bed.

Or onto the cinema-room chair, she thought grimly.

He stood and so did she, their movements stiffened by that special kind of awkwardness shared by people who've gone too far, too fast.

He cleared his throat. "Thank you for...I mean...This was..."

"I'll see you tomorrow," she interjected, her cheeks burning.

"Right. Tomorrow."

He started toward the door but she beat him to it. "I'll let myself out. Try to get some rest."

"I will. *Chau,* Eva."

"*Hasta mañana.*"

She bolted out of the room, up the steps, across the high-ceilinged atrium and through the front door. Only once she was safely behind the wheel of her car and pulling out of the driveway did she release the breath she'd held since she turned her back on him.

Chapter 11

"Rio, bzzzbzzz—"

As he crossed into the dressing room Rio held up a hand to silence Roland, Eva, and anyone else who wanted to talk to him during halftime. Without acknowledging any of his teammates he walked directly to his locker, tugging off his shirt as he went. Then he plugged his headphones into his phone and took his grandmother's rosary off the hook where it hung.

Headphones on, he sat down in the corner of the dressing room and rested his head against the angle where the two walls met. He scrolled to a song and pressed play, closed his eyes, and rolled the worn beads between his fingers.

The first half against the Bluffs had been the worst forty-five minutes of his career at Skyline. He was a mess, missing opportunities, losing possession, constantly finding himself in the wrong place at the wrong time. At one point Deon had jogged up to him and gestured to ask if he was all right or if he wanted to be subbed out.

He ran his hand over his eyes, pressing his forehead harder against the wall. His performance was so bad his captain had given him the out to excuse himself. He'd never been more humiliated in his life.

Bold action by Deon had put them up to one-one for about ten minutes, but then Paulo fell in the area and managed to handball an own goal. The Bluffs had celebrated as much as if they'd scored on their own, knowing full well this meant they could sit back and defend, forcing Skyline to attack to level the score. Rio had no doubt Memphis would sub in the big Ghanaian, and he'd be spending the next forty-five minutes trying to avoid getting trampled by the elephant herd that was the Bluffs' defense.

He knew exactly why he couldn't focus on the pitch, and the reason was just over five feet tall with dark hair and secretive eyes. Yesterday she'd rocked his world, then drop-kicked it into orbit with her revelation that their first time together would also be their last if he couldn't make a commitment.

He didn't blame her, and he valued her honesty. He'd never hesitated to get serious with women before, having no qualms about monogamy or faithfulness or whatever else seemed to be amorous hurdles for many in his profession. Anyway it's not like there was anyone else in the picture, or that he had any reservations about Eva herself. Just the opposite, in fact.

So why had he tossed and turned all night long, trying and failing to decide what to do next?

Because despite his perpetual motion on the pitch and what sports writers referred to as his feverish style, he wasn't reckless. He took risks, but they were calculated. He knew his limits and those of his teammates, and even his most outlandish shots on goal had deep method behind what looked like madness.

But Eva wasn't just a regular-season point, she was the final penalty in a World Cup shootout. He didn't have the courage to take his shot yet, and he couldn't afford to miss.

He exhaled slowly, turning up the volume on his phone.

The song he played on repeat had been a club anthem during the last World Cup. The team sang it on the bus on the way to what turned out to be their last match, and the night after they were knocked out he danced to it in a Brazilian nightclub, buoyed by his personal performance despite the team's loss.

He sank into the beat pulsing through his headphones, focusing his mind on the memory of that night. So many women had approached him, half of them taller than he was, all of them extraordinarily beautiful. He'd danced to this song with a voluptuous Colombian, but in his imagination he danced with Eva.

In his mind's eye she smiled up at him, the multicolored lights shimmering across her hair, her eyes bright with joy. They moved together in perfect harmony, their bodies fitting close, her soft curves pressed against his hard lines.

The club heaved around them, the beat was so loud it shuddered through his body, but when she leaned in to whisper in his ear he heard every word with perfect clarity.

"Go out there and win. I know you can do it."

When Rio jogged out of the tunnel with his teammates five minutes later, he put all of his mental energy toward preserving the almost meditative state he'd achieved during halftime. He saw only the ball, heard only the song repeating in his mind, felt only its thudding beat pumping through his veins.

The whistle blew and he exploded into action, mentally repeating the lyrics over and over and over so nothing else could distract him.

He snatched the ball away from Memphis within seconds of hitting the pitch and drove hard into their half. Their defenders crowded around him like bees on a flower and he passed to Nico, who promptly lost possession.

He briefly heard Laurent swear behind him before blocking him out, recovering his complete submersion in the music and the moment.

He had to wait a while for his next chance to take the ball, but when it finally came with a received pass from Guedes he knew he had to make the most of his opportunity.

He stormed into the Bluffs' half and their defenders charged toward him, and within seconds he was surrounded by three giants in black shirts. He darted left, pivoted right, bouncing back and forth in the triangle they'd created around him. He heard the song, saw the ball, and when one of the defenders pushed him squarely in the chest he pitched forward to stay upright and shot out between the other two, the ball stuck to his feet like he had duct tape on his toes.

He sprinted down the pitch, leaning to avoid a tackle on his left, then swerving to avoid another on his right. Deon was near the area, fighting with a Bluffs defender, and Rio passed to him at an angle that had the nearest Memphis player slamming his fists on his thighs in frustration.

Deon leapt above his opponent and headed the ball into the goal.

The scoreboard flicked to two-two.

Rio didn't celebrate with his teammates. He stood on the pitch, muttering the lyrics of the song under his breath as he waited for play to resume. When the ball was back in motion he watched it like his life depended on it.

The Bluffs were on the attack and there were several minutes of scrabbling in Skyline's half before the keeper caught the ball and booted it to the halfway line. Laurent and one of the Memphis midfielders jumped to head it, colliding in midair and sending it wild.

Rio watched the ball sail toward him, aware of yet totally unbothered by the defenders storming in his direction. When it got low enough he leapt for it, controlling the ball on his chest before bouncing it to his feet.

Two Bluffs defenders crowded him, forcing him to hop behind and over the ball to keep it away from their grabby boots. He purposely broadcast wrong moves, looking left while he jumped right, trying to buy a few extra feet in the direction of the goal but struggling to make much ground against his opponents.

He saw red jerseys clustered beyond the defenders, most of his teammates unmarked and eager while Memphis's players focused on him. There were six boots stabbing at his two. He knew he should pass, but he couldn't see how. They were all over him, blocking out the light, pushing the limits of the rules as they tried to knock him off his feet.

He started singing.

"*Y solo baila,*" he sang at the top of his voice, feeling the beat pulse with every thud of his heart.

One of the defenders was so bewildered he stopped short, staring at Rio with a perplexed frown.

"*Solo baila,*" he repeated, letting the rhythm pervade his body, loosening his muscles, his veins throbbing with the music in his mind. He saw Eva smiling up at him on that imagined night, swiveled his hips in time with the song, and broke free from the defenders.

The crowd roared as he tore down the pitch, running as fast as he could, his legendary speed carrying him past his black-shirted opponents.

He slowed just outside the area, checked the offside flag, met the keeper's gaze, and slammed the ball into the left corner.

The huge, brick-red flag went up behind the goal. The score was three-two, Skyline.

Rio dropped to his knees, closed his eyes and held his palms toward the sky. *Thank you, Eva. Thank you.*

* * * *

"Jesus, slow down." Eva's grip on the edge of her seat was white-knuckled as Rio gunned his sports car down the highway.

"Don't worry, I can smell a cop from five miles away." He flashed her that infectious grin and she couldn't help but return it. He'd just pulled Skyline back from the brink of defeat. He deserved to let off some steam.

Although maybe not at the cost of wrapping them around a light pole, she countered, gritting her teeth through one of his hairpin turns.

"Did the tow guy say when your car will be fixed?" he asked over the roaring engine.

Her happiness deflated as she remembered the gut-punch feeling of leaving the stadium to discover that someone had backed into the front of her car, helpfully leaving a gas-station receipt with a sad face drawing and the word "sorry." She'd been even more miserable when she discovered the impact sensors had tripped and the engine wouldn't start, but her spirits lifted decidedly when the head of stadium security told her he'd review the closed-circuit footage and do whatever it took to "nail the bastard."

"I don't think the garage will even be able to assess it until Monday. My insurance will cover a rental in the meantime."

"Good thing I was still around to give you a lift. Now you get to be chauffeured home in high-performance German luxury instead of a busted-ass taxi."

She tilted her head and fluttered her eyelashes. "My hero."

Her tone was joking, but she spoke the truth. Never mind the flustering arousal of watching him slice up the pitch, knowing in detail what lay between those swift legs, or the pride that swelled in her throat when he answered a simple, post-match interview question in halting but reasonably coherent English. Nothing compared to the relief of seeing that his car was still parked in the lot, having him answer his cell with a cheeky, "*Aló,* Eva," then rushing out to meet her with his hair still wet from the shower.

At the time she'd been grateful not to have to wait for a taxi or awkwardly beg a ride from another member of Skyline staff, but as they sped toward her condo in Brookhaven she began to wonder if she was making a mistake. After all, she'd more or less thrown down the gauntlet last night and he had yet to pick it up, or even acknowledge it.

Did he think he could switch on the charm, hoping she'd forget about her commitment caveat and offer a repeat performance?

It wouldn't be like him, but then again, this blatant avoidance of the issue wasn't the Rio she knew either.

Maybe she didn't know him at all.

He turned up the volume on the radio and sang along, reasonably on key but clearly totally unaware the lyrics were about a messy breakup.

"You know there are probably already a thousand cell-phone videos of your musical interlude on the pitch making the rounds on the Internet," she teased. "Have you ever considered a career as a recording artist?"

"Good to know I have something to fall back on if this soccer thing doesn't work out." He shifted gears and left the highway, easing onto the four-lane road that led into her neighborhood.

"This is it, on the left." She guided him into her condo complex and along the quiet streets to her front door.

He pulled into her short driveway and cut the engine.

"Thanks for the ride." She put her hand on the latch but he was already sliding out of the driver's seat. He rounded the front of the car and opened her door, tugging her up from the bucket seat.

"I should walk you inside. Check for squatters, stray cats, that sort of thing."

She propped her hand on her hip. "Is that your best line?"

He shrugged. "I'm tired."

"Smooth." She motioned him toward the door. "Come in."

He followed her through her two-bedroom townhouse as she flicked on lights, kicked off her ballet flats and led him to the sitting room with its open-plan access to the kitchen. She indicated for him to sit on the couch as she moved to the fridge.

"Can I get you something to drink? Juice, tea, coffee, tequila?"

"What're you having?"

"Wine. It's been one of those days." She pulled a half-full bottle of white from the fridge and filled a glass, glancing at him over the island counter that separated the two rooms. He sat forward at one end of the faded gray sofa, his elbows on his knees and his head on a swivel as he took in his surroundings.

She peered over the rim of her wineglass, trying to see her familiar home from his perspective. It was small, sure, but reasonably modern, built less than ten years ago. She'd decorated in neutral gray and lilac, and watched enough home décor shows on TV to be deliberate in her color and layout choices. The furniture was comfortable, the bookshelf overflowed, and every Friday she treated herself to a bouquet of fresh flowers, plunked in the center of her coffee table.

She hoped he liked it. If not, she concluded with a sip, too bad for him.

He stood up and crossed the room, picking up a framed photograph from the mantel. "Is this your mom?"

"Yup. Sure you don't want something to drink?"

"How old were you here?"

"Seven." She circled the island and flopped onto the couch.

"I'm pretty sure my mom had this exact same haircut at one point. Must've been a Nineties thing." He replaced the photo, taking care to angle it exactly as she'd had it.

He sat sideways on the couch beside her, his arm flung over the back. "Where was that taken?"

"At the hotel restaurant where Juana worked. It was my birthday. All of the kitchen staff were Mexican and they made a big fuss over me, baking me a cake and singing *Las Mañanitas*. Do you sing that in Chile?"

He shook his head. "What is that?"

"A silly song you're supposed to sing on the morning of someone's birthday."

One side of his mouth quirked in a smile. "My mom bakes pineapple cake for our birthdays. One year she dropped mine on the way to the table, but we all pretended not to notice and ate it anyway."

"That was nice of you."

He shrugged. "It's really good cake, even when it's been on the floor. Have you had any news from the private investigator?"

"Just more invoices."

"Is he expensive?"

She took a stalling sip from her wineglass, wishing she hadn't gone there. "I can afford it, but it's annoying to keep paying him for zero results."

He stretched his left leg in front of him, careful to keep his shoe off the couch, and idly rubbed his knuckles into his thigh. "How did it get to the point that you had to hire a private investigator? It sounds like your mom really went off the grid."

"I know, who would've thought that in the Internet age it could be this difficult to find someone? But it is, apparently."

She put her wineglass on the coffee table and leaned into the cushions. "I think I told you, when I was younger she used to write to Juana. E-mail was just becoming a thing then but my mom wasn't in a position to have a computer, let alone know how to work one, so all of her correspondence was handwritten. She moved around a lot, trying to earn money and find places to stay, so there was a new return address with almost every letter. She wrote regularly, once or twice a month, until suddenly the letters stopped. We kept sending things to the last address she'd given us, but never got a reply. Then we moved, and sent our new address to the last one we had for her, but who knows if she ever got it."

"And you couldn't call her?"

She shook her head. "We only spoke on the phone a few times a year, and then the calling card usually ran out after ten minutes or so. These were the days before cell phones and every time she moved she changed numbers. Sometimes she was in a boarding house so shared a phone, sometimes she gave us a number for somewhere she worked. It was all pretty chaotic, and hard to know who would answer when you called."

He studied her for a few seconds, his face dark with concern. "What do you think happened to her?"

"The million-dollar question." She smiled bitterly, flopping back against the couch and tilting her face toward the ceiling. "To be honest, I have no idea. Whatever it was, it can't have been good."

"Was she the type to…" He paused, clearly choosing his words carefully. "Get into trouble?"

"Maybe." She exhaled. "Of course when I was young I didn't want to believe that, but who really knows? I'm fairly confident she was on the straight and narrow when she was raising me, but maybe there were demons in her past, or maybe her later circumstances forced her into bad situations. The fact is that I was twelve when my mother disappeared, and I don't know what kind of woman she was before I was born, or what kind of woman she became after she went back to Mexico. But I'll do whatever is necessary to find out."

Her statement hung between them for a few moments, heavy and sad.

"I hope you find her," Rio said finally.

"Thanks. I do too."

"Can I tell you a secret?"

She nodded.

"My dad wasn't my dad."

Her eyes widened. "Really."

"My siblings are his, but my biological father is someone else. A dock worker, my grandmother thinks. She didn't know for sure. My mom admitted it to her after I was born."

"Your grandmother told you this?"

He nodded.

"When?"

"A few days before she died. I was ten."

She whistled. "That is serious baggage to lay on a kid that age."

"She hated my dad—the guy I thought was my dad. I think she wanted to help me, to free me, in a way. She didn't want me to end up like him."

"A miner?"

"An alcoholic." He smiled tightly. "Another secret you'll never see in the rags-to-riches, full-color sports-page version of my background."

"Wow, Rio." She shook her head at the weight of it all. "Was your grandmother right? Did it help to know you were different from him?"

"Maybe a little." He shrugged. "Mostly it felt like justification for why my brother and sister are so smart and successful and I kick a ball for a living."

She held up a palm. "Hold on. You can't seriously tell me that you feel inadequate. You're, like, a national hero."

"For now. Soccer fans have short memories."

"And you'll have a bulging bank account either way, so who cares?"

"I think I should've taken you up on that tequila."

She ignored his weak attempt to change the subject, and he continued with a sigh. "I've never talked about it with my mom, and she's never raised it with me either. I get the sense it was hugely shameful for her, and that it's a secret she'd like to take to her grave. So I feel like I owe it to her to be the best at whatever I can be, to prove that although she might be ashamed of what she did, she doesn't have to be ashamed of who I am."

"Rio," she said softly, simultaneously astonished and not at all surprised that he was so hard on himself.

She sat up, retrieved her wineglass, and raised it in a toast.

"To families, their secrets, and their imperfections."

He leaned forward and tapped her glass with his index finger. "To not making our parents' mistakes."

"I'll drink to that." She swallowed a mouthful before replacing the glass on the table. "Here's the real question. Why are you telling me all of this?"

"I trust you."

She waited, and after a few seconds he continued, "I want you to know me."

She held his gaze, keeping her expression neutral despite the increasing pace of her heartbeat. "I want to know you, too."

He smiled. "I hope you like what you find."

"I already do."

He leaned forward and gripped her legs, tugging until she unfolded them, and then he pulled her feet into his lap. Strong fingers massaged her ankles, slipping under the hems of her tight jeans.

"I thought about what you said on Thursday," he murmured, rubbing his thumbs along her Achilles tendons. "Maybe I shouldn't have needed to think about it, but I did."

"That's fair," she assured him quietly, although at the time it certainly hadn't felt that way.

"I guess I wanted to be sure. Not how I felt about you—I think I've made my interest clear from the beginning." He cracked a half-smile. "I wanted to be sure I was good enough for you. Tonight I convinced myself."

She stared at him, wide-eyed and unblinking, incredulity tangling with astonishment as she processed what he'd just told her. "Why wouldn't you be good enough for me?"

He lifted a shoulder, avoiding her gaze. "You know I've been struggling on the pitch, not quite finding my rhythm with my teammates, and it doesn't help that I can't communicate with them, and—"

She pressed a silencing finger to his lips. "I'm not interested in your assist stats or your attempts on goal. I'll show you what interests me."

She replaced her finger with her mouth, bending forward over her knees. One of his hands rose to her jaw while the other found her waist, dragging her onto his lap.

His kiss was different from Thursday. Still hot, still hungry, yet warmer. Slower. Like he knew she wasn't going anywhere and there was no need to rush.

His lips were soft, his tongue gently curious. She inhaled sharply, filling her senses with tea tree oil and saltwater as she raked her fingers through his hair.

She could've kissed him all night, yet when he pulled back she wasn't disappointed. She knew as well as he did that this wouldn't be the night they took the next step. She didn't mind—they had plenty of time.

"You have to go," she acknowledged quietly.

He nodded. "I need to sleep. And I want to do this properly, take you out somewhere, go on a real date."

"I'd like that."

They shared a smile, and then she slid off his thighs and he stood up. They walked toward the door in silence, and as they passed into the entryway he took her hand. She squeezed, then opened the door.

"Will I see you at Mass tomorrow?" she asked.

"I guess you'll need a lift."

"I will."

"I'll be here at nine-thirty."

He leaned down and brushed a kiss over her lips, tracing his forefinger along her cheek. Then he crossed the threshold and she shut the door. She pressed her hands over her heart, listening to the engine of his car start, rev, and then recede as he drove away.

She raised her palms to cover her face. She could still smell him on her skin, her clothes, her hair.

Quickly, before the feeling dissipated, she jogged up the stairs to her bedroom and pulled a notebook out of the bottom drawer of her dresser. She sat cross-legged on the floor and opened it, suppressing a pang of sadness when she noted the date of the most recent entry.

Eight months ago.

She pulled the pen out of the spiral binding, wrote the date in the top-right corner, and began to write.

Hi Mom,

It's been a while since I've written to you in this notebook—I guess there was nothing I thought you needed to know.

Tonight there's something I want to share with you.

I've been working as a translator for a new Skyline player. His name is Rio Vidal. He's handsome, and kind, and I think you would like him a lot…

Chapter 12

"Are you sure you don't want to come in?"

She did, but she shook her head. "You need to rest."

She'd repeated those four words time and time again, but she meant it now more than ever. He looked exhausted. On top of the hours of travel to and from Oregon for the midweek match against the Eugene Pines, during the second half of the goalless game he'd taken a late tackle and twisted his knee as he fell. He sprang back up, but by the time the whistle blew he was visibly limping.

He insisted he was fine, but at breakfast that morning he'd confided to Eva that he'd struggled to sleep after the game. He muttered something about the hotel bed and the thermostat, but she suspected pain had kept him awake.

They sat together on the plane and he slept through the entire five-hour flight, slumped against the window. She longed to adjust his pillow or run a soothing hand over his thigh, but she couldn't. It had only been a few days since their agreement to turn their attraction into a relationship, and between her commitments at the church and his training schedule they'd barely had a moment alone.

Which is why, as he smiled at her from the passenger seat of her rented car, it was so hard to turn down his offer to come inside.

"Call me if you change your mind."

He leaned over and kissed her, a lingering press of his lips that had fireworks exploding behind her eyes. She pulled back before she lost her nerve.

"Go to bed," she instructed firmly.

"Only if you come with me," he countered teasingly, but grabbed his Skyline-branded duffel from the backseat and climbed out of the car. He waved as he made his way to the front door, and as soon as he shut it she backed out of his driveway.

Back at her own home she was restive, tired from the daytime flight but not yet adjusted to the Eastern time zone. She unpacked the small suitcase she'd taken for the short trip, answered a few e-mails and unloaded the dishwasher. She sent some texts, scrolled through Facebook, and finally settled on the couch and clicked through her DVR to find a TV show requiring as little thought as possible.

She was ten minutes into an episode of a dating reality show when her phone rang. She glanced at the screen, then fumbled to mute the TV.

"Miguel, how are you?" she greeted the private investigator.

"Are you sitting down?" he asked in his characteristically curt manner.

Her heart beat so fast she felt nauseous. This was it. The day had finally arrived. After eighteen years apart she'd finally get to see her mom again.

Her eyes brimmed with tears as she replied, "Yes."

"Your mother died in August 2003. I'm sorry."

She blinked, her unshed tears hovering uncertainly on her lower lids. What did he say?

No, she must not have heard him correctly. "Sorry, can you repeat that?"

"Your mother is dead. Her body was found in the desert outside Juarez. I'll send you the full report."

"No, that can't be right." It couldn't be. Not after all this time. Not after everything she'd been through, all those prayers, all that hope. No, that was ridiculous. Impossible.

"I'm sorry," he repeated.

"Maybe it's someone else. There must be a lot of women named Maria Torres. Are you sure you've got the right person? Because she usually went by her middle name—"

"Dolores, shortened to Lola. I triple-checked. It's her."

Belatedly she realized she'd been shaking her head since he delivered the news, and it was making her dizzy. She stopped, with effort, and forced herself to exhale slowly.

"What else can you tell me?"

"She was working in one of the factories and still resident at the address you gave me. The reason her contact stopped so abruptly was probably because—"

"I get it," she interjected, not wanting him to say the words again. "Could you find a reason why?"

She practically heard his shrug over the phone. "You know what that part of the country's like. Juarez was up to a hundred murders a day at one point."

"So you don't know if it was a drug thing, or…" She braced herself. "A prostitution thing?"

"There's nothing in the police report. That she was identified at all is lucky. Most of the bodies they find in the desert aren't."

She squeezed her eyes shut, the heavy finality of the moment settling on her shoulders like a fifty-pound weight. "I guess I'll probably never know more than I know now."

"I'll complete the paperwork and e-mail it to you in the morning, but the answer is no. Probably not."

"Okay. Thanks for calling."

"I wanted to let you know as soon as I found out. I'm sorry I couldn't bring you a better outcome, Eva."

It was the first time in all their interactions that he sounded remotely human, and that made things worse. *I paid you for answers, not a fucking apology*, she wanted to scream. Instead she thanked him again and ended the call.

Then she dropped her phone, sank to the floor, and covered her face with her hands.

She couldn't even weep. Her devastation was so consuming it was like a black hole opened below her ribs and was sucking everything inside, swallowing the air from her lungs and the thoughts from her mind.

She wasn't stupid or carelessly optimistic—she'd known this might be the ending. But on some level she'd always believed that she'd know if her mom died, that she'd have some kind of physical sensation or sixth sense the moment it happened. She often talked to her mom in her mind lying in bed late at night, and imagined that somehow, in some way, her mom knew she was thinking of her.

Evidently she'd spent more than a decade talking to a ghost.

Suddenly she needed movement, escape. She jumped up from the floor and paced the open-plan ground floor, but it wasn't enough. She couldn't breathe, she needed air—she had to get out.

She walked up and down her driveway, in circles around the car, through the gate to her small yard and back again. She went back inside and picked up her phone, put it down, picked it up again. She tried to scroll through her list of contacts to find Juana's number, or Lulu's number, but her hand shook and she dropped the phone a second time. She didn't want their comfort or their empathy or their tears where she had none.

She wanted Rio.

Blindly she shoved her phone in her purse, grabbed the car keys from the counter and sped off in the rental, her stomach lurching, her breaths short and tight.

She drove slowly, fully aware she wasn't at her attentive best, but the empty Thursday-night roads made it a short trip despite her extra caution.

She cruised down Buckhead's leafy streets, glancing enviously at lights shining in curtained windows in the neighborhood's large houses. She imagined a happy, perfect family behind each one, homework finished, dishes cleared, baths drawn. They weren't worried about money or jobs or what to do with their lives. They didn't know her mother was dead, had quietly been dead for years, and they didn't care.

She parked at a sloppy angle across Rio's driveway and stumbled up the steps, her knees weak, her vision fuzzy. She felt drunk and sick and utterly without hope as she pressed the doorbell, not daring to wonder what she would do if he didn't answer—or what she would do if he did.

She waited, resting her forehead against the door. After what felt like a sufficient amount of time but could've been anywhere from two to ten minutes she pressed the bell again, and heard it resonate inside the house.

She squeezed her eyes closed, barely staying upright, and then the door opened and he was there, white T-shirt, dark skin, mussed hair, bare feet.

She sobbed in relief and sagged against his chest. His arms locked around her waist as the roaring in her ears became unbearable. Her knees buckled as the dark spots before her eyes swum and swelled and swallowed her whole.

Someone's fingers were in her hair. Rio's fingers—she could smell him, rainy asphalt and saltwater. She opened her eyes. She was on his couch. He crouched on the floor in front of her.

His eyes were narrow with concern. "What's wrong, *querida?*"

The endearment burst the dam. She turned her face into the cushion and wept.

Vaguely she registered Rio saying her name and then he was beside her, tugging her into his lap, wrapping his arms around her. She cried against his chest, clutching the soft cotton of his shirt, finding some solace in his solidity and warmth.

"Please, tell me what's wrong," he pleaded against the top of her head.

She closed her eyes, dragging in a shuddering breath. "Did I faint?"

"And scared the shit out of me, yes."

"For how long?"

"As long as it took me to carry you to the couch. Less than a minute, probably."

"I'm sorry I missed that," she told him genuinely.

"I'll carry you anywhere you want if you tell me what happened."

Tears tingled afresh as she remembered the horrible, irrecoverable turn her life had just taken.

"The private investigator called. My mom died in 2003, in Mexico."

He swore brutally. "I'm so sorry."

"Her body was found—I think she was—"

He hushed her, tightening his grip as she dissolved into sobs. That was it, now—she'd made it real by telling him. She could've lied, told him she was still waiting for news, told him the investigation was taking longer than expected, and then at least her mom would've been alive in his imagination.

Now her death felt much more final than it had a minute earlier.

She cried for a long time, until his shirt was soaked with her tears and she was sure his arms must've ached. She cried for her mother, for her short, fraught life and its violent end. She cried for her younger self, the girl who hadn't known she'd never see her mother again as she left for school, who'd always believed it was only a matter of time until they reunited. She cried for her future self, the woman who would never hear her mother's voice again, never show her mother an engagement ring, a wedding dress, a newborn grandchild. And she cried for all the mothers and daughters and sisters whose stories ended in that brutal desert, the ground hard and indifferent as their bodies cooled, their names forgotten.

She wasn't sure why she slowed, but eventually she did. And then she stopped.

She sniffed and turned her head to rest her cheek below his collarbone. He smoothed her hair and wiped the wet trails from beneath her eyes.

"Come on." He urged her to her feet, letting her lean against his side for stability.

"Where are we going?"

"To bed. You need to sleep."

It was the best idea she'd heard in years.

He led her up the stairs to the second floor which, she realized with a jolt, she'd never seen despite having been to this house more times than she could count when she worked with Hector.

The landing was as grandiose as the rest of the place. She followed Rio to the far end of the hall, where he ushered her through a half-open door.

She took in the crumpled white sheets, the clothes on the floor, the shoes peeking out from beneath the bed. "Is this your room?"

"None of the other beds are made up. Go ahead, I'll sleep next door."

She turned begging eyes on him. "Stay. I don't want to be alone."

He hesitated, and for the first time since she'd left her house she second-guessed her decision to come here.

Was this pushing their fledgling relationship—if it could even be called that—too far? Where was all the self-assured aloofness she'd shown him until now? Where was her self-control, her strength, her prized independence?

Had she really just sobbed a wet patch onto the T-shirt of her not-even-boyfriend who also happened to be a millionaire professional athlete?

Humiliation fisted in her stomach. Rio didn't want a hysterical mess of a girlfriend. He'd be kind to her tonight, because he was a kind man. Then he'd leave her. Just like so many other men before him. Like her dad. And now, like her mom.

This is why she'd spent so long avoiding commitment. It never ended well.

He opened a drawer, pulled out a T-shirt, and tossed it on the bed.

"You can sleep in that, if you want. I'll be right back."

Her throat tightened with fresh sorrow as he left the room, certain she'd just screwed up the best thing that'd happened to her in a long time. She undressed and pulled on the T-shirt, which was the same flat gray as her mood. Then she climbed into the bed, pausing briefly to savor his scent in the sheets before sliding over to the other side, where the pillows were smooth and untouched.

Rio reappeared carrying a glass of water, which he set on the bedside table next to her. He shut the door, yanked off his shorts to reveal the red boxers he wore beneath, and slipped under the covers.

She rolled onto her side, unable to look at him. Then the mattress dipped and the sheets whispered and he tugged her into his half, spooning her, looping his arm around her waist and sliding one leg between her knees.

"Everything will look brighter in the morning, *querida*," he murmured. "It always does."

She couldn't even find the energy to thank him. She slid her arms over his, snuggled back against his body and fell into a heavy, dreamless sleep.

* * * *

Rio jerked awake as a sharp pain shot through his knee. He half-sat up, then sank back into the pillows as he shifted his leg and it subsided.

Someone was breathing next to him. There was a woman in his bed.

Eva, he recalled with a sigh, folding one arm behind his head and running his other hand down her spine.

He'd never felt as helpless as when she'd told him about her mother. He'd cursed his lack of education, his lack of language, his lack of anything that might help him make her feel better. There were probably a thousand things he should've said, clever words of comfort and understanding, but like an idiot he'd just held her in silence.

He rolled his eyes at the memory. He had plenty of lines when he wanted to seduce her, but when she really needed him? Nothing.

She stirred in her sleep, rolling over to face him. He slid his arm beneath her head and scooped her onto his chest, stroking his thumb over her temple.

"I'm sorry," he whispered. "I'm sorry you won't see your mom again, and I'm sorry I can't do anything about it."

Her lashes fluttered. She opened her eyes.

"Are you talking to me?"

"Go back to sleep," he urged, glancing at the clock on his bedside table. Five o'clock in the morning. His alarm would go off in an hour so he could train at home before training with Skyline.

When he looked back Eva stared up at him, eyes big and round and mysterious in the semi-darkness.

"Rio," she murmured, and leaned up to kiss him.

He kissed her back—he couldn't help himself. She was so soft and warm, her scent a welcome disruption in his familiar surroundings.

She turned onto her side and he followed her, already so hard he hurt. He touched her bare legs, followed the curve of her thigh, traced the edge of her panties and swept his palm over her stomach.

Her hands were beneath his T-shirt and he echoed the movement, trailing his fingers up her abdomen to the space between her breasts.

He hadn't touched her breasts yet, he realized with a throb of arousal. He waited a second longer, savoring the anticipation, then covered her breast with his palm.

She moaned into his mouth and he pressed his erection against her hip, teasing her taut nipple with the pad of his thumb. She grabbed his wrist and pulled his hand off her breast, guiding it between her legs.

He swept his fingers over her panties, already wet to the touch. She took his wrist again and shoved his hand beneath the silky garment, bucking against his palm.

She was soaked, so hot and ready for him that he almost stopped breathing.

Which is why he pulled back from her with a tremendous force of effort, tugging down the shirt she wore and pulling the duvet back up to her waist.

"We can't, Eva, not now," he ground out between clenched teeth. "You're grieving, it wouldn't be right for me to—"

She sat bolt upright, scowling at him through the pre-dawn gloom.

"I'm perfectly capable of consenting," she snapped.

"Slow down," he urged, raising a steadying palm. "It's not that, I just don't want the first time between us to be—"

"Then I should leave."

"What? Why?"

But she was already out of the bed, yanking on her jeans and stuffing her bra into her purse. "I'm sorry. I shouldn't have come here."

For several seconds all he could do was watch her, so bewildered he had no idea what to say. Only when she had shoved her feet into her shoes and was on her way to the door did he realize he had to do something.

"Wait, stop." He rushed to his feet, ignoring the twinge of pain in his knee as he put weight on it. He beat her to the door and put his hands on her shoulders, forcing her to turn toward him. "What's going on? What did I do?"

She wouldn't meet his eyes, her gaze fixed on the carpet. "You didn't do anything. It's my fault. I should've dealt with this like an adult, not dumped all my shit on you."

She pushed past him into the hallway and he hurried after her. "You didn't dump anything on me, and there's no right way to deal with the news you just got. Please," he pleaded, chasing her down the stairs. "I don't want you to leave."

But her stiff shoulders and determined chin told him the woman he'd worked so hard to catch was already slipping out of his grasp.

He caught her by the arm as she reached the front door. When she turned to him her eyes glistened with unshed tears.

"Don't do this," he urged. "Stay with me. I want you to."

She shook her head, the sadness in her expression like a knife in his heart. "I can't be with you or anyone right now. I have a lot to think about, and I need space to do it."

She shouldered her purse and opened the door, and when she looked back at him she was all business. All of her warmth and softness had gone, replaced by the cool detachment he'd seen on his first day in the country.

"I'm going to take some time off from work, but I'll call a friend of mine to fill in. She's American, but she lived in Nicaragua for years with her ex-boyfriend. She just moved back to Atlanta after finishing a job translating for a baseball player in New York. You'll like her."

"No, I won't," he insisted. "Not like I like you."

She didn't speak, didn't look at him as she slipped outside and shut the door behind her. He heard her car door slam, and then the whine of its small engine as she drove away.

His knee throbbed and he shifted his weight onto his right foot. He took in the house's grandiose entryway, the chandelier hanging from the double-height ceiling. He thought about his sports car in the garage, the money he'd wired to his mother last month, the zeroes in his bank account.

Why did it all feel meaningless in comparison to the woman who'd just walked out the door?

He wandered into the kitchen and took a bottle of water from the fridge. Outside the pre-dawn sky was still dark, but he knew he wouldn't get back to sleep.

Should he call her? Text her? Get in his car and go after her?

She said she needed space. Should he let her have it?

"*Huevón*," he muttered harshly, cursing his own stupidity. He thought he knew a thing or two about women, but damn if Eva hadn't taught him otherwise.

At least there was one thing he was good at. He grabbed a second bottle of water and headed toward the gym.

Chapter 13

The sound of the doorbell roused Eva from her half-sleep. She rolled over and squinted at the clock. Who could be at her door at six o'clock on a Sunday evening?

Probably Jehovah's Witnesses. She shut her eyes and pulled the duvet over her shoulder.

It had been ten days since she'd fled from Rio's house in the early hours of the morning, and they'd been ten of the worst she could remember.

At first she felt justified in taking time off to grieve, even though the loss occurred more than ten years ago. Skyline's HR manager gushed her sympathy, encouraging her to take as long as she needed. Her fellow church volunteers had also fallen over themselves with condolences, and assured her they could handle the drop-in program until she felt ready to return.

She'd had long, tearful phone calls with Lulu and Juana, and a much briefer but equally comforting one with Eriberto. Olivia sent her flowers and Father Diego made a personal visit to remind her he always had time if she wanted to talk.

Rio called and texted and e-mailed and called again, but she didn't respond. She couldn't face him yet, not until her head cleared and she figured out how to let him know it was okay for him to move on in a way that preserved both their dignities. After all, she still wanted to keep her job. She just didn't want him to think she expected anything more.

The weekend passed. She didn't watch Skyline's home game on Saturday night, but she saw on the news that they lost. She wasn't surprised—they were playing one of the top teams in the league.

Then came Monday, and Tuesday, and Wednesday, and she grew restless. She drafted e-mails to a few of her closest friends about her mom, then discarded them, feeling sheepish about what felt like looking for sympathy for something that happened a long time ago—and which she probably should've guessed anyway.

She began to regret asking for time off and making a fuss about such an old tragedy. She phoned the HR manager at Skyline and offered to come back early but was kindly shushed as the woman assured her Chelsea—her replacement—was doing just fine translating for Rio.

Then she phoned her co-coordinators at the drop-in center and got a similar answer. Everything was great, they were managing with no problems, and there was no need for her to rush back to help.

At a loss, she called Juana and suggested flying down for a visit, maybe even timing it to be present at Eriberto's court appointment. Juana had been grateful but firm in her refusal. She encouraged Eva to focus on all the successes she'd had with her career and the good work she was doing at the drop-in center, and not to get bogged down by the past. She and Eriberto would be all right, she insisted, and she'd see Eva when Skyline next brought her to West Texas. As Eva put down the phone she wondered whether on some level Juana had known all along that her mom wasn't coming back, that the friend whose child she'd raised was gone forever.

And so she'd gone to bed. No one needed her, apparently, so what was the point in getting up?

She'd spent the last three days in a bizarre nocturnal suspension, sleeping through most of the day, then watching television through the long nighttime hours when her brain refused to quiet down. She'd left the house for groceries and little else, eventually succumbing to the temptation of pizza delivery more often than not.

Saturday afternoon Skyline played in Miami. The Miami away fixture was one of her favorites. In years past Hector had dismissed her early so he could enjoy a Floridian bacchanal. She used the free time to walk on the beach, meet her old grad-school friend for dinner and many drinks, and once she'd even gotten lucky with a hot Cuban-American sales executive.

This year she didn't watch the match on TV, and she didn't wait for the score to flash up on the news. She didn't reply to the late-night text from her friend, who'd just realized Skyline was in town and wanted to know whether she was with them.

She did, however, spend most of that night imagining Rio in one of the city's famed salsa clubs, twirling women who were prettier and sexier and much better dancers than she would ever be.

Sunday morning she forced herself up and into the shower, vaguely contemplating a trip to church. But as soon as she'd gotten out and realized how much effort would be required to blow dry her hair she gave up, pulled on clean pajamas, and crawled back between the sheets.

Now, eight hours later, the doorbell rang again. It was so long after the last ring that she decided it couldn't be Jehovah's Witnesses—they wouldn't bother waiting for an answer.

She got up with an exasperated sigh and pulled on a hoodie to hide that she wore no bra beneath her cotton T-shirt. Maybe the women from church had brought her dinner. Or, even better, maybe the pizza delivery guy was so accustomed to her order he'd brought her one for free without her having to call.

She grabbed her wallet before she answered the door. Even if the pizza was free, she owed the guy a tip. She pulled out a couple of single-dollar bills and swung open the door.

Atlanta Skyline's multi-million-dollar Chilean winger stood on the threshold.

He grinned.

She panicked.

"Rio, oh my God," she gushed, running her fingers through her hair and realizing unhappily that she wasn't wearing any underwear beneath her size-too-big running shorts.

"Can I come in?"

"I guess, but—"

He stepped inside and shut the door behind him before she could object. His smile, his perfect teeth, his voice, the narrow length of him in jeans and a thin black sweater—it was almost too much to bear.

She'd missed him so Goddamn much.

He held up his palms. "I know you don't want to see me, but there's something I wanted to show you in person."

She hesitated, unsure how to play this. She should probably demand that he leave, but she wanted to see him, too. "Can I run upstairs and change my clothes first?"

"Why? You look great."

"No, I don't."

"You do," he insisted.

What was it she'd told herself she wanted? A man who appreciated the real her, un-brushed hair and all. She had to at least give Rio his chance.

She sat down on the couch and gestured for him to join her. "All right, what do you want to show me?"

He cleared his throat, his expression suddenly shy. Then in thickly accented, halting English he said, "Hi. My name is Rio Vidal. I am from

Antofagasta, Chile. I come to Skyline. I will want to win many title. Today we have a good match. I receive well from my teammates. Thank you."

He beamed proudly.

She was speechless.

Reverting to Spanish, he said, "Chelsea taught me that. Pretty good, right? I've been working hard on my lessons this week and I think I'm finally getting somewhere."

She stared at him.

Skyline didn't need her, because they had Chelsea.

The drop-in center didn't need her, because they had other volunteers.

Juana didn't need her, because she had Lulu.

Her mother didn't need her, because she was dead.

Now even Rio didn't need her.

She burst into tears.

Rio's eyes widened in horror as he slid closer and put his arm around her shoulders. "What did I do? I'm sorry, Eva, I keep trying to make you happy but I seem to screw it up every time."

She shook her head, inhaling slowly to calm her emotions. "You do make me happy."

"You're crying, so apparently I don't."

She sighed, swiping at the wet trails on her cheeks. "I'm not, and you do. And I'm very impressed by your English. That was excellent."

"Then what made you upset? Remember I'm not smart like you are, so spell it out clearly, because I'm lost."

"You are smart," she assured him, taking his hand in both of hers. "So smart that you'll crack this English thing in no time. Then you won't need me at all."

Comprehension dawned on his handsome face. "Is that the problem? You think I don't need you?"

She nodded.

He clucked his tongue in disapproval. "The only reason I worked so hard this week was to show you that soon you won't have to be my interpreter, you can work for someone else, and then you won't need to worry about whether you can be my translator and my *polola*."

Her heart softened with his words, and his distinct slang for *girlfriend*. He put his index finger under her chin to raise her gaze to his.

"I'll do anything to be with you. Don't need me. Want me."

"I do. More than anything," she confessed.

"So what happened last week?"

She exhaled. "I was embarrassed. I didn't want you to see that side of me."

He frowned. "Which side?"

"Emotional. Irrational. Weak."

"I haven't seen any of that yet. I saw a strong woman who's survived a hell of a lot get the devastating news that a long journey had ended, and ended badly. That's all."

She managed a shaky smile, her heart tripping over itself as she absorbed his words. He wanted her. He cared about her. Whether he still would tomorrow, or next week—it didn't matter. Tonight he was hers.

"Dammit, you're going to make me cry again."

"Please don't."

She laced her fingers through his. "Does this mean I'm not getting fired and replaced by Chelsea?"

"Only if you get fired for sleeping with me. Should we test it and see?"

She couldn't help but return his cheeky grin. "Does that mean I'm allowed to change my clothes now?"

He shook his head. "No point. I'm planning to take them all off in a minute."

She rolled her eyes teasingly but his expression was dead serious. When he spoke again the intent in his voice sent shivers across her back.

"Where's your bedroom?"

"Upstairs."

"Show me."

She led him up the stairs and into her bedroom, wondering if her house seemed tiny in comparison to his, trying to remember when she'd last shaved her legs, hoping he didn't ask her to turn on the light because this would be so much easier if—

He flicked on the light switch.

She shot him an accusatory look.

"I want to see you," he said simply.

"Just give me a minute." She glanced around the room, frantically thinking about how she could MacGyver herself and her surroundings into something sexy. And considering she was too young to have ever watched an episode of MacGyver, she wasn't off to a great start.

She snatched up her brush with one hand and tugged it through her hair while she used the other to sling errant pieces of clothing into a vague pile in one corner. She straightened the bottles on her vanity, stacked the papers strewn across the top of her dresser, and kicked a pair of shoes under the bed. She was fighting with a particularly stubborn knot in her hair when Rio's laughter drew her attention.

"*Querida*, what are you doing? You're not hiding anything—I've already seen it all."

She chucked the brush onto her vanity with a sigh. "This is not how things would've looked if I knew you were coming over."

He moved to where she stood and wrapped his arms around her waist. "Do you really think I'm the type of guy who'd pass up a night with you because you had some clothes on the floor?"

He was already hard. She could feel it through his jeans. Suddenly the tidiness of her bedroom was the last thing on her mind.

"Show me what type of guy you are, then." She leaned up on her toes to kiss him.

The fierceness of his response took her breath away. No man had ever kissed her with so much need, his tongue seeking hers, his hand cupping her jaw as if their joined mouths weren't enough.

To be fair, they weren't. Not nearly enough.

She pulled away from him and stepped back. He grinned, starting toward the bed, but she put a palm against his chest to stop him.

"I want to undress you."

His eyes brightened. "I'm all yours."

She started with his shoes, unlacing what she was sure were expensive sneakers and tugging them off his million-dollar feet.

"Your socks don't match," she observed, pulling off one, and then the other.

"No, they don't," he replied, sounding as if it was news to him.

She straightened and rolled the hem of his sweater up his chest, then up and off his obligingly raised arms. He wore a cotton undershirt beneath and she took a moment to admire its bright white contrast against his dark-olive complexion before slipping it over his head and piling it on top of his sweater.

Then she stepped back to admire the view.

He let her look her fill, his posture relaxed and unself-conscious. Then again, with a body like his, what was there to be self-conscious about?

He was, in a word, perfect.

Suddenly giddy with the realization that he was hers, she began her exploration of his flawless torso.

She knew the trend among soccer players was to wax, but the fine, soft hair on Rio's forearms suggested his smooth chest was entirely natural. She pressed her palms against the hard planes of his pecs, then slid them down to his taut six-pack. His jeans bulged tellingly a few inches below but he stood still, giving her what she wanted.

She moved her hands to his wrists and swept them upward, taking in his corded forearms, rock-hard biceps, and the chiseled muscles of his shoulders.

She slung her arms around his neck, marveling that he was the smallest player at Skyline and probably one of the shortest in the league. To her, he seemed like a giant.

She kissed him once, lightly, and without dropping his gaze she reached between them and unzipped his jeans. Although he said nothing his jaw tightened, and her smile grew.

In one motion she dragged his jeans down to his ankles, and he stepped out of the bunched garment. Kneeling, she worked her way back up his long, powerful legs, smoothing her palms over his calves, gently squeezing his rock-hard thighs. He wore tight, black briefs, his erection distorting the designer name printed across the waistband.

She trailed her thumbs along his inner thighs, lingering, enjoying the anticipation. Then she yanked down his briefs, exposing his manhood in all its vital, unapologetic glory.

When she could tear her gaze away she raised it to his face, expecting to find his trademark back-teeth grin.

The concentrated desire she saw instead tripled the pace of her heartbeat.

He leaned down and tugged her to her feet, the force of his grip stating that it was his turn to take control. Normally she bristled when men became too alpha in the bedroom, but she trusted Rio. She knew he would follow her lead and never try to push her somewhere she didn't want to go.

She was motionless as he raised the hem of her sweatshirt, luxuriating in the way his eyes widened when he realized she wore no bra beneath the T-shirt he found underneath. He wasted no time removing that as well, and it was her turn to stand proudly as he drank his fill.

For several moments he simply looked, eyes bright and eager, unconsciously running his tongue along his lower lip.

He moved as if to touch her, then changed his mind as his gaze drifted to her shorts. She smiled to herself, knowing what he didn't as he hooked his thumbs beneath the waistband.

He tugged the shorts down her thighs, his hands faltering when he realized she wore nothing underneath.

"Eva," he growled, hooking his arm around her waist and dragging her backward to the bed. He pulled her shorts past her ankles and eased on top of her, his mouth devouring hers as one hand cradled the back of her head and the other explored the rounded terrain of her breasts.

She moaned against his lips as his firm, confident fingers kneaded her flesh, his thumb finding her nipple and coaxing it into a taut peak. She squirmed beneath him, her body colliding with what felt like a wall of solid muscle as she tried to soundlessly encourage him and slow him down at the same time, torn between her urgent need and her longing to make this experience last forever.

He propped himself on his elbows and smiled down at her. "Tell me what you want."

"You."

"Be specific."

"You," she repeated, guiding his hand between her legs. "Here."

His erection pulsed where it pressed against her hip. He slipped one finger inside of her, pressing the heel of his hand against her clit.

The sound that wrenched from her throat was so primal it took her several seconds to realize it had come from her.

The movement of his chest against hers betrayed the quickened pace of Rio's normally slow breathing. He shifted onto his side, using his free hand to stroke her face while the other worked her into a throbbing frenzy.

He brushed his lips over hers. "Ready?"

"What do you think?"

He plunged a second finger into her slick heat. Then he grinned.

She flopped back on the pillows as he bent over the edge of the bed, rummaged for his jeans and produced a foil-wrapped condom. He tore it open with his teeth and then she plucked it from his fingers, and took her time rolling the thin latex over his hard length.

By the time she finished a sheen of sweat covered his forehead. He urged her back down on the bed, shifting her onto her side and then, to her surprise, moving into position behind her.

"What are you doing?" she asked over her shoulder.

He nodded to the full-length mirror on the wall opposite the bed. "I told you, I want to see you."

She cringed as she caught a glimpse of the two of them, of the Latino equivalent of a Greek god sliding his hand over her decidedly not-flat stomach. She wasn't usually self-conscious about her appearance, but Rio's perfection seemed to illuminate and multiply all the ways she wasn't.

"I can't, it's too embarrassing," she muttered, squeezing her eyes closed.

"You're beautiful. Look," he insisted.

She did. She saw him part her knees and raise her leg, tucking her calf behind his thigh. She saw him smile as he touched her sodden core one more time, his fingers wet when they came away. She saw him line himself up, felt the head of him just begin to part her folds, watched him push inside her with a single, smooth thrust.

Then she saw stars.

He was big, bigger than she expected, and he stretched and filled her with his hot length. Once inside he paused, his lips pressed against her temple, and she could tell he was gathering his self-control, fighting his completion and working to make this last.

The eroticism of the moment—their naked bodies joined in the mirror, his brow furrowed in concentration—nearly overcame her, and her internal muscles clenched him inadvertently. He groaned, closed his eyes, and began to move within her.

His first stroke sent her to heaven, and when his fingers found her clit she plummeted into hell.

She fought to hold on to what little restraint she had left, but soon she was powerless against the runaway train of her desire. She met each of his thrusts hard, driving herself down on his shaft, alternately opening her eyes to soak in the image of them in the mirror and then slamming them shut when the sight nearly sent her over the edge.

He muttered a string of filthy, sexy Chilean slang, only half of which she understood, but that half was more than enough to have her writhing against him. She ached for release yet dreaded it, doubtful she could ever feel this good, this whole, again.

Rio moaned her name and began to tremble against her. She knew he was close, and she knew she wanted them to finish together.

She bucked her hips and arched her back, drawing him in as deeply as she could. He swore vehemently, his fingers working her clit, his lips on her neck, and as she raised one arm to bury her fingers in his hair she looked into the mirror.

Their reflected gazes met and locked. Rio's brown eyes were wide open, round with excitement, and shimmering with an emotion so intense she didn't dare give it a name. It was honest, and sincere, and made her feel so cherished she nearly burst into tears.

The moment passed and he squeezed his eyes shut, gritting his teeth as he held his breath and throbbed within her.

Watching his release, knowing she'd driven him to that point was the final push she needed. Her entire body went rigid with her orgasm, her legs straightening and her back arching. As waves of pleasure rolled up and down her flesh she called out to no one in particular, shouting her joy, sharing her triumph, sighing her bone-deep happiness.

* * * *

"Your turn."

"Let me think." Eva propped herself on one elbow, idly trailing her fingers through Rio's hair as she considered. He was pleased to see she was taking their post-coital question-and-answer game fairly seriously. There was so much more he wanted to learn about her, and in the afterglow of one of the most mind-blowing sexual experiences of his life she was finally opening up.

"I've got it. What's the best purchase you've ever made?"

"Easy." He bared his teeth.

She frowned. "You bought your teeth?"

"I paid to have them fixed," he explained. "And my mom's, and my siblings'. I was seventeen the first time I went to the dentist."

Her expression seemed too neutral. "Is dentistry expensive in Chile?"

"You already had your question. Now it's my turn."

He stared up at the ceiling, eyes narrowed in thought. Then he turned to her with a smile. "Here's something I've wondered about. How did you get interested in soccer?"

"Good question. I can't give you the exact moment I fell in love with the game—it was gradual, throughout my childhood. It started with living in an immigrant community, where most kids' parents were from Mexico or Central America. There was always a match on someone's TV, or on a Spanish-language radio station, and the boys played in the courtyard of our apartment complex. In junior high I tried out for the team but I was cut pretty much immediately, so I guess my interest shifted from playing to watching."

"You wanted to play?"

"That's another question," she chided teasingly. "But yeah, although I genuinely wasn't any good—the coach was right not to let me on the team. I joined an intramural team in college and I think they would've benched me every match if they hadn't been desperate to make up the numbers, but I had fun anyway."

"Intramural?" He carefully repeated the unfamiliar word.

"All the teams are students at the same university, as opposed to competing against teams from other universities."

"Oh. What position did you play?"

"Defensive midfield. I was terrible." She nudged him. "My turn."

"Go for it."

"Before your neighbors bought you that first pair of cleats, what did you play in?"

"Nothing. I played barefoot."

She winced. "Seriously?"

"When my agent was negotiating my first professional contract in Chile, he told the manager my quick, tight style came from playing barefoot on

the street. That I had to navigate around rocks and pieces of broken glass."
He smiled fondly. "That guy is so full of shit."

"Good at his job, though."

"The best. After all, he got me to Atlanta." He pulled her against his chest
and raked his fingers through her hair. "Are you ready for my question?"

"Sure."

"What kind of guy was your last boyfriend?"

She tried to jerk away but he held her tightly, not letting her run
from him this time.

"You didn't tell me we were getting heavy with these questions." She
laughed unconvincingly. He said nothing, waiting for her answer.

She exhaled and flopped back down. "It's been a long time since I called
anyone my boyfriend, since that's a word that implies mutual commitment.
But I guess the last one was in grad school, about five years ago."

"And? What was he like?"

"He was all right." She raised one bare shoulder. "Boring. Safe. Punching
above his weight to the point I figured he wouldn't dare leave me."

"What happened?"

She smiled bitterly. "He left me."

"Idiot."

"It's my curse." She sighed. "Some women attract bad boys, some can
never learn what's good for them—you know the usual stories. Mine is
always being left. No matter how well things go or how serious things get,
in the end they always leave. For a long time I gave up on asking them to
stay, but I'm trying to turn that around."

"Good. Their loss, my gain. And I'm not going anywhere."

She murmured something that sounded like "we'll see," but before he
could protest she asked, "How was Miami?"

"Is that your question?"

"Yeah, why not?"

Because he was hoping to keep talking at the level they were only just
beginning to explore, but the rules were the rules. "It was okay. We drew,
one-one. I got the assist, but I screwed up an attempt on goal in the second
half. The keeper was nowhere but it went wide about six inches." He shook
his head in disgust, recalling the moment he realized the ball was on the
wrong side of the bar.

"They're a good side. One-one is not a bad result."

"Anything other than a win is a bad result."

"Spoken like a true professional." She rolled onto her back and examined her nails, which he'd learned was a telltale sign that she was worried or uncomfortable about something. "What did you do after the match?"

He scooped her into his side. "Went back to the hotel, why?"

"Miami's usually a big party destination for Skyline. For some reason the fixture keeps falling ahead of the break for the international schedule, plus the weather's good. The players typically like to blow off some steam in the clubs."

"I think a bunch of guys did go out, but I ordered room service and watched Telemundo. I was tired."

"What did Chelsea do?"

He rolled his eyes. "How many questions have you had in a row, now?"

"Does that mean you don't want to answer?"

"I don't know what Chelsea did. We said goodnight in the lobby and I didn't see her again until breakfast."

"Do you like her?"

"Not as much as I like you."

The way her face lit at his simple, obvious praise tore at his heart. Who were these morons who'd walked away from her in the past?

"I know. I'm being immature and jealous. It's just that Chelsea is so tall and blond and skinny, and—"

"And her language skills aren't as good as yours, and her sense of humor isn't as quick as yours, and she doesn't know as much about soccer as you do. And the truth is I spent most of Saturday night worrying about you, deciding to turn up here tonight and praying you didn't slam the door in my face."

"I would never do that," she admonished, brushing a welcome kiss over his lips. "I would call the police, have you arrested for harassment and then sell my story to the tabloids, though."

"Thanks, that's good to know."

She smiled sweetly. "No problem."

"If you're done taking way more turns than you're due, I have a question."

"I'm listening."

He braced himself, having been turning over this request in his mind for days. "Will you come with me to the international qualifier on Friday?"

"The international qualifier?" she echoed, half-laughing. "But that's in Chile."

"I know."

"You want me to go with you to Chile," she repeated.

"The flight leaves tomorrow night. The plan is to go straight to Antofagasta, spend a couple of days with my family, then fly down to Santiago on Thursday morning. We'll be back in Atlanta by Monday afternoon."

She shook her head, scoffing, "I don't think you need an interpreter in a Spanish-speaking country, Rio."

"This is not a professional invitation. I'll pay for your flights personally. You're already booked off with Skyline anyway, right?"

"Right," she agreed slowly.

"And they wouldn't expect you to come back to work while I'm away."

"But the Chilean press, they'll be all over us and no matter what we—"

"I've thought about that," he interjected. "We can try to limit being seen together, but frankly I think it's easier if we're open and honest about the fact that we're dating. I asked my agent and he says there's no reason why we can't be involved, that it's not a conflict of interest."

"You asked your agent?" she screeched, bolting upright.

"Relax." He urged her back down to the mattress with his hands on her shoulders. "He's so discreet I could tell him I had a fetish for animals and he'd start figuring out how to sneak me into the zoo at night."

"That's disgusting," she decreed, but settled onto the pillows.

"To be honest, I think he was disappointed. I've never been the subject of any major scandal and I think he was hoping for something juicier than announcing my intention to start a relationship with my interpreter."

"He's sure it's fine?"

"One-hundred percent."

"And he doesn't think Roland will mind?"

He shook his head. "No one cares."

Her brow furrowed in thought and a crushing notion careened into his brain. He debated briefly, then decided to put it out there. "Unless you don't want people knowing you're with me?"

"You know that's not it," she assured him. "An interpreter dating her client isn't the most professional scenario in the world, but it's not unheard of. And you say my job is safe?"

"Definitely."

"And the same conditions I mentioned before still apply. I'm not looking for a fling, so don't commit unless you're serious."

"I'm serious," he promised.

She exhaled. "Okay. Let's go public."

"Really?" he asked, unable to keep the disbelief from his tone. After all her protests about professional boundaries, he was astonished she'd relented so quickly.

"Really. I was using my job as an excuse to push aside my feelings for you. The truth is"—she paused to take a deep breath—"I was scared."

He clucked his tongue, trailing a finger down her cheek. "Scared of what, *querida*?"

"What's every woman who's attracted to a man like you afraid of? Rejection. That you wouldn't feel the same way."

"I think I made my intentions pretty clear." He moved one leg over hers beneath the covers, remembering that kiss in the salsa club, their escapades in the theatre room. He stiffened against her smooth thigh, rapidly losing interest in this discussion.

"And I came around in the end, didn't I?" She smiled coyly, slowly pushing the duvet down to her waist.

He didn't bother to reply, lowering his face to her breasts and taking her nipple in his mouth. He rolled his tongue around the hard peak, teasing her, while he slipped a hand between her legs. The slippery heat he found there sent a shudder through him, and he eased his body over hers, grateful he'd had the optimism to bring more than one condom.

"Hold on." She planted her palms on his chest and pushed him off. "You called the shots last time. This round, I'm in control."

He lay flat on his back and crossed his arms behind his head. She stroked him needlessly—he was as ready for her as if she was the first woman he'd taken to bed after five years of abstinence. She rolled on the condom and settled herself above him, positioning the tip of him between her legs.

He closed his eyes as she slid down and took him deeply. For the first time since he arrived in the United States, he finally felt at home.

Chapter 14

"If you wouldn't mind, please bring your seat into position for landing, Señor Vidal. We're starting our final descent. Welcome home."

Eva didn't miss the flight attendant's lingering smile at Rio, or her wink as she moved down the aisle. It had been the same throughout the nine-hour journey, as Rio was offered extra drinks and pillows while Eva dodged the magazine practically thrown at her head.

She couldn't fault Rio's polite but impersonal responses, nor could she blame the woman for giving the only celebrity in the relatively empty first-class section a little extra attention, she supposed. But as the plane circled low over Santiago, the unease that had followed her all the way from Atlanta grew stronger and stronger.

The last forty-eight hours with Rio should've been blissful. Finally honest about her feelings for him, she should've lounged by his side in bed, indulged in his body, looked forward to her unexpected trip to a foreign country, and basked in the commitment that his invitation represented.

That first night had been everything she imagined. Monday morning he left early to train in his home gym, and after showering and packing a bag she drove over to join him and prepare for their flight that evening.

He was finishing what looked like a grueling sequence of deadlifts when her phone rang.

"Are you with Rio?" Roland asked without preamble. "Chelsea says he's not with her and he's not answering his phone."

"I am," she confirmed cautiously, wondering if that was the wrong answer and briefly indulging a paranoid fantasy that Rio's agent had it all wrong and this would be the moment she lost her job.

"Put me on speaker."

She gestured Rio over as she propped the phone on the bench press and pressed the speaker button. "He can hear you."

"Tell him I've talked to the medical team and we've reconsidered. I'm happy for him to travel for the match in Chile, but I don't want him to start. He can be subbed in if they're losing, but his exhaustion showed in Miami. He needs to rest this week."

Rio watched her expectantly. She bit her lower lip, considering how best to relay Roland's message.

"He thinks maybe you should start on the bench on Friday. He's worried about you."

Rio snorted. "The country's best player, sitting on the bench in an international qualifier? Not a chance. Tell him to fuck off."

She turned back to the phone. "He...disagrees."

"I bet he does," Roland muttered. "Eva, between you and me, try to get him to see reason. Venezuela haven't qualified since the seventies. Chile should run away with this match. I know the decision comes down to him and the national-team manager, but he should take advantage of the opportunity to let some of the younger guys get playing time while he has a break."

The Swede sighed audibly. "He's killing himself with this overtraining. He practically staggered off the pitch on Saturday night. Can you talk to him? He might listen to you. He sure as hell isn't listening to me."

"I'll try," she promised, disconnecting the call. Rio rolled his eyes and resumed his deadlifts.

"That man worries so much, sometimes I think he's my grandmother instead of my manager," he scoffed.

"Maybe he has a point," she ventured. "Why not give the younger players a chance, and come on if they need you? If a game can ever be as good as won before the first kick, this one's a victory."

"Nothing's won until the last whistle." He dropped the dumbbell with a clatter, circling his arms and flexing his shoulders. "Let's get some lunch. I want to go for a run before we leave for the airport."

Roland's words echoed in her mind as the plane bumped onto the runway. She agreed with him—this was a good chance for Rio to rest and recuperate. But what chance did she have of convincing him?

Absolutely none, she concluded when they emerged from customs and were greeted by a surging mass of people barely contained by metal barriers and a line of security guards. Press cameras clicked and flashed, women screamed his name, teenage girls wept, and a huge homemade signed poked up from the crowd showing his name and jersey number beside the Chilean flag.

She knew Rio was famous, but she had no idea he was *this* famous.

He waved and smiled, barely acknowledging the black-suited security detail that ushered them past the horde, down what looked like a service corridor and into a luxury SUV with tinted windows. By the time the car pulled away from the airport Eva felt like she'd run a marathon.

"Oh my God," she exhaled. "You did not prepare me for that."

"I'm so used to it, I guess I forgot."

"It's always like this?"

He shrugged, sheepish. She looked out the window, shaking her head.

It turned out to be a short car ride as—instead of going to a domestic airport as she'd assumed—they pulled up to a private airfield not far from the international terminal.

She eyed the small, lone jet parked on the tarmac as Rio helped her out of the SUV. "We're going in that?"

"I can't fly commercial between Santiago and Antofagasta. There'd be a riot on the plane."

"I have a thing about really small aircraft."

"What sort of a thing?"

"A nagging awareness that they crash way more often than big planes fear-sort-of thing."

"You'll be fine. Wait 'til you see inside."

He was right. As soon as she saw the luxurious leather seats, the fully stocked minibar, and the basket of freshly baked pastries, she forgot all about statistics. She buckled herself into a seat opposite Rio, smiled as the flight attendant poured her a mimosa, and enjoyed the view as the plane arced up into the sky.

Two hours later they touched down on a private strip outside Antofagasta. The seaside city looked like an urban oasis in the surrounding Atacama Desert, and viewing it from the air, she understood why it served as a crucial industrial port.

Excitement edged out anxiety as they took another luxury car to a grand hotel with an ocean view. It had been years since she'd traveled outside the States, and Chile had long been on her list of someday destinations.

To be visiting in five-star style with a famous footballer on her arm— well, that had never even entered her imagination.

"Just one room," she observed after they finished checking in and rode the elevator to the top floor. "You're feeling confident."

He shot her a cheeky smile as the elevator doors slid open. "It's a three-bedroom suite. I'll even give you first pick."

The suite was bigger than her condo. She drifted to the wall of floor-to-ceiling windows overlooking the ocean. She blinked, trying to shake the surrealism of the moment and convince herself it was real, that she was, in fact, thousands of miles from normality, living the soccer wives-and-girlfriends dream she'd only ever read about. Yet here she was, dropped into a three-dimensional version of the gossip-page photos and Instagram posts.

Rio was a whirlwind—he played like one, lived like one. She never imagined she would get so caught up his dizzying orbit. Or that it would feel so much like home.

She was so absorbed in the view that she barely noticed Rio moving to stand behind her.

"Welcome to Chile," he murmured against the crown of her head.

She whirled, unable to contain her delight. "This is amazing. Thank you for inviting me."

"Thank you for accepting."

She clapped her hands together. "What's our plan? Can we sit on the beach, or will you be mobbed? Is your family meeting us here?"

"We'll meet my mom and my brother for dinner later. They're both at work."

"Your mom still works?" She gaped.

"She likes her job. She's a secretary at the university. I send her money and built her a house, but she says she'd get bored sitting at home all day."

"Fair enough. So what are we doing next?"

He laughed, slinging his arms around her waist. "I'm going to bed. I only got a couple hours' sleep on the plane."

"Rio," she whined. "We've flown thousands of miles to a different country and you want to sleep?"

"Yes. Although I could be persuaded to do something else first."

She arched a misunderstanding brow, and he clarified by tightening his grip to pull her closer, lowering his face to hers and pressing a long, greedy kiss to her lips.

When he released her mouth she only had one activity on her mind.

"Pick a bedroom," she instructed, and followed him into the first one they found.

"So my colleague rushes in and says there's a big commotion at the school, she thinks it must be burning down as the whole fire brigade is parked outside. I panic and race over, worried something's happened to the kids. As soon as I arrive a teacher hurries toward me, saying she's so glad I'm there, they didn't know what to do. I ask, what to do about what? Rio, she says. I say, what about Rio? She looks at me like I've just asked her what day it is. Rio, she shouts, has been up a tree all morning and he refuses to climb down!"

Rio rolled his eyes as Eva joined in the laughter at his mother's oft-repeated story. He shook his head in mock embarrassment and disapproval.

In truth he couldn't remember the last time he'd had so much fun.

He stretched his legs in front of him on the floor of his aunt's house. Normally this dilapidated, aluminum-roofed shack in the village on the outskirts of the city where he'd lived as a child wouldn't have been the first impression he'd chosen for a woman like Eva. He'd thought as much that morning when his mother called to tell him his aunt was hosting dinner. He loved his family, but he didn't relish having to ask Eva to cope without indoor plumbing for a few hours.

He'd been nervous all afternoon, cautiously trying to prepare Eva for the trip out to the village, but now as he watched her listen attentively to yet another of his mom's embarrassing tales he realized he shouldn't have doubted her. She hadn't so much as blinked at the dirt roads, the crammed-in rows of shacks or the way they all filled their plates in the kitchen and then sat on the floor to eat in the sitting room, which was the only one big enough to accommodate all ten people.

"Where is your family from, Eva?" his aunt asked from her perch on an overturned crate.

"Mexico, originally."

"You're really good at understanding our crazy Chilean accents," his cousin Rosario commended.

Eva smiled. "Rio's teaching me all the slang."

"It's her job," his mother announced proudly. "Eva told me she spent a lot of time studying Chile and the way we speak so she could do a good job for our Rio when he arrived."

Everyone murmured noises of approval, except for his brother, who remarked, "It must be a hard job trying to make this guy sound smart and funny."

Rio half-stood, intent on giving Julio a punch on the arm, but Rosario beat him to it.

"Ignore him," she advised Eva. "We all do."

"Do your parents also live in Atlanta?" his aunt asked.

He saw the flash of sadness that clouded Eva's eyes and got to his feet, extending his hand for her to join him.

"Sorry everyone, this interview is over. Eva is sick of hearing all your humiliating and seriously exaggerated stories from my childhood. Come on," he urged, pulling her upright. "Let's go for a walk before it gets too cold."

She glanced uncertainly toward the kitchen. "Oh, no, let me help clean up first."

"Don't worry," his cousin Alfredo chimed in with a wink. "We'll save you some dishes."

He breathed easier once they were outside, away from his family's well-meaning but prying questions.

"I hope that wasn't too painful," he said, wincing.

She shook her head, her smile radiant under the solar-powered lamp mounted above his aunt's front door. "I'm having a great time, actually. Your family is amazing. Everyone is so nice and welcoming, and I love hearing the stories about when you were a kid."

"Don't believe everything you hear," he muttered, but he couldn't suppress his answering smile.

He took her hand and together they walked down the main road that ran through the village. There were no tall buildings to break up the wind this far out toward the desert, and the breeze whipped up dust from the streets and swirled it around their ankles. Most of the dwellings they passed were shacks as shabby as his aunt's. The flashing lights from TV screens illuminated windows covered with everything from handmade curtains to threadbare towels, as the handful of streetlights flickered over their heads, illustrating how unreliable the electricity supply was this far out of town.

"I've never brought anyone else out here," he told her quietly.

She looked up at him in surprise. "Really? Not even Mercedes?"

He shook his head.

"But you were with her much longer than you've been with me."

"I never saw the point. We dated for over a year, but I always knew I'd never..." *Marry her. Spend my life with her. Fall in love with her like I think I'm falling in love with you.*

"Never what?"

"I knew we were mostly having fun. It was never going to become too serious," he amended. "Anyway, she wouldn't like it out here. She used to complain if the tables were too close together in restaurants, so I don't think she would've coped with cramming onto the floor."

"Then she missed out," Eva replied matter-of-factly.

"Maybe."

"Definitely."

They walked in silence for another few minutes, dirt crunching under their feet.

"You look like your mother," Eva remarked.

"And my brother looks like his father," he replied, referencing Julio's three-inch height advantage and overweight build.

"I would never say anything, in case you were worried. Your secret's completely safe. I promise."

"I know."

They continued down the road, the noise of his thoughts filling in the void left by their lack of conversation.

He thought about this village, his family, the real reason he'd never brought any other girlfriends to the place he'd been born, or even to the high-rise apartment building in the rough part of town where they'd moved after his father died.

Was he embarrassed? Not exactly. His youth was a matter of public record—anyone could look up his biography on the Internet and learn the circumstances in which his life began.

He wasn't ashamed of his background, but maybe he hadn't been ready to own it yet, either. He hated players who wore their impoverished childhoods like a badge of honor, and he didn't want pity or praise. He wanted to be judged on where he was today, not how he'd gotten there or where he'd started.

But now, as they passed a wheelless car propped up on cinder blocks, he realized he wanted Eva to truly know him. All of him.

He stopped as he realized he'd subconsciously led her to the cemetery gate, two timber poles vaguely marking out the entrance to the headstone-dotted field on the edge of the village.

He tightened his grip on her hand. "My dad is buried here. The man I thought was my dad, I mean."

She smoothed her thumb over his knuckles. "Do you want to go in?"

He shook his head. "I don't even know where his grave is. My mom never brought us to visit. This is why we're here." He indicated a vacant patch of land beside the gates, where a row of metal cans for burning trash lined the rocky, rutted ground.

He led her onto it, shifting a large stone with his toe. "This is where I learned to play soccer."

He watched her look around, taking in the rusted, jagged-edged cans littering the periphery, the ripped tire tossed haphazardly in one corner, the pieces of broken pipes jammed into the ground to demarcate the goals.

He wondered what she was thinking. Was she imagining the boy running barefoot, ignoring the cuts on the soles of his feet as he shot for goal? Did she pity him, mentally clucking her tongue at how little he'd been born into? Was she changing her mind, reconsidering their whole relationship, questioning whether she could ever build something long-term with someone from somewhere like here?

After a moment she slipped her arm around his waist and leaned into his side. When she spoke her voice was hushed and thoughtful.

"Thank you for bringing me here."

"Thank you for coming."

They were talking about more than this patch of dirt, or his aunt's house, or the village. He slid his arm across her shoulders and held her tightly, looking at the dusty earth, the field dotted with headstones, the stars in the clear black sky overhead.

The revelation hit him like a free kick to his chest.

He loved her.

"Rio! Hey, it's Rio Vidal!"

They turned to see two brothers—if the resemblance and height difference was any indication—jogging over to greet them.

"I know you, you're Rio Vidal," the taller one confirmed. His declaration seemed to have set off a secret kid alarm system, as within seconds they were joined by another four boys and girls of varying ages and sizes.

One of the boys produced a grubby, semi-deflated soccer ball. "Will you play with us?"

"Why don't you guys play on that nice pitch I built for you?" He gestured toward the fenced-in sports field all the way on the other side of the village. He'd paid for its construction five years ago, maintained the salary of a groundskeeper, and annually donated a fresh batch of boots and balls.

"The groundskeeper locks the gates at eight o'clock," a barefoot boy explained.

"Come on, just a few minutes?" the ball-bearer whined.

He looked at Eva. She nodded encouragingly.

"Okay," he agreed. "Let's play keep-up. Highest number of touches wins."

Over the next hour he showed off his ball skills, bouncing the ball from his feet to his knees to his head and back again, daring the kids to take it off him as he kicked it around the lot, and heading it as many times in a row as he could. The kids took turns demonstrating their own tricks, and soon the encounter developed into a game of four-a-side with Eva ably leading the girls' team. His knee protested the activity in thin-soled sneakers on an uneven surface, but he ignored it, relishing the chance to play under the same weak lamplight that had overseen almost every game of his childhood.

The girls were up two-one when his mother appeared on the edge of the lot, having wandered down the road looking for him and evidently unfazed by the crowd of children gathered around him.

"Time to come in, Rio," she called. "Your tea is getting cold."

Chapter 15

"GOOAALLL!"

Eva joined the other forty-five thousand fans in the stadium as she leapt to her feet, punching the air. The huge screen over the pitch showed Rio raise his fists in celebration, then pull on the front of his shirt to kiss the national-team badge. The noise in the stadium tripled as the crowd cheered for the goal that raised the score to three-nil.

She sank bank into the massive leather armchair that served as her seat to the international qualifier. She'd had a frisson of excitement when she'd followed Rio's mother—who insisted that she call her by her first name, Yolanda—his aunt, brother, brother's girlfriend, and assorted cousins into the VIP box bearing a sign that said *La Familia Vidal* on the door. She'd never even set foot in any of Skyline's private suites, and the plush seating, endless supply of food and drinks, and stunning view were instantly novel.

As the match wore on, however, she became uncomfortable with her distance from Rio. She was used to watching him from the dugout, within shouting distance, and certainly close enough to make eye contact. Now she might as well be at home on the couch for all the support she could give him.

As much as the setting wasn't ideal, nothing could've made her miss this chance to see him play for his country. At Skyline he was a midfielder, but as he lined up to sing the national anthem alongside his teammates his jersey number was nine.

Striker.

His performance did that number proud. He was a head shorter than every other player on the pitch, but his skills were a cut above.

Even greater than his skill was his passion. Rio was by nature a dedicated player, but she'd never seen him play with such soul, such ferocity, such palpable devotion that in moments it nearly brought her to tears. He hurled himself after the ball, sprang up every time a Venezuelan player tackled him to the ground, and took the sorts of audacious shots that could only come from a man playing more with his heart than his head.

He was a joy to behold. With every evaded challenge and ballsy steal she marveled at how much she'd discovered about this man in only a few short days—and how much more infatuated she became with every layer she uncovered.

She'd been less surprised by the facts she'd already more or less known— that he was ridiculously famous, that what he described as the village where he grew up was more accurately called a slum, and that he'd given back more to his community than he would readily admit—than by her own reaction. She already knew, intellectually, that Rio was kind and humble and generous. Seeing him in action was something else entirely.

On Wednesday, she accompanied him on a visit to the children's ward of a public hospital in Antofagasta. After dragging behind Hector, watching him smile insincerely in a dozen cancer wards and foster agencies and soccer academies for underprivileged kids she'd been wary of what felt like a classically choreographed PR stunt. She didn't say anything to Rio beforehand, but prayed the outing didn't undermine her impression of his good nature.

She shouldn't have worried. From the minute they arrived at the hospital and she realized there wasn't a camera or publicity professional in sight, she knew things were different.

The nurses greeted Rio warmly, and he asked each of them personal questions that bore testament to the frequency of his visits. When the all-female staff eyed her with emotions ranging from curiosity to suspicion, he introduced her as his *polola*, and explained that she was his voice in English-speaking America.

Whatever nervousness she'd had about the visit—she had zero rapport with children—was quickly dispelled by Rio's easy charm with patients and parents alike. Some people he'd already met, and others were delighted by his unexpected appearance.

"We'd heard rumors that he likes to pop into the ward, but I'd never actually seen him," a mother mentioned to her as they watched Rio play peek-a-boo with her toddler. "I guess he really is as nice as everyone says."

"I think so," Eva replied, her heart clenching as she watched Rio gently push the toddler's pacifier back into his mouth.

Apart from the many selfies and cell phone pictures taken by staff and parents there was no public record of his visit. Astonished by his total disinterest in leveraging the opportunity for publicity, as they climbed back into the chauffeured SUV she asked, "Don't you think you should tweet something to tell your fans what you got up to today? Remember, the Skyline PR manager said you need to have more of a personal presence on social media, not just retweet things posted by your sponsors."

He shrugged absentmindedly, scrolling through his e-mails on his phone. "You know how I feel about that stuff. It's not really anyone's business but mine, is it?"

That attitude pervaded the entire trip. His phone rang constantly as his agent's PA called to pass on requests for TV interviews and magazine shoots, but he turned them all down. His standard response was a joking line about being home on a social visit, not a professional one, but for all intents and purposes it was true.

They spent Wednesday afternoon in a housewares store where he failed to convince his mother to let him buy her a high-end espresso machine and sighed in exasperation as he plopped a cheap filter coffeemaker on the counter and handed over his credit card. Wednesday night they toured the new apartment Julio and his girlfriend had recently moved into before taking the couple out for dinner at a nearby steakhouse. Thursday morning they piled into the private jet down to Santiago accompanied by his extended family, and Thursday night the two of them ate dinner alone in their hotel room, naked, both famished after an afternoon spent pushing the limits of the in-room hot tub.

Friday morning she pressed a good-luck kiss to his lips as he left to join the team to prepare for that evening's match. Now here she was, physically separated from him for the first time in almost a week—and what a week it had been.

The rest of Rio's family had resumed their seats after his goal, but she wandered closer to the floor-to-ceiling windows, peering at the action below. Down on the pitch Venezuela were consolidating their efforts to halt Chile's advance, although at three-nil they probably should've focused more on attacking. Instead their style had become bullying and aggressive, almost as if they'd decided that if they were going to lose, they were going to take out as many of Chile's players as they could.

Rio had the ball, and two of the opposition's defenders were in such a hurry to tackle him they nearly collided with each other. He nipped between the two of them in a way that made her think of Moses sauntering through the two halves of the parted sea, full of confidence and utterly without fear.

A second later he was tackled, and the late challenge sent him rolling across the pitch. The culprit threw up his hands, insinuating Rio had dived, and a cluster of players from both sides gathered around the ref to argue.

The referee waved his hand to dismiss the incident and play resumed, but tensions were so high she could practically feel them all the way up in the box.

Venezuela took possession and for a few minutes the action centered in Chile's half. Eva was checking the time on the scoreboard—seventy minutes—when a collective intake of breath from Rio's family summoned her attention to the pitch.

Rio had stolen the ball and was powering toward Venezuela's goal, his lightning-quick speed carrying him away from the bulk of the players. Immediately a defender sprinted after him, driving him toward the edge of the pitch and away from his teammates. Rio glanced over his shoulder to see who could receive a pass, and in that the split second the defender stuck out two hands and shoved him in the back.

Rio fell head over feet, slamming into the row of pitch-side photographers and catching his knee on the edge of the wooden barrier in front of them.

"Come on, ref, fucking book him! Violent conduct!" Eva screamed at the glass, only realizing after the words had left her mouth that she'd spoken in Spanish, not English. She cast a sideways glance toward Rio's mother but if she'd heard, she made no acknowledgement. She was also busy hurling vulgar language at the referee.

There was no replay on the big screen in the stadium, but as Rio gingerly extricated himself from the mass of toppled camera equipment the TV in the VIP box—which was tuned to a network simulcast of the match—showed a slow-motion repeat of the incident.

The foul was as blatant as any she'd ever seen, and one of the most malicious. Yet on the pitch below the defender had his arms up to declare his innocence, and the referee gestured for Rio to rejoin the action.

"No fucking way," Julio shouted, punching the arm of a chair in disgust. "He could've broken Rio's neck."

"I hope they have some kind of performance review system for referees," his girlfriend, Martina, remarked hotly. "Because that was clearly an error."

Eva quirked a smile at Martina. "I think that's the most polite response to a bad call I've ever heard."

"Fire that halfwit scumbag!" Rosario demanded, proving Eva's point.

Never one to enter into protracted arguments with the referee, Rio waved to the fans, who cheered vigorously as he re-entered the pitch. He broke into a jog to catch up with his teammates and it was clear he was favoring his left leg.

Eva checked the time. Fifteen minutes to the whistle.

"He needs to come off," she murmured to no one in particular.

"What did you say?" his mother asked, moving to her side.

"They're up three-nil with only fifteen minutes on the clock. Venezuela have to score four goals to win—it'll never happen. The game is as good as won, Rio should be subbed out and checked for injury."

Yolanda squinted at the pitch. "You're right. He's limping."

"He needs to come off," she repeated, panic rising in her throat. The VIP box began to feel more like a prison than a privilege.

Why was he still playing? Didn't anyone else notice that he couldn't move properly? Was she the only one who cared?

She tried to calm herself down, certain the manager would pull him off. A minute went by, then another, then another, and he was still the central target for the rest of the team's passes. His pace had visibly slowed and his limp seemed to be worsening.

She wondered if Roland knew the Chilean national coach, or if they'd ever spoken. Maybe he wasn't aware that Rio was under medical caution from Skyline. Who was she kidding, of course Rio would never disclose that unless he had no choice.

She owed it to Roland to try to intervene.

No—she owed it to Rio.

He'd taken better care of her over the last two weeks than, well, any other man in her life, ever. He was there for her when she got the news of her mother's death and persisted in his efforts to support her no matter how often or how hard she pushed him away.

Now it was her turn to take care of him.

She rushed over to the waiter who'd been pouring their drinks for the last hour and a half. "I need to speak to the manager. Can you get me a line to one of the coaching staff on the sideline, please?"

To his credit, he concealed his are-you-crazy expression within a second of its appearance. "I don't think that's possible, *señorita*. They're all busy with the match."

She rolled her eyes. "Look, I'm not just *la polola*, okay? I work for Atlanta Skyline as the personal liaison between Roland Carlsson and Rio Vidal. I have vital information to communicate to the manager—or someone on the coaching staff, at least—regarding Rio's physical condition."

Recognition dawned in the man's eyes. "Ah, yes, I saw the article in the paper. You're his translator, I believe?"

"The article?" she echoed, bewildered.

He held up a finger to ask her to wait, then rummaged in the fanned spread of newspapers and magazines on a low table near the bar. He picked up one of the Chilean national dailies, flipped to a back page and handed it over.

Her jaw dropped halfway to the floor.

In the center of the page was a classic paparazzi photograph of Rio walking through the airport, head ducked, holding the hand of the woman by his side. She'd seen images like it a million times—there were usually at least three airport-crossing celeb photos on the sidebar of the Internet tabloid she surfed daily.

But this was the first time she'd been *in* one of them.

"What a score!" the headline announced. "He moves as fast with the ladies as he does on the pitch—Rio Vidal brings his American girlfriend home to Chile after just three months in the United States."

The opening paragraph speculated about whether his activities between the sheets would tire him out for the match against Venezuela, and she slammed down the paper as her mind reeled.

Of course she knew when she agreed to go public that there would be press coverage as word of their relationship would get around. Clearly she'd been naïve, because she hadn't considered that it would happen this fast. They'd only confirmed their commitment on Sunday, and less than a week later there was a photo of her looking disheveled and wide-eyed in a tabloid with national circulation.

She put a steadying hand on the bar as the waiter watched her expectantly. She couldn't deal with this right now—she had to get Rio off the pitch. Then she could quietly freak out.

"I am his translator," she agreed slowly. "And part of my job involves representing the wishes of his manager. Roland Carlsson had concerns about Rio's fitness and now he appears to have picked up a potential injury. It's critical that I speak to a member of the national-team staff in case they aren't aware of the preexisting concern."

Yolanda had moved to her side and was giving the waiter a narrow-eyed glare.

He glanced between both of them, then reiterated, "The entire staff is occupied with the match. I can try to arrange something afterward, but—"

"Quit wasting time," Yolanda snapped with the authority of a woman who'd raised three children on a shoestring by herself. "Call someone to take her down to the pitch. Now."

"Of course, *Señora* Vidal. Right away."

Yolanda rolled her eyes as he busied himself on the internal phone system. "Everyone assumes the players' girlfriends are all idiot lingerie models. They should know Rio would never bring a woman here unless she had a good brain in her head."

Eva gaped at what she was pretty sure was Yolanda's tacit approval of their relationship, and the waiter spoke before she could muster a response.

"Let me show you to the elevator. Someone will meet you on the other end."

With a quick wave to Rio's family, Eva followed the man down the corridor. He swiped his security pass and entered a code for stadium access, then nodded goodbye as the doors slid shut.

She unlocked her phone screen and scrolled through her contacts list as she rode the elevator down to the pitch. Should she call Roland and have him speak directly to someone from the national team? Or was she about to cause an international incident?

She checked the time and guessed at how long was left in the match. Around ten minutes, plus at least four for injury time. Maybe it didn't seem like much to make a fuss over, but it only took a second for a muscle sprain to be aggravated into a tear. She had to say something to someone and save Rio from himself.

The elevator came to a halt and the doors opened, revealing a young, pretty blond woman with big blue eyes. She looked up from her phone to greet Eva, who knew immediately what her borderline patronizing smile signaled.

She wasn't a member of the coaching staff. She was from the PR department.

"Hello, you must be Eva Torres?" She extended her hand. "Francisca Figueroa, one of the publicists for the national team. I understand you have a message you want to relay to the coaching staff? I'm afraid they're all quite busy with the match, but I can—"

"I get it." Eva sighed, exasperated. "Clearly no one wants to take me seriously."

"That's not the case at all," Francisca soothed in a placatory tone. "The whole team appreciates your commitment to Rio and his welfare. It's just that—"

"Do you ever feel like your colleagues don't take you seriously because you're a woman? Especially the training staff?"

Francisca blinked. "What?"

"Which did you love first, PR or soccer?"

"Soccer, but—"

"Have you ever noticed how most of the women working for elite-level soccer clubs are in the publicity, marketing, or HR departments? And even then, the directors of those departments are usually men. Is your boss a man or a woman?"

"I really don't see how this—"

"Just answer the question."

Francisca dropped the hand holding the phone to her side, her expression now totally devoid of its professional gloss. "He's a man. And I should've gotten the job over him two years ago." Her smile returned, only this time it was genuine. "What can I do to help?"

Minutes later they were greeted at the entrance to the tunnel by a man in a Chilean national-team tracksuit. His youth and politeness suggested he was a very junior member of the coaching staff, but Eva had reached the point where she would take what she could get.

"I'm Eva Torres, I work with Atlanta Skyline," she introduced herself. "I'm not here to undermine anyone, but I did want to let someone know that there's been concern at Skyline that Rio Vidal has been overtraining and may be more prone to injury than usual. I noticed he took quite a tough tackle there, and I wondered whether given this additional context—"

"I appreciate your raising this, but he had a full medical review before taking the field today and everything was clear." His smirk suggested he was already on his way to becoming a self-important manager. "I can assure you we're entirely capable of assessing our own players' match readiness."

She opened her mouth to argue, then closed it. Forget being seen to undermine the national-team manager—was this whole escapade undermining Rio?

She'd reacted with her heart when she saw him shoved into the camera, and now her head was catching up.

Did Rio always do what was best for him? No, he didn't. But he was an adult, capable of making his own choices. No matter how much she cared for him, or how convinced she was he would downplay any potential injury, she couldn't tell him what to do and she certainly couldn't meddle in his career.

She woke up to the situation like she'd startled from a dream. What the hell had she been thinking?

That she could save him. Protect him. Help him like she couldn't help her mother.

"Glad to hear it, and of course I trust the judgment of your staff," she replied, fighting to conceal the embarrassment, regret, and borderline hysteria raging behind her eyes. "I know inter-club communication sometimes breaks down when players move overseas, so thanks for taking the time to hear me out."

The young man nodded, indicating the conclusion of their conversation, and hurried back to the sideline.

Eva met Francisca's gaze reluctantly.

"That's it?" the publicist demanded. "Do you know what I had to do to get you that conversation? You know he's not going to pass on a word you said to—"

A raucous cheer echoed from the stadium, drowning out their conversation.

The ref had blown the final whistle. Chile were victorious. Even if the coaching assistant had listened she would've been too late.

Again.

Francisca glanced at her phone and rushed away as she typed furiously on the screen. Alone and unsupervised, Eva lingered in the tunnel, not sure she could find her way back to the VIP box if she wanted to. Instead she wandered toward the entrance to the pitch, thankful the security guards were too occupied with getting the players off safely to care about a five-foot woman in flats and a tangerine sundress.

She'd never been to an international qualifying match before, let alone one in soccer-mad South America. The atmosphere was electric, the stands an undulating sea of red and blue as supporters waved and sang to celebrate their nation's victory. On the pitch the players shook hands and swapped jerseys, and—judging by Rio's bare torso gleaming under the lights—his was one of the first to be claimed by the opposing team.

She peered at him from the shadows of the tunnel. He looked so happy, he practically radiated delight. He grinned at the fans, gave them two thumbs up, and then raised his arms to applaud, expressing his gratitude for their support.

Something stirred in her heart as she watched him. Had she ever been as blissfully, sublimely happy as he was at this exact moment? Had she ever known such uncomplicated joy? Had she ever had his absolutely clear vision, known exactly who she was and where she was going and what on earth she was doing with her life?

No.

Actually, yes. She knew she wanted to be with Rio, no matter the consequences. She liked who she was when she was with him.

Actually, scratch that—she'd always been a pretty big fan of herself. She liked that *he* liked who she was, exactly as she was.

Actually, "like" no longer entered into it. She was falling in love with him.

The fact insisted on itself once more, clearly and simply, before submitting to being tucked away deep in her heart. She was falling in love with Rio Vidal. Of course she was.

The players began drifting into the tunnel. Too late to sneak away she stepped out from the wall, bracing herself for Rio's reaction when he saw her. She hoped he wouldn't guess she'd been down here acting out some subconscious, unfulfilled savior urge.

His back-teeth grin the second he saw her assured her he hadn't.

He called her name and rushed over, sweeping her off her feet in a spinning hug before setting her back down with a kiss. "What are you doing down here?"

"It's a long story."

"Tell me later." He didn't even look at the equipment manager who handed him a fresh jersey, which he pulled on over his head. "They need me for the post-match interview."

She nodded. "Then I'll see you back at the hotel."

"Come with me." His smile seemed to banish every shadow in the concrete tunnel.

She wrinkled her nose. "Do you think that's appropriate? Players' girlfriends don't usually—"

"I don't care." He grabbed her hand and dragged her to the edge of the pitch, where a press board with the sponsors' logos had been set up in the sight-line of a television camera.

Her throat tightened and her eyes went wide as she stared out at the stands, barely able to see past the super bright lights illuminating the pitch. She felt like an ant under a microscope, hyperaware of all those eyes staring down from tens of thousands of seats. She squirmed just standing under their anonymous scrutiny. She couldn't imagine being expected to deliver goals as well.

The gray-haired, suited channel correspondent raised an eyebrow but said nothing as Rio took his place in front of the board. Francisca appeared beside the reporter and indicated for Eva to stand off to the side, which she gratefully obeyed.

Rio answered a few questions about events during the match, his voice echoing through a loudspeaker in the stadium. Fans cheered whenever he mentioned Chile, their shouts escalating as he declared it was good to be home.

The reporter seemed to be wrapping up the interview, thanking Rio and commending him on his victory. Eva relaxed minutely, relieved she hadn't had to face the camera.

Then Rio grabbed her and pulled her into the shot, pinning her to his side.

"One more thing," he interrupted. "I want to introduce Eva Torres, who translates for me at Atlanta Skyline. I would be lost in America without her, and whatever success I've had in the Championship League is owed at least in part to her support."

Her face was so hot she was sure it could burst into flames. She braced herself for a chorus of boos from all the adolescent girls who'd be ripping Rio's posters off their walls tonight.

Instead the Chilean fans redoubled their applause, chanting Rio's name as he waved at the crowd.

She'd never stood in the middle of a packed stadium before. The noise of the fans was immense, overwhelming, heady in its surround-sound intensity. No wonder Rio loved playing for his country. The cheering alone was downright addictive.

As much as she enjoyed her ten seconds in the spotlight, she exhaled her relief as they walked off the pitch and back into the privacy of the tunnel.

"I'll let you get showered," she told Rio, taking his hands and swinging them playfully. "I should go make sure your aunt isn't scandalizing the waiter in the VIP box."

"He should be more worried about how many bottles of liquor she's snuck into her purse."

"I'll offer to carry it for her and see how loudly it clinks."

She started to turn away and he tugged her back. "I meant everything I said just now. I don't know what would happen to me at Skyline if you weren't there."

His gaze pinned her to the spot with such sincerity she had to look down. She traced the number nine on his chest and then pulled out of his grip, starting in the direction of the elevator.

"See you later, striker," she called over her shoulder, just catching his cheeky, answering smile.

"Oh, God. Just like that. Don't stop."

Eva increased the pressure on the ball of his foot, running her thumbs along the arch. "You're sure I can't undo whatever the physiotherapist did earlier?"

Rio sank lower into the hot tub, closing his eyes as she worked her fingers along the soles of his feet.

"Even if you do, it'd be worth it."

"I'm not sure about that. How much are these things worth?"

He opened his eyes and grinned, gesturing down the length of his body. "Ten million for the whole thing, according to the insurance company."

She arched a brow. "Chilean pesos?"

"United States dollars."

"Way out of my price range." She shoved his feet off her lap and sat back, sloshing some of the soapy water over the side of the tub.

"I told you, they're insured. Keep going." He propped his foot on her thigh.

"Haven't you ever heard the phrase, you break it, you buy it?" But she drew his foot against the smooth, slick surface of her stomach and worked her knuckles into the muscles of his calves, the undersides of her breasts brushing his toes as she leaned forward.

He groaned in sheer ecstasy. Two goals to win for his country and the woman of his dreams massaging his legs. Could life get any better?

His eyes lit up with an idea. "Let's order room service."

"Again? You eat more than anyone I've ever met."

"I'm a man with a healthy appetite, that's all."

"And a healthy ego," she teased.

He smiled a response, but her words reminded him of the nagging concern he'd planned to discuss with her before their libidos took over.

"Anyway," he began, trying to keep his tone light. "We've gotten a lot of attention in the last couple of days. How are you feeling about it?"

She shrugged, her eyes downcast. "Fine, I guess."

He waited for her to elaborate. When she didn't, he leaned forward and brushed his finger beneath her chin, encouraging her to meet his gaze. "Really?"

She flashed him a hesitant smile. "I think so. I was never the type to fantasize about having a rich and famous boyfriend. It takes some getting used to."

"What did you fantasize about?"

"I don't know."

He straightened where he sat and reached for her, guiding her through the warm water to lean back against his chest. "Everyone has dreams when they're young." He combed his fingers through the damp ends of her hair. "What were yours?"

"Even as a teenager I was practical to a fault. My wildest ambition was to work in professional soccer and travel internationally. And look, here I am."

"What about law school? Do you still want to do that?"

She sighed. "I don't think so. The more I think about it, the more I realize it was a stupid, childish fantasy. When I was a kid I used to think, if I can get an A on this essay, then God will bring my mom back. I just have to do the right things to please Him and He'll give me what I want. Except whenever I achieved something and she didn't return, I had to find something else. The A-plus essay didn't work, so I had to make the honor roll. That didn't work, so I had to win an academic award—or all of the academic awards. The targets got higher and bigger until I didn't consciously realize they were targets anymore. Being a lawyer was the last one—if I could study super hard and spend all this time and money to become a powerful immigration lawyer, doing loads of good for people, she'll come back."

She shook her head. "Except now I know she won't, no matter what I do."

He frowned at the uncharacteristic ambivalence in her words. "But you love the drop-in center and the work you do there."

"I used to," she agreed. "They're coping just fine without me, though, and it's going to be hard to celebrate the success stories without thinking about my own sad ending. I think it might be time for me to take a step back and let someone else take the reins."

This definitely wasn't the woman he knew. He paused as he considered his response, trying to get his words exactly right before he spoke them.

"You didn't fail your mom, Eva. There was nothing you could've done to bring her back."

She splashed him with the sharpness of her turn, her eyes wide and surprised. Then she resumed her relaxed posture with a heavy exhalation.

"I did fail her, Rio. I should've hired a private investigator earlier, when I was in high school."

"You know that's a ridiculous thing to say," he replied gently. "You told me you worked at a frozen yogurt shop in high school. You never could've paid the fees."

"I could've tried. Maybe I could've made a deal," she countered glumly.

"What kinds of deals do you think border-crossing PIs make with adolescent girls?"

She lifted a shoulder. "I could've found an honest one."

"Everything you could've done, you did," he told her firmly.

She said nothing. He shifted slightly beneath her.

"You weren't at Mass last week, but I went. I stopped by the drop-in center, too."

"Good for you," she muttered.

"Virginia was there. Remember her? From Honduras, her son was facing deportation?"

She nodded. "We met her together. Your first Sunday."

"She had good news that she wanted to tell you in person. Her son's deportation order was lifted."

"Then she should thank her lawyer. I didn't—"

"But she wanted to thank you. Maybe the lawyer is the one who booted it into the net, but she couldn't have done that if you hadn't crossed her the ball in the first place."

She rolled her eyes at him over her shoulder. "What's your point? That I'm the midfielder of legal advice?"

"Everyone has their part to play, that's all. Don't leave the pitch because you've decided you don't want to wear the number-nine jersey."

"Maybe I would be happier in the midfield." She raised her arms in a lazy stretch, giving him a clear line of sight to her breasts. He couldn't help himself—he cupped their supple heft, his thumbs teasing her nipples.

She purred her delight and he was instantly hard, his erection jutting against the small of her back.

The cloud of lust was encroaching on his thoughts like a thunderstorm, but he still had something he wanted to say.

He brushed his lips along the line of her shoulder, up her neck, stalling beside her ear. "With all this media attention, the articles in the tabloids—you know your job at Skyline is safe, right?"

She stiffened in his grip, pulling away, then repositioned herself so they sat perpendicular to each other.

"I have to tell you something."

Worry increased his heart rate but he kept his voice even. "What?"

She quit. Or she lost her job. If that Swedish asshole fired her, I swear—

"Roland asked me to keep an eye on you down here. You know, make sure you weren't overdoing it."

He exhaled slightly. So Roland was an intruding busybody with no boundaries. That wasn't news.

"That's okay," he assured her. "He shouldn't put you in the middle like that, but you didn't do anything wrong."

She spread her hands in front of her, examining her nails. "You found me in the tunnel today because I forced my way down there. I thought they should've subbed you once the score hit three-nil. I even considered calling Roland and having him speak to the national-team staff."

Rio took several slow, deep breaths to quell the rare anger blooming in his chest. He must've misunderstood. She couldn't—she wouldn't dare. His manager's meddling was one thing, but he couldn't deal with her interfering on his behalf. Not in his own country, with his own team. Not after everything he'd shown her. Not after he'd seen her on the sideline and forgotten about the crowds and the match and everything except her face. Not after he realized he was falling in love with her.

"You didn't, though, right?" he clarified, hoping to verify his disbelief. "You didn't put Roland through to anyone on the coaching staff."

She shook her head. "I thought better of it at the last minute. I'm sorry, Rio. It was a mistake, and it won't happen again, but I wanted to be honest with you."

He drew her back to his side with a sigh, pushing down the flare of indignation and fury that still fought to rise up through his ribs. "I'm glad you told me. My career is the only thing I have. I'm not smart like you. If I screw this up, I can't go get a job in an office. While you dreamed of working in soccer, I dreamed of playing it. It's the only thing I've ever wanted, and I'm doing the best I can to keep it going for as long as possible." He brushed her hair back over her shoulder. "Next time Roland tries to go behind my back, I want you to tell me right away. We're a team, you and I. Okay?"

She nodded. "Okay."

He squeezed her, then reached over the side of the tub for a towel. "The water's getting cold—my muscles are locking up. Let's order dessert and I'll show you the best of Chilean TV."

She stood, water cascading down her body as she watched him with a coy smile. "How about we warm up those muscles in bed and you can have me for dessert."

He threw the towel across the room, running his hand up her thigh instead. "Done."

Chapter 16

Eva's eyes were already wide open when the alarm squealed on Rio's bedside table.

He silenced his beeping phone and rolled over, pulling her against his stomach and wrapping his arms around her waist. She slid her legs between his and closed her eyes, unable to stop reliving the moment that occurred two hours earlier.

A strange sound jolted her awake sometime after four o'clock in the morning. It took a few seconds for her to get her bearings—Rio's bed, early Saturday morning, no, she wasn't late for work—and then register the source of the odd and distressing noise.

Rio was whimpering in his sleep, his brow furrowed with pain.

She whispered his name and ran her hand down his arm, hoping to redirect him from what she assumed was a nightmare without waking him up fully. He mumbled something unintelligible, then rolled over with an anguished groan and opened his eyes.

He shut them again almost instantly, wrapping his hands around his knee and flopping onto his back.

"What's wrong?" she asked, smoothing her fingers over his forehead. It was damp with cold sweat.

"Nothing," he replied through gritted teeth. "Just a cramp."

"In your knee?"

He nodded, eyes squeezed closed.

She wasn't a doctor, but she was pretty sure knee cramps weren't really a thing. "Are you sure it's not something else? Do you want me to call Tony?" she asked, naming Skyline's medic.

He shook his head forcefully, dragging himself upright and swinging his legs over the edge. "I just need to walk it off. Can you give me a hand?"

"Of course." She hurried to meet him on the other side of the bed, and used all her strength to support him into a standing position.

His left leg buckled the second he put weight on it. He caught himself with a hand on the bedframe as she dove to prop him up from the other side.

"I'm calling Tony. Sit down," she instructed, but he refused, slowly putting weight on his left knee.

"See? I'm fine. Took some warming up, that's all. No need to get Tony out of bed at this hour."

His words were tight and breathless with pain. She sighed disapprovingly as he hobbled across the room, then held out his palms as if to say, *voila.*

"Not impressed," she informed him flatly.

He reached into the bottom drawer of his dresser, pulled out a roll of athletic bandage, and dropped into a chair in the corner of the room.

"You've heard of the magic spray," he said, referring to the topical aerosol anesthetic used by pitch medics as he wrapped his knee. "This is my magic bandage. Works every time."

She crossed her arms. "That's the side you were favoring after you fell into the cameras on Friday."

"So?"

"You can be honest with me. I'm not your manager."

"No, but you might go running to him with whatever I tell you," he snapped.

"Don't you dare," she shot back, concealing her shock at his uncharacteristic sharpness. "I'm trying to help you."

"I know. I'm sorry." He rubbed a weary hand over his eyes. "Match-day nerves."

"You can't play if you're injured."

"I'm not injured."

"You look injured."

"I'm not," he repeated firmly. "I get nighttime muscle cramps all the time. It's not a big deal."

She pursed her lips, debating whether or not to voice the sentence forming in her head.

She had to. She'd hate herself if she didn't.

"Obviously I'm not a doctor, but I've spent enough time with Hank to know that knee pain usually means there's something wrong with the joint or the ligament—not muscle. If you're having an issue with the knee you pretty blatantly smacked against a wooden barrier, you should have him look at it before you make it worse."

"You're right, you're not a doctor." He made his way back to the bed, his tight expression betraying his effort to conceal his limping progress. "Which is why you need to trust me to make good decisions about my fitness. You know I would never jeopardize my career."

She slid under the covers beside him, stroking the side of his face as he settled onto his back. "My concern is that you'd rather bet on yourself to play through a minor injury than run the risk of being replaced in the first team if you don't start."

His sharp glance told her she'd hit the nail on the head, but within seconds he smoothed his keen gaze into a charming smile.

"I know what I'm doing. Trust me, *querida*."

He kissed her lightly on the lips, then lay back and drew her into his side. Within a few minutes he'd gone back to sleep.

She never managed to join him.

Now she squinted resentfully at the light glowing around the edges of the curtains. She began to prop herself up on her elbow but Rio pinned her to the mattress. He was more awake than she'd realized.

She opened her mouth to remind him of his match-day schedule, but the words stalled and died in her throat as his hand slid beneath the waistband of the boxers she wore—his boxers.

While his left arm kept her tight against him, the index finger of his right hand slipped between her legs. First he gently probed her sex, exploring her slickness until she was so wet she practically leaked onto her thighs. Then the pad of his finger found her clit, and began a series of slow, merciless circles on her hypersensitive flesh.

The sounds she made were primal, her efforts at movement wild, but he held her fast, his lips against the back of her neck and his erection pressed between her buttocks as he perfectly maintained the steady, agonizing rhythm.

He slipped his middle finger inside her and she bucked against his hand, a fine sheen of sweat breaking out across her torso. She moaned his name as her vision blurred, losing herself to the frenzy that preceded release.

She grabbed his wrist, rocked against his fingers, desperate to push him harder, deeper, delirious with the nearing brink of ecstasy.

"I want to make you happy." His whispered words barely registered above what sounded like a freight train rushing through her ears. "I love you, Eva."

Her orgasm was like crashing her car into a brick wall. Sudden, jolting, bewildering, the neck-whipping force of impact and the trembling surge of adrenaline. It took a long time for the dust to settle. And when it did, she knew she would never be the same.

"You can go in now."

Eva nodded her thanks to Roland's PA as she crossed the reception area to the manager's office door. She knew Roland hadn't called her in to tell her what a great job she was doing, and she braced herself for the worst as she stepped inside.

"Eva," Roland acknowledged her flatly, gesturing to a chair in front of his desk. "Sit."

She did, her posture straight as an arrow. She hadn't done anything wrong, and if he dared suggest she—

"I'm worried about Rio."

She said nothing.

"He passed his medical this morning," he continued. "I have no reason not to start him in a couple of hours. Except my gut instinct."

"I don't know what you want me to say," she replied.

"Is he really fit to play?"

"That's between you and him. I'm not his doctor, I'm his—"

"Girlfriend," Roland supplied, momentarily stopping her heart. "And probably the only one he'll tell the truth."

You'd be surprised, she thought tightly, waiting for the backlash. She would take whatever he wanted to throw at her, then apologize profusely. Or maybe she didn't owe him an apology at all. It wasn't her fault she and Rio had fallen for each other, and anyway, who was Roland to—

He sat back in his chair, adjusted his trendy waistcoat and crossed his arms. She held her breath, determined to stand up for herself.

"I called his old manager on Monday, in Chile. I asked him if he had problems with Rio overtraining or if it was related to the move to the CSL. He said there was only one thing the two of them ever fought about—Rio's refusal to self-report his injuries. He loves to play so much—and is so paranoid he'll lose his spot on the team if he doesn't keep up this insane work rate—that he trains until he physically can't anymore. Apparently he had a recurring hamstring strain a couple of years back, and Rio got so depressed that his manager used to put him on the subs bench even though he had zero intention of letting him on the pitch."

She blinked. Was that it? No mention of professional boundaries? Nothing? Well, she wasn't about to bring it up if he didn't.

"That sounds like Rio," she acknowledged.

"My point is, even his manager had to learn how to save Rio from himself." He leaned forward, his expression beseeching. "Lord knows I hate seeing any of my players injured, but I couldn't forgive myself if Rio pulled up with something serious because I played him when I shouldn't have. On the other hand, I don't want him going through the psychological stress of being benched when he's fit to play. You saw what happened in Tucson—he could barely sit still." Roland threw up his hands. "I need your help, Eva. I don't want to put you in a position to betray Rio's confidence, but I'm at a loss."

She studied the edge of Roland's desk, and then the hem of her red Skyline polo.

Dammit. Why couldn't Roland be more of an asshole, someone she could readily hate and defy? Why did he have to be so fair and understanding and...sincere?

She understood the manager's perspective. He'd never been interested in policing his players' personal lives, as long as they didn't affect their performance. Hector's relentless sexual appetite was the perfect example. If Roland hadn't felt he could intervene then, why did she expect him to intervene now?

On the same point, it was hard to trust a player with a history of injury concealment, but at the same time there was no point in benching someone—and losing his contribution to the match—if he was good to play.

Nevertheless, Rio had made it abundantly clear that his readiness to play was a matter for him and his manager. She'd already come close to undermining him once, and couldn't—*wouldn't*—do it again. She wasn't his doctor or his nanny. It wasn't her job to inform his manager that knee pain was waking him up at night, making him sweat and grit his teeth in his sleep...

"He insists he's fit to play," she said finally, if somewhat uneasily. "If I could tell you more, I would, but I can't."

Disappointment etched Roland's face, but he nodded. "Thank you. And I want you to know I trust you implicitly. You did great work for Hector no matter how much he made that difficult, and now you have Rio's best interests at heart. I know you'll do what's right for him if it comes to it."

She left his office and headed for the staff lounge, her thoughts running a mile a minute. What should she do about Roland? What should she do about Rio? What should she do about what he'd said to her that morning?

She poured an umpteenth cup of coffee and slumped at one of the café-style tables lining the back wall of the lounge. She hadn't reacted at all to Rio's revelation that morning. By the time she'd recovered her wits and basic control of her extremities, the moment had long passed, and she didn't know how to respond. No one had ever said it to her before.

She could guess the appropriate reply, and it wouldn't have been a lie to say she loved him too. She did, and she loved him more with each minute that passed. Recognizing that was a challenge in itself. Saying it aloud was another hurdle entirely.

If he was hurt by her lack of reciprocation he didn't let on. But she knew he had to be thinking about it. Maybe even at this exact second, as he warmed up alongside his teammates, his thoughts were of her. Processing how he felt about her. Wondering how she felt about him.

She cringed into her coffee cup, wishing she'd had the courage to be honest and tell him the truth, that she felt exactly the same.

Had she fallen through a wormhole to an alternate reality? She'd always been confident and sexually fearless, not to mention resilient in the face of successive relationship failures. Now she'd bagged an international soccer star, a man tens of thousands of women would climb over her dead body to date, and she went tongue-tied.

Ugh.

"That's not the face I would expect on someone just returned from a sexy getaway to Chile." Olivia dropped into the chair on the other side of the table. "Everything okay?"

"Not really. But what are you doing slumming it with the staff instead of lounging in a VIP box?"

"The PR department needed extra hands with a sponsor photo shoot. One of the assistants called out sick. I was bored—and standing nearby—so I got roped in to holding a light meter."

"In that case, shouldn't you be off trying to convince Guedes not to look so homicidal in the team photos?"

"You've noticed that too?" She rolled her eyes. "It's like he's auditioning for a movie called *Straight Outta the Favela.*"

Eva laughed, and Olivia pulled her chair closer to the table. "Seriously, I have time. What's up? And before you say anything, I love Deon with all my heart, but that doesn't mean I don't occasionally fantasize about taping his mouth shut."

"Rio has his moments," she agreed. "But this is about me, not him. My boundaries, my ethics."

Olivia whistled. "A little more serious than forgetting to pick up his dirty socks, huh?"

"A little."

She exhaled. "I'd offer you advice, but quite frankly, I made more wrong moves than right ones."

"Did you know they were wrong when you made them?"

"Sometimes," Olivia admitted. "Other times only in hindsight."

Eva propped her chin on her hand. "I'm not used to not knowing exactly what to do and when to do it. It sucks."

"Welcome to the swamp of ambiguity that is love." Olivia raised her cardboard coffee cup in a mock toast. Eva joined her, trying not to panic at Olivia's use of the l-word.

Love. It wasn't a concept she'd spent a lot of time thinking about. Even her most romantic fantasies were practical and usually material, dreaming of a husband who had an Ivy League degree, wasn't paying off a car loan, and had a Series 7 license. The emotional angle was assumed—of course love would be a prerequisite—but never explored.

Did that make her shallow? Maybe. More likely it said something about her priorities and how they were changing the longer she and Rio were together. He had greater personal wealth than anyone she'd ever remotely imagined dating, his net worth so high it became more theoretical than comprehensible. And despite that—or maybe because of it—she had to face up to all the emotional complexities she'd ignored until now.

So here she was, uniquely unprepared for what she realized was more important than a bank balance or an IQ score: the raw, unforgiving, unrelenting push-and-pull of love.

"I've got to head off, make sure the PR guys don't need me again," Olivia said, jerking Eva from her reverie. "Providence brought their mascot. Apparently he has a tendency to start fistfights."

"Good luck."

"Let's go Skyline." Olivia stuck a thumb in the air, already typing on her phone as she walked out of the lounge.

"Or something," Eva muttered, swirling the remains of her coffee in the cup. In a few minutes she'd have to walk down to the dressing room and sit in the row of chairs outside the door, ready and waiting should Roland and Rio need one more pre-match conversation. It was an element of her job she normally adored—being part of the match-day machine, moving amongst the high-energy players, finding exactly the right way to communicate the manager's most important pep talk.

Today she would've rather scrubbed stadium toilets.

She sighed, crumpled her cup, and chucked it in the recycling bin. Who knew being in love would be so miserable?

Rio had never been so grateful for the half-time whistle. The ache in his knee that had previously only bothered him at night and at the end of training sessions had decided to make its first match-day appearance for Skyline as they took on the Providence Colonials.

Inevitably his knee couldn't have chosen a worse time to give him grief. Skyline's first team had returned from the international break with a slate of injuries, and to say the talent on the field was thin was generous.

Brian was playing for Nico, who'd injured his hip in Argentina. Swedish defender Oz was out with a hamstring sprain, Paulo had pneumonia, and their third-string goalkeeper looked suspiciously ready to be subbed on. Brian's careless own goal equalized Deon's one-nil lead, Providence's striker had two near-miss attempts, and Roland looked like he was on the verge of a heart attack.

Supposedly soccer players ran about seven miles during a ninety-minute match. As he trudged off the pitch, Rio felt like he'd run at least fifteen.

His spirits lifted when he saw Eva on the sideline. Instead of making waves, news of their relationship had barely rippled the sea of Championship League gossip, which was preoccupied by the pregnant mistress of a French forward who played for Cleveland. He was almost disappointed—if he so much as looked sideways at a woman in Chile it made the tabloids—but for Eva's sake he appreciated the lack of fanfare.

He paused in the tunnel to take her hand before following his teammates to the dressing room. Her eyes were soft with sympathy.

"That first half was brutal. How are you holding up?"

"Fine," he said automatically.

She didn't need to reply—her expression reminded him in no uncertain terms that she expected honesty.

She was right. She deserved the truth.

"My knee's a little sore," he confided quietly.

"The same one as last night?"

He nodded.

"Was it that tackle from the big blond guy?" she asked, referring to one of the Colonials' defenders.

"Maybe."

Her fingers tightened around his. "Do you want to see the medic?"

He did. Desperately. He wanted Tony to wrap his knee, work the muscles above and below, give him a batch of painkillers and send him home to bed. He was tired and sore and terrified that his throbbing joint was going to end his career with Skyline. He'd only had a couple of months to prove himself—no way would Roland renew his contract if he spent the same time again on the injury list.

Which is why he shook his head. "After the second half. It's not that bad."

Her tilted head said she didn't believe him.

"Roland's already used half of the subs' bench," he protested.

"And he'll have to keep using them if you overdo it and hurt yourself."

"I wouldn't play if I didn't want to."

"You wouldn't play if you *couldn't* play," she corrected. "Even then I think you'd try it on one leg."

"You know me too well, *querida*." He flashed her his big grin, but wasn't too surprised when it failed to charm away her palpable concern.

She nodded down the tunnel. "Come on, or you'll miss Roland's rousing half-time team talk."

"Promise?"

She rolled her eyes and he backed her against the wall, indulging in a single, lingering kiss that he didn't have time for yet couldn't resist. He should be stretching, rehydrating, changing out his soaked undershirt. He should be icing his knee, refocusing his mind, readying himself for the second battle of this ninety-minute war.

All he wanted to do was take her to bed and show her how much he loved her.

"This morning—"

"We have to go," she urged, dragging him down the tunnel toward the changing room. "You've only got ten minutes and Roland's going to be furious."

"I don't care." He halted their progress, anchoring her in place with his hands on her upper arms. "Did you hear what I said this morning?"

"I heard you."

"And?"

She glanced over her shoulder, ensuring they were alone. "Can we talk about it later? You need to—"

"The only thing I need is for you to tell me three words."

She hesitated. His heart stalled.

Then she smiled.

"I had five words in mind, but I guess I can lose two."

"I'll take as many as you want to give me."

She planted her hands on his chest, leaned up to press her lips beside his ear and whispered, "I love you too, Rio."

"Vidal!" Ross appeared at the end of the tunnel. "Bzzzbzzzbzzz Roland bzzz!"

Eva dropped back onto the soles of her feet. "He says you—"

"I can guess."

"Have a good second half." She squeezed his hand once more before dropping it.

"I will," he promised, to her and his team and the fans and anyone who'd ever believed in a scrawny kid from the strip of civilization between the ocean and the desert. He would make his country proud to call him a native son. He would make his mother proud to have borne him despite his paternity. He would make every poor child kicking a ball in bare feet proud to be starting from the same place he did.

He would make Eva proud to love him.

He charged onto the pitch for the second half with the energy of a tidal wave sweeping up the shore and consuming everything in its path. His knee hurt but he didn't care, too buoyed by adrenaline and excitement to feel anything except pure joy.

She loves me. He drove the ball down the pitch and shot it to Laurent.

I'm in love—we're in love. He received a pass from Brian, negotiated around one of Providence's defenders, and sailed the ball to Guedes.

Holy shit, she loves me! He tackled a Colonials defender, took possession and crossed to Deon, who made an attempt on goal.

The crowd exhaled collectively—the shot went wide. Still they were off to a good start, and the momentum was on their side.

Laurent jogged nearby as the goalkeeper booted the ball back down the pitch. He pointed toward one and then another of Providence's midfielders, using the crude but effective form of communication they'd developed as they played together.

"You, left, push right," Laurent suggested, employing a couple of the words in Rio's growing English vocabulary.

Rio nodded, replying in English, "It's okay."

As they charged down the pitch to put their plan into action, Rio was overtaken by an unusual sense of contentment.

For all his success, his life had never felt perfect—until now. He was still sailing on the high from his trip to Chile, where playing for his country gave him more bone-deep satisfaction than any degree of fame. He'd found his place at Skyline, had earned the trust and respect of his teammates, and was on his way to league title contention in his first season in the Championship League. His brother and sister were secure and happy. His mother was taken care of. Even the void that was his real father's identity had stopped bothering him.

And of course there was Eva. Her Virgin's eyes and all the secrets they contained. Her confidence and strength and gentle core. Her laugh. Her smile. Her tender, noble heart.

He lifted his eyes to the heavens, offering his gratitude to God or the Virgin or whoever happened to be listening. Then he sprinted toward the midfielder he was marking, one eye on his target and the other on the ball.

His knee gave out.

His hands hit the grass before he could fully process what happened. It came back to him in a disjointed sequence: a sickening *crunch*, a tilting view of the stands, a wave of pain so intense he felt nauseous.

He rolled into a sitting position and stretched his leg in front of him, shivering from the stabbing ache that rolled up his thigh from his knee. Laurent knelt beside him, frowning his concern.

"Bzzzbzzz, okay? Bzzzbzzzbzzz."

Rio shook his head automatically. "It's nothing, I'm fine."

But Laurent raised his hand for the medic. Providence kicked the ball out of play as Tony jogged to meet him, Eva at his side.

"What's wrong?" she asked.

Rio gritted his teeth against a shock of pain as Tony probed his knee with rubber-gloved hands. "I twisted my knee, but it's all right. I can get up."

To prove his point he started to push himself back to his feet, but Tony stopped him with a hand on his shoulder.

"Bzzzbzzzbzzz," the medic said, then turned to Eva. "Bzzzbzzz bzzz bzzzbzzz."

"He wants to know if you heard or felt anything in your knee, like a pop or a crunch."

Rio shook his head.

Tony studied the joint, then spoke to Eva. "Bzzzbzzzbzzz. Bzzzbzzz?"

"Can you bend it? Does it feel stiff or loose?"

"It feels fine. It hurt when I first fell, but it's getting better by the second." Rio hauled himself into a standing position, trying not to let the agony show on his face. He wasn't completely lying—it did feel more stable than when he first went down. He could put weight on it. Barely.

Eva translated for Tony, whose expression was unreadable. When she spoke again he knew her words were meant only for him.

"Tell me the truth. Are you injured? Do you need to come off?"

"One more goal," he confided. "We look good to push it up to two-one but it won't happen with me on the bench. One goal. Then I'll be done, I promise."

"It's not worth it."

"It won't take long."

"You don't know that."

"Trust me."

She darted an anxious look at Tony, who watched their exchange with interest. "Don't put me in this position. Don't ask me to lie so you can be reckless."

He blinked away the sting in her words, her revelation of what he was asking. He couldn't worry about that now. One more goal. His knee would last until then.

"I'm not asking you to lie. I'm telling you I don't need to come off."

The look she shot him was black as fresh tar and twice as hot.

He didn't care.

He turned his back on Eva and Tony and limped toward the center of the pitch. He was dizzy from pain and adrenaline and anxiety, but he forced himself to jog toward the direction of play.

Cold sweat broke out on his forehead. His knee felt loose and wobbly. He wouldn't last another half-hour. He might not even last another five minutes.

Suddenly he was ten years old again, raw with grief at his father's death, bewildered by the revelation he wasn't his father at all, peering through wary eyes at his teammates. He was the newest, the smallest, and by far the best player on his school soccer team. His outsider status had been obvious the day he'd turned up to practice without boots—a boy from a rural slum trying to make his way among the city kids. In the classroom he was held back, barely able to read and write, but on the pitch the coach pushed him forward until he was playing against thirteen-year-olds twice his size.

Every time he stepped onto that patchy grass he had something to prove. Whether it was about soccer, or money, or that his very existence was evidence of his mother's shame, those ninety minutes carried so much more weight than the score on the board at the end. He had to win. Otherwise he was nothing.

"Rio." Guedes called his name to get his attention, then pointed toward the sideline.

The fourth official raised the digital substitution board. Number seventeen was in red.

His match was over.

He scowled as he hobbled off the pitch, frustration and disappointment and panic at the implications of his departure building into uncharacteristic rage. He didn't thank the fans, he didn't acknowledge the second-team player who would take his place, and he refused to look at Roland, shaking off the manager's attempt to grab him by the arm.

Instead he limped over to the giant plastic bucket full of water bottles and kicked it as hard as he could, sending bottles rolling into the tunnel on a wave of melted ice as the bucket ricocheted off one of the concrete walls.

"Rio!" Eva came up beside him, her hands on her hips. Fans seated in the stands above the tunnel had their phones out, and he was sure his outburst had already gone viral.

Whatever. His reputation wouldn't matter if he had no career.

Tony and two members of the training staff tried to usher him into the tunnel but he jerked out of their reach, whirling on Eva.

"Did you do this? Did you tell Roland to take me off?"

"Damn straight I did," she shot back, eyes flashing.

He slammed his hand through his hair, so angry he shook. "That wasn't your call to make. You had no right."

"You can barely walk. If it hadn't been me it would've been—"

"But it was you," he interjected, his own words registering bleakly as they left his mouth. "After everything we've talked about, everything you've seen, this is what you do to me?"

Her fierce expression faltered. "Rio, I didn't—"

But he was on a roll, carried by the momentum of his fury. "You're the only person who understands the weight on my shoulders. I've never trusted anyone else with what I showed you in Antofagasta—my story, my legacy, the stakes I play for every time I set foot on the pitch. And how did you reward my trust? By undermining me. Interfering with my career. Telling my manager exactly what I told you not to. You betrayed me, Eva." He practically spat the word. Then he pivoted on his good knee and charged into the tunnel.

Tony rushed to join him, and as the pain in his knee overcame his receding frustration, he allowed the medic to put a comforting hand on his elbow.

Tony indicated his bad leg. "Bzzzbzzz bzzz?"

Automatically he glanced around for Eva. She stood at the entrance to the tunnel, staring after him, her expression so stricken he almost had a pang of regret.

Almost.

Tony looked between him and Eva, and raised his brows as if asking whether they should wait for her.

Rio shook his head and continued forward without her.

Chapter 17

Eva opened the kitchen cabinet, took out a wineglass, plunked it on the counter. She moved to the refrigerator, picked up a mostly full bottle of white wine, put it on the counter, changed her mind, put it back and shut the fridge door. She replaced the wineglass in the cupboard and walked back to the couch, but didn't sit down.

"Fuck it. Desperate times."

She returned to the kitchen and repeated the same sequence, again changing her mind at the last minute and shutting the door to the refrigerator without pouring the wine.

She'd been home from the match for over an hour and this was her third round of to-pour-or-not-to-pour. A whole evening of this and she'd wear grooves into the tile floor.

This time she sat on the couch instead of standing in front of it, and the relief of being off her feet was so instant she flopped down onto her back. She stared at the ceiling, resolved to finally replace that light that had burned out, and wondered what the hell she was going to do about Rio.

She didn't regret telling Roland he was injured, not for a second. Tony would've done it anyway, but that wasn't the point—she wasn't going to lie to protect his crazy self-destruction. She cared about him too much to do that.

His insistence on continuing when he was obviously hurt wasn't only crazy, it was stupid. When your body is your career, why jeopardize it? Why push yourself so far beyond your limits that you risk losing everything?

She recalled that match against Tucson, when Rio practically vibrated with nervous energy on the bench and begged to be allowed to play. Visions of him in the gym flashed through her mind, as did his ongoing arguments with Roland about overtraining. She thought of his reception at the airport in Santiago, the inches of height separating him from the rest of the national team, the pure bliss in his expression when he scored for his country.

Maybe he was blind to the danger he put himself in by playing through an injury. Maybe he couldn't see past his fans' adoration to the reality that they were as invested in him as a player as in the numbers he put on the scoreboard. Maybe he was still that barefoot kid in the slum, jostling his friends for possession of a half-inflated ball beside the gates of the cemetery.

She flattened her hands over her eyes with a sigh. And maybe she didn't even need to waste her time thinking about it. After their exchange on the sideline she could very well be out of his life and out of a job.

That was the unspoken angle she'd been too in love to consider. Sure, her job would be safe if she was keeping her player boyfriend happy. But what happened when it all fell apart?

Unemployment was the last thing she needed on top of a broken heart. The emotional implications of breaking up with Rio—no. She couldn't even go there yet. That was the huge, droning wasp in the bedroom she was too afraid to approach, let alone kill.

She stood up and walked back to the kitchen. She would have that glass of wine after all.

She was reaching for the glass when her phone buzzed on the counter. She glanced at the screen.

Tony.

Her heart leapt into her throat and her breaths came fast and hot. Was Rio okay? Did he want to talk to her? Was everything about to be restored to the way it was or ruined forever?

She snatched up the phone. "Hi, Tony."

"Can you come to the hospital? I'm here with Ross and Rio."

She closed her eyes, trying to interpret his uncharacteristically serious tone. "What's wrong?"

"We're struggling to explain the situation to Rio, and it's important that he understands. It's not good news."

She swallowed hard. "Does he want me to be there?"

Tony paused. "He needs you to be here."

"I'm on my way."

She never felt less safe behind the wheel than she did on the drive to the hospital. Her hands shook and her lungs clenched, and she used all of her energy to focus on the road ahead. Whenever her thoughts veered in Rio's direction she reined them in without mercy.

There was no point in speculating before she had all the details.

There was no point in breaking up with him in her mind before he'd said the words.

And if he said the words...

She shook off that line of thinking as she parked, then followed Tony's instructions to find the right room. She knocked lightly before opening the door.

The mere sight of Rio took her breath away. He'd changed into a white undershirt, training shorts and Skyline flip flops, and even semi-reclined on a hospital bed with his knee wrapped in athletic bandages, he was the most exquisite man she'd ever laid eyes on.

Which is why the darkening of his expression as she entered the room hurt more than she could imagine.

Ross and Tony greeted her with palpable sympathy. If his averted gaze was anything to go by, she guessed they had a hard time convincing Rio to let her come.

Well, he could get over it. She had a job to do.

Thankfully the doctor arrived within moments, saving them all the awkwardness of sitting in silence while they waited. She swept into the room with a manila folder, from which she plucked several printouts of what looked like a scan.

"Are you the interpreter?" she asked, not impolitely.

Eva nodded.

"Great. Let's not waste any more time."

The doctor clipped one of the scans onto a light box and launched into a lengthy explanation of the results of Rio's MRI. Eva concentrated intensely, trying to memorize everything the doctor said while simultaneously figuring out how to translate such technical medical terminology. Some of the words were unfamiliar to her in English—how would she find a Spanish equivalent?

But this was what she did, and she did it better than anyone. The doctor finished and put the printout back in the folder.

"Did you get all of that?"

"I did." She turned to Rio, taking a minute to finalize exactly what she was going to say.

He watched her intently. She took a bracing breath.

"You've torn a ligament in your knee. The tear is severe, and requires surgery to fix, which she recommends scheduling immediately. It'll be at least three months before you can play again."

He stared at her blankly for so long she began to wonder whether she'd mistranslated something. The room was a tense tableau, no one daring to move, waiting for his reaction.

When he finally spoke his voice was hollow with disbelief. "Three months? Is she sure?"

"She is."

"Surgery," he echoed, his gaze drifting to his lap. "I've never had surgery before. I've never even been in a hospital overnight."

She wanted so badly to comfort him that she ached with the urge to take him in her arms. Instead she kept things professional, asking, "Do you have any questions for the doctor?"

He shook his head. "Actually, I'd like to be alone for a while."

She relayed this to the doctor, Tony and Ross, who dutifully filed out of the room. She hesitated in the doorway while the two Skyline staffers took seats in the waiting area down the hall. She'd heard what he said, but his shell-shocked expression worried her. She didn't think his own company was really what he needed right now.

She shut the door, staying inside the room. She'd already defied his wishes once today, how much worse could it get?

He looked up at her sharply. "I said I wanted to be alone. Jesus Christ, Eva, when are you going to quit interfering and learn to respect what other people want?"

Okay, so it could get worse.

Too late to turn back now.

She gave in to her instincts and moved to his side. She put one hand on his arm, which he snatched out of her reach, and ran the fingers of the other hand through his hair, her thumb smoothing his temple.

He didn't look at her, but he didn't flinch from her touch either.

"Go on, say it," he grumbled. "You were right. I needed to be taken off."

"Is that what you think I care about? Being right?"

He shrugged, toying with the tape holding the bandage on his leg.

She sighed as she perched on the edge of the bed beside him. "I won't apologize for telling Roland you were injured, but I take no happiness from making the right call. I'd rather be wrong a million times than see you in pain."

He still refused to look at her. "Did the doctor say when she can do the surgery?"

"She can do it tomorrow if you feel ready. If not, it can wait a few days."

"I just want it done."

"I'll tell her." She dropped her hand from his hair to his wrist. This time he didn't pull away. "Do you want me to phone your mom, tell her what's happening?"

He shook his head. "I'll call her in a minute. Soon the press will get the story and then everyone will know."

"Being injured is nothing to be ashamed of. Almost every player will—"

"For all your apparent soccer expertise, you clearly have no idea what a long recovery period can do to a player's career," he snapped, jerking out of her grasp. He finally raised his gaze to hers, his eyes shimmering with anger.

"You won't lose your spot on the first team," she assured him, trying to keep her tone soothing as she eased off the bed to stand. "This is going to be a bigger problem for Roland than for you. You're by far his best midfielder."

"Today I am. Tomorrow, it could be anyone."

"Like who, Brian?" She shook her head. "He'll never be as good as you."

"Three months is a long time."

"He's already had years."

"Roland could make a transfer, or recall a loan."

"He won't. He wants you."

"You don't know that."

"I do," she insisted. "Why else would he—"

"Stop," he shouted, making her jump. He held up his palm. "Just stop. I can't take any more of your deluded optimism, okay? This is reality."

She stiffened. "My what?"

He threw up his hands. "This is the problem with you, Eva. For someone who claims she never had big dreams, you can't seem to step out of your fantasy world and put your feet on the ground. Guess what? Injuries don't always heal. Careers can't always be salvaged. And mothers don't always come back, no matter how many good grades you get or deportations you stop or how often you go to Mass and pray to your silent stone Virgin. Your mom is dead—her story is over. The story of my career is over. Now our story is over too."

The air rushed from her lungs like she'd fallen backward off a swing. Tears welled in her eyes but she blinked them back, straightening her spine as she dug up the strength to respond.

"You don't really feel that way."

"There you go again, refusing to see the truth," he muttered, but his gaze had dropped.

"What you said to me this morning—what I said to you at half-time— what was that?"

"A mistake."

She placed a steadying hand on the edge of the bed. He didn't mean it. He was frustrated and hurting and angry. He'd come around. Everything would be as it was.

Or she should cut her losses and leave now.

"Don't say something you'll regret," she warned him, battling to keep her voice from breaking.

His eyes found hers, dark and hard. "I already did. This morning."

She whirled away from him, unable to bear any more cruelty from the man who'd shown her more sincerity and affection than any other. Three hours ago she wouldn't have believed he was capable of such malice. Now she wondered if she'd ever really known him at all.

She balled her fists at her sides. It would be easy to storm out, blame him, and write him off. It would be easy to go home, drink wine, and draw a thick black line through this whole episode. It would be easy to tell herself she could stop loving him, she would get over him, she never loved him anyway.

It would be so easy.

And it would be a lie.

She forced herself to turn around and face him, lifting her chin until their gazes locked. She breathed deeply, calming herself. Bracing herself. *This is going to hurt.*

"I love you, Rio." The words were strong and confident, her voice unwavering. "I didn't make a mistake when I said that, and I don't regret it."

He sighed exasperatedly. "Again, you won't face up to the reality that—"

"This *is* my reality. My love for you is as real as the earth I'm standing on. I'd fight for it if I had to, but I won't fight you." She unclenched her hands and straightened her shoulders. "If this is over, then tell me it is. I'll leave. We won't see each other again."

She didn't dare breathe in the silence that followed. His expression was inscrutable, eyes narrowed with an emotion she didn't recognize. He didn't move, didn't speak. The ticking second hand on the wall clock behind him seemed to boom every time it twitched around its circle.

"I love you," she repeated, disappointment beginning to overtake hope. "But I won't wait forever."

Every molecule in her body screamed at her to go to him, to embrace him, to kiss him until he understood she meant every word. This could be her last chance. This could be their end.

But she'd made herself clear. He had to decide whether to take the hand she offered, or leave her like all the rest.

"Go," he said finally, his eyes black and cold.

She lifted her chin, turned her back on the first and only man she'd ever loved and walked out the door.

"Rio? Bzzzbzzzbzzz, Rio. Bzzzbzzz."

There was an urgency to his need to be awake, to open his eyes, but he struggled. His head felt like it weighed a hundred pounds, his arms even heavier, but someone was speaking very close to his face and shaking his shoulder and it seemed very important that he pry open these stuck-fast eyelids as soon as possible.

"What? What's the problem?" he slurred, finally opening one eye and then the other.

A woman he didn't recognize leaned over him, smiling and speaking quickly in a language he didn't understand.

"Bzzzbzzzbzzz bzzz bzzz bzzzbzzz. Bzzzbzzzbzzz?"

He shook his head, panic swelling his in chest. Where was he? What was going on? Where was Eva?

"Rio, bzzzbzzz?"

"I don't know what you're saying," he replied, more alert now, taking in his surroundings. Bright lights, gray walls, speckled linoleum floor. Tubes—bedding. He was in a hospital.

Of course, his knee. The surgery. The anesthesia. He flopped back on the pillow, breathing more easily as the pieces came together.

"How did it go? Is everything okay? When can I play again?"

The woman—a nurse, probably—frowned. Had she asked him a question? He hadn't answered it.

"It's okay," he managed in English. "Eva? Eva Torres." He pointed toward himself, hoping the woman understood she needed to get his interpreter before he could answer anything too complicated.

The nurse nodded and moved out of his line of vision. He could hear other people in the vicinity but took advantage of the nurse's brief absence to close his eyes again, giving himself over to the grogginess pinning him to the bed.

Eva would be here soon, with her warm smile and soft hands. She'd explain everything. In the meantime he'd just have a little rest.

"Rio, bzzzbzzz."

Reluctantly he opened his eyes.

A blond woman who looked familiar gave him a big smile. "Hi, Rio. The surgery's finished. They're going to take you to your room in a minute. How are you feeling?" she asked in Spanish.

"Chelsea?" The name came from some deeply buried place in his subconscious. "What are you doing here? Where's Eva? Is she all right? Is she sick?"

He'd pushed himself up on his elbows in his anxiety, and for the first time he realized his left leg was bandaged from thigh to mid-calf, immobilized in a brace and elevated on a foam block.

At least it didn't hurt. Yet.

Chelsea bit her lower lip, then offered an artificial smile. "You said you didn't want to work with Eva any more, remember? So Tony arranged for me to be with you today."

"That's ridiculous," he scoffed, his thoughts coming clearer with each second, although he still felt half-drunk. "Why would I fire my own *polola*? I love her, not to mention her Spanish is much better than yours. No offense," he added quickly, his mouth running faster than his brain.

"It's fine," she replied primly, although clearly it wasn't. "But you did fire her. Yesterday. After the match against Providence."

"Was that yesterday?" He dug through his memory like it was an overfull toy box, discarding most of what he found, setting a few snapshots aside for closer examination.

The hollow *thwack* as he kicked over the plastic bucket on the sideline. He couldn't believe he'd done that. So childish and embarrassing. He hoped it hadn't gone viral.

Three o'clock this morning, alone in his house—Hector's house—scrambling eggs in the kitchen before his pre-surgery fasting period kicked in. Scrolling through his phone as he poked disinterestedly at his food, his stomach twisting with regret. Wanting to call Eva, deciding against it, unable to convince himself he deserved her forgiveness even if she offered it.

Yesterday, again—probably twenty-four hours ago. The shame burning through him when she translated the doctor's diagnosis. The overwhelming sense of unworthiness, the automatic instinct to push her away as fast and hard as possible. The horrible things he'd said, the lies he'd told. The door closing behind her.

He collapsed back on the bed, gripping his head in his hands. Holy God, what had he done?

The nurse leaned in again. "Rio? Bzzzbzzz bzzz?"

"She wants to know if you're in pain," Chelsea explained. "They can give you drugs if you are."

Oh, he was in pain—he was in agony. And there was no drug in existence to fix it.

He had to get her back—could he get her back? *Should* he get her back? Or had he proven once and for all that he didn't deserve her?

"Shit, shit, shit," he moaned into his palms. He'd screwed up. He'd lost her. He'd had his shot at a World Cup penalty and he'd hit the bar. Now he had no choice but to own his failure and try to move on.

Except he didn't want to move on. He wanted Eva, more than anything in the world.

He shifted his hips and pain shot through his leg, so hot and sudden he gripped the raised sides of the bed as he clenched his teeth.

The nurse's expression sharpened, and she spoke to Chelsea in a prompting buzz.

"They want to move you into your room now," Chelsea explained. "Do you want more pain medication first?"

He nodded fervently. "Yes. Definitely."

Chelsea said something to the nurse, who fiddled with the IV pole above him. Within seconds his body relaxed, but while his thoughts moved more slowly they were no less intense.

A minute later—or maybe ten, he wasn't quite sure—a couple of orderlies wheeled him out of the operating theatre and down the corridor. Chelsea walked briskly alongside and he closed his eyes, unnerved by the multi-colored blur of unfamiliar walls.

He tried to take his brain to all the calming places he visited to gather his nerves before corner kicks or at half-time. He envisioned the sea in Antofagasta, the aquamarine water, the light sand, the tall buildings along the coastline. He thought about the springy, bright-green grass on the pitch in the stadium in Santiago, the smart red and blue of his national-team uniform. He heard the punchy *thwack* of his boot hitting the ball, the resonant *swish* of the net as he found his target.

He exhaled in exasperation, opening his eyes as the orderlies turned a corner. Who did he think he was fooling? This visualization crap wasn't going to work right now. It might never work again.

Because none of those images could overpower the one that had soothed him the most, and now ripped his heart in two: Eva smiling at him from the sideline, happiness lighting up her face.

He pressed his forearm against his eyes, blocking out the light, the pain in his leg, the wreck he'd made of his life

"What did you do yesterday?" Chelsea asked in English.

"I will going store," he replied distractedly, glancing at the clock over her shoulder.

"I *went to* the store," she corrected. "Past tense. Try another activity. What did you do yesterday?"

Weary, he used the one English phrase he'd perfected. "I don't know."

"Yes you do," she prompted. "What did you do yesterday?"

"I eated the food."

"You *ate*. And can we find a better word than food? More specific?"

"I don't know."

"Come on, Rio," she chided exasperatedly, reverting to Spanish. "We just did food words yesterday."

She wore that pinched expression that usually preceded one of her lectures about his slow progress and lack of effort. His knee throbbed beneath the kitchen table. Overwhelmed by defeat, he crossed his arms on the wooden surface and lowered his face into them.

He heard Chelsea's sigh of irritation and ignored it. The week since he'd woken up in the hospital had been the worst of his life.

Although the doctor anticipated good results from the operation, she kept him in overnight for observation. The following morning he was in the middle of exchanging texts with Nico, arranging a time for the Uruguayan to pick him up, when Roland arrived with Chelsea in tow.

"You can't go back to Hector's house—too many stairs," she translated, and although he couldn't understand Roland's words specifically, he could tell the manager's tone brooked no argument. "The guest cottage at Roland's house is single-story, so he's arranged for your stuff to be moved there. For the next couple of weeks he wants to oversee your recovery personally."

"He wants to make sure I'm following the rules," Rio filled in.

"Can you blame him?" she asked.

He couldn't, and in the end Roland had no need to worry. Rio felt like the doctor had removed his spirit while she was fixing his knee. He was constantly tired, listless, cowed by his pain and immobility. He complied docilely with Chelsea's lessons, the doctor's instructions, and the exercises guided by the physiotherapist who came to the one-bedroom cottage twice a day. He didn't always agree with all of them, but he didn't care enough to argue.

He didn't care about anything except Eva.

He felt her loss more keenly than the ache in his knee or the uncertainty of his career. He missed her so much it surprised and bewildered him, and he couldn't summon any of the anger with which he'd sent her away to mitigate it. Even worse, he had no idea how to fix the situation—and doubted he could, no matter what he tried.

Sitting at the table with his head in his arms was exactly where he deserved to be, he decided, pressing his forehead lower. His recklessness had finally caught up with him, just like everyone told him it would. He refused to listen, and now he had no career, no Eva, no future. He was useless and unloved, and probably always would be.

He heard Chelsea get up from the table, round the breakfast bar and turn on the kettle. She was probably going to make more of that herbal tea she was always drinking, some sharp-smelling concoction of ginger and lemon. She must get through a gallon of that stuff a day. And then she'd be running off to the bathroom all afternoon, leaving him waiting.

God, she was so annoying.

A five-rap knock sounded on the front door. Roland. The last person he wanted to see.

Rio dragged up his head as he heard the manager's footsteps, but he was too slow—Roland's expression showed that he'd seen his star winger's defeated posture.

"Bzzzbzzz bzzz." Chelsea spoke to Roland tartly from her place by the sink. Rio dropped his head again. Let her complain about him—it made no difference.

A chair scratched against the floor, and then Roland's hand was on his shoulder, the Swede's voice rumbling incomprehensibly at his side.

Chelsea's pause before she offered her translation was unusual, and when she finally spoke Rio understood why. "He came by to tell you Skyline's made a deal for a new defensive midfielder to join in the midseason transfer window. He's Argentinian. Doesn't speak much English."

Slowly Rio raised his head. "And?"

Roland spoke again, and Chelsea explained, "Eva Torres has agreed to serve as his translator. She was just here, at the house, to finalize the terms. She asked about you."

Rio locked eyes with his manager. Roland said nothing more—he didn't need to. His face told the story, and Rio read the ending loud and clear.

Eva wasn't going anywhere—her future was at Skyline. But if he wanted to be part of it, he had to pull himself together and make it happen.

Hope surged in his chest, radiating energy through his body like he hadn't felt since he'd woken up in the recovery room. She didn't hate him. She hadn't forgotten him. Maybe he still had a chance.

If he lost the ball, he did everything he could to get it back—and nine times out of ten he succeeded. Why was he giving up on something far more important than any pass he'd ever intercepted, any goal he'd ever scored?

He was Rio Vidal, Goddammit—the bastard of Antofagasta who grew up into *el Príncipe de Chile*. It didn't matter whether his first season at Skyline turned out to be his last, or whether the rest of his career petered out on the bench of a second-tier Chilean side. He loved Eva more than he knew he had the capacity to love anything. If she was through with him, fine—but he wouldn't let her go without a fight. Not him. Not Rio fucking Vidal.

Roland squeezed his shoulder, then stood and walked back out the front door. Chelsea resumed her seat across the table, wrapping two hands around a mug of tea.

"Where were we?" she asked in Spanish. "Food vocabulary, I think. Do you want to review the lesson from yesterday, or try the past tense again?"

He shook his head. "Actually, I have another idea."

Chapter 18

"And instead of *appreciated*, I'd use *honored*. It's more polite."

Nico nodded, amending the printed copy of a speech he'd asked Eva to review.

"That's it. A couple of tweaks and you're good to go." She sat back in her chair, regarding the Uruguayan across the table. They sat in the Regal Terrace, King Stadium's VIP restaurant and viewing suite, which was shuttered and empty on this Thursday afternoon.

"Great. Thanks for your help."

"I didn't contribute much. Your English is almost perfect." She crossed her arms. "You didn't really need me to look this over, did you?"

He shrugged, shuffling the piece of paper back into a manila folder. "It's nice of this Latin American association to give me an award. I want to make sure I thank them appropriately."

"You don't need me," she confirmed. "But I appreciate what you're trying to do."

He sighed and leaned back. "Rio's going through a rough time, but he'll get through it. I thought I could help ensure you're still around when he does."

Her smile tightened. Nico was trying to be nice, so she didn't want to offend him, but for Christ's sake, she was sick and tired of talking about Rio to everyone and anyone who wasn't him.

It had been a week and a half since they'd parted at the hospital, and while she'd had radio silence from the man himself, she couldn't seem to get through more than five words without his name arising in conversation.

First there was the awkward discussion with Roland, in which she thought she conducted herself with flawless professionalism. Roland's response, however, was to mutter obscenities under his breath and assure her she still had a job at Skyline. They were expecting an Argentinian transfer during the midseason window and he was happy to float her on the payroll until the new player arrived. She informed him that wasn't necessary, she had plenty of freelance jobs lined up and she was sorry she'd overstepped her professional boundaries, but he insisted.

She'd thanked him, then glanced around his home office as she gathered the courage to ask her next question. "How is Rio?"

"Physically he's improving every day," he answered without hesitation. "Psychologically he has a long road to travel. I think he'll get there, though. And I'm hopeful he come through this a better, more mature player."

She absorbed the manager's words, and he seemed to interpret her pause another way.

"Do you want me to tell him anything?"

She shook her head. "He knows where to find me."

"Rio's misguided stubbornness has already lost me my midfield powerhouse for three months," he explained. "I'm not about to lose you, too."

Then Olivia had taken her out for cocktails on Monday evening, and the conversation immediately focused on the med student's good-natured but unhelpful efforts to cheer her up.

"He's an idiot," Olivia asserted. "He'll never find another woman like you."

"Probably not," Eva agreed. "So he'll go back to dating lingerie models."

To her credit, Olivia only gaped for a second before recovering. "Then I hope they're all a foot taller than him in heels. Cheers." She raised her glass for a toast.

"Cheers." Eva brought in her glass for a clink, but her smile was forced, knowing full well Rio couldn't care less.

Last night she'd had the least likely expression of sympathy of all. She'd hesitated before answering the call from a number with a Chilean country code, and when she recognized Rio's mother's voice she considered pretending the line was bad and hanging up.

Instead she listened politely as Yolanda thanked her for ensuring Rio got the medical attention he needed.

"I hope we'll have the chance to welcome you to Antofagasta again," Yolanda concluded.

"I hope so too," she replied, admiring Yolanda's deft acknowledgement that Eva did the right thing without too obviously throwing her son under the bus.

That sentiment seemed to be the predominant one. Ross, Tony, and now Nico had found opportunities to assure her she'd done right by Rio and that eventually he'd do right by her, too.

It was nice of them all to say so, and if she'd needed reassurance she would've been grateful.

But she didn't. She knew she was right and Rio was wrong, if it had to be broken down that way.

Being right didn't ease her pain. It didn't dampen the resonant silence of her phone when he didn't call. It didn't warm the empty half of the bed. It didn't close the wound of having opened her heart to someone like she'd never done before, only to have that most vulnerable part of herself balled up and tossed aside like yesterday's newspaper.

She didn't care about being right. She wanted to be loved.

And she didn't want to have any more discussions about Rio, she decided exasperatedly, refocusing her attention on Nico.

"Your speech is perfect," she told him. "And my job is safe, but thank you for thinking of me."

He flattened his palms on the table. "The midseason transfer window is on its way. Should I tell Rio he needs to move quickly or he's going to lose you to another player?"

"You don't need to tell him anything."

"Are you sure?"

"He had surgery on his knee, not his fingers. I'm sure he's perfectly capable of dialing my number if he wants to."

Sadness tinged Nico's answering smile. "I wish it were that simple. An injury like his is tough to swallow, not just for a player like Rio—for all of us. Three months is a big chunk of the season, and sometimes it takes longer to get back to full fitness. Some players never recover from a gap like this. They can't regain their speed, their hunger, their focus. Rio's in a dark place. It can be hard to see the light."

She arched a brow. "If you want me to feel sorry for him—"

"I don't." He raised placatory palms. "Just don't give up on him. That's all."

Eva mulled over Nico's words as she made her way through the labyrinthine stadium complex to her car.

Logically she knew Rio had spoken out of anger the last time she'd seen him. He was frustrated and hurting and absorbing terrible news—fine. She got it. And if he'd called her a day or two later she would've brushed off his apologies and chalked the whole thing up to stress.

But he didn't call her a day or two later. Or five days later. Or a week later. Nearly two weeks on she hadn't heard a word. With every hour that passed her detachment hardened while her hope faded.

After all, why should he be different from the rest of the long list of people who'd left her? He was richer, more famous, and better looking than any other man she'd dated. Why on earth had she ever thought he'd be the one to break the mold and stay committed?

Because he told me he loved me. And I believed him.

She sighed as she unlocked her car and slid into the driver's seat. She'd gotten over plenty of hurt in her life. In time—a long time—she'd get over Rio, too.

She'd just put the key in the ignition when her cell phone rang. She glanced at the screen, saw Father Diego's number, and picked it up.

"Hello?"

"Eva, are you busy?"

"No, why?"

"Come to the church. There's something I want you to see."

He hung up, and she stared at the phone for a few seconds before shoving it back into her purse. Father Diego had never been a man of many words, but it was unusual for him to sound so excited. Whatever it was he wanted to show her, it couldn't be too bad.

She speculated wildly on the drive to the church. Had an infant been abandoned in the nave? Had the trailer's leaky roof been fixed overnight? Had the water in the baptismal font turned into wine?

The answer stared at her from the church steps as she pulled into the parking lot, and she muttered a few deeply unholy phrases as she parked and got out of her car.

Rio.

He sat on the third step from the bottom, his left leg in a brace, a pair of crutches at his side. Father Diego sat on the step above him, rising in greeting as Eva approached.

"There you are," the priest said warmly, but her attention was focused on Rio. He was clearly surprised to see her, and she tried to smooth the shock out of her own expression as she finally turned to Father Diego.

"Look what Señor Vidal has given us." He showed her a check.

Her jaw dropped. She'd never seen so many zeroes in her life.

"Holy—" She clamped her hand over her mouth, catching herself just in time.

"It's for the drop-in center," Father Diego explained, grinning widely. "He was so impressed with the good work you do here, he's given us enough funding to add additional sessions and start a legal aid fund. And look," he unfolded a set of what looked like architectural drawings. "He's hired a firm to replace the trailer with a real, brick-and-mortar auxiliary building."

She couldn't speak. She glanced between the check, the priest's smile, and Rio's stony silence and back again, a bewildering triangle of conflicting emotions.

"Isn't this great?" the priest prompted, then put an understanding hand on her shoulder. "I know, it's a huge surprise."

"Yes. It is," she agreed.

"Father!" One of the ubiquitous church ladies appeared in the doorway, her face bright with excitement. "Phone call for you—it's the diocese!"

"Probably returning my call about the donation. Excuse me." He jogged up the steps and disappeared into the church, leaving the two of them staring at each other.

Eva cycled through her emotional options like items on a menu. Joy, relief, gratitude, indignation, anger—no, indignation would do just fine.

"What the hell do you think you're doing?" she demanded, hands on her hips. "Did you think this would impress me? Buy back my favor?"

His brown eyes widened hopefully, and she cursed her betraying heart for skipping a beat. "Did it work?"

"Of course it didn't," she insisted, clutching tightly to her anger. "I don't hear from you for ten days, and now you're trying to anonymously fund the drop-in center. I'm lost. Explain."

He held up placating palms. "It was supposed to be anonymous. I didn't know Father Diego called you until you pulled up." She looked at him—really looked at him. He was a mess. Shadows ringed his eyes, he wore a button-down shirt over training shorts, and he was at least two days overdue for a shave.

Despite everything he'd done—and hadn't done—her heart ached for him. She flopped down on the step beside him.

"What's going on, Rio?"

Any trace of humor disappeared and he sighed, scrubbing a hand over his eyes. "I've had to move out of Hector's house and into Roland's guest cottage, because it has no stairs and he wants to personally oversee my recovery. I can't play, I can't train, I can't even walk. And Chelsea is so Goddamn annoying."

Don't smile. It's not funny.

Eva bit her lower lip. "Why is she annoying?"

"She comes out with all these weird facts about Chile that she reads on the Internet, and she's started reading Chilean newspapers online and trying to talk to me about politics." He rolled his eyes. "I didn't even know who the president was until I met her when we won the South American Cup."

She opened her mouth to offer polite encouragement, but he raised a hand to stop her.

"I know, it's my own fault. I've created this whole, miserable situation myself. I deserve it. Trust me, I know."

"Rio," she murmured, giving into the urge to touch him as she rested her hand on his wrist. "You don't, not at all."

"Of course I do." He propped his elbows on his thighs and dropped his head into his hands. "I'm so sorry, Eva. I hate myself for what I said to you. I was scared and ashamed and I wanted to push you away so you wouldn't see me fail. I don't expect you to forgive me—I don't deserve it. But you deserve everything you've ever wanted, and the money and the new building for the drop-in center are my way of trying to give you just a fraction of what you deserve. They don't obligate you to anything, and if you tell me you never want to see me again I'll respect that. But I hope I'll have at least made you happy. That's all I've ever wanted."

She stared at him, eyes wide, struggling to process his words.

Then she inched closer and slid her arm across his lower back.

He turned to her in surprise, and she squeezed his wrist where she held it.

"You deserve more than forgiveness, more than joy. You deserve to be loved for the remarkable, good-hearted man you are. And as it turns out, today's your lucky day. Because I love who you were, who you are, and who you'll become."

Disbelief rounded his eyes. "Really? Even after what I said?"

"Oh, I'll expect you to make it up to me."

"I'll do anything. I didn't realize how much I need you—no, *want* you—until I had to face a future without you." He raised his palm to her cheek, his gaze soft and beseeching. "I love you, Eva. And I'll love you forever, I swear."

"Kiss me," she instructed, her heart so full and heavy she could barely breathe.

His mouth quirked into his trademark grin. "Right here? In front of God's house?"

"He won't mind."

"If we get struck by lightning I'm blaming you."

But he risked it, bringing his mouth to hers in a kiss so perfect, Eva was sure divine intervention was involved.

She thought of the statue of the Virgin inside the church, that poker-faced saint who'd patiently endured hours and hours of Eva's silent prayers, her begging gaze, her longing for something she couldn't define.

For a while she thought fulfillment would be in her career. Then, in making an impact on her community. Finally she decided she could only be satisfied when she found her mother.

She'd been wrong every time.

Now, in Rio's arms, she'd found it. She loved him, he loved her. And she was whole.

She imagined her stone Virgin's lips curling in a knowing smile.

At last.

Epilogue

"Left—number fifteen. I go straight, mark number nine."

Laurent nodded at Rio's instructions, delivered in choppy but steadily improving English.

It was only his second match since he'd returned from injury, and the first one in which he'd started, but he felt great. Better than ever before.

This home match against Tucson was symbolic in ways only he and Eva understood. Tucson was where they'd danced, where they'd kissed, where they'd covertly tried on their relationship for size.

Now he was on his own turf, his own terms. Their relationship was public, but he intended to make sure everyone knew the score.

It turned out a three-month recovery period wasn't so bad when you had the love of your life at your side. Watching Skyline play without him was a twice-weekly frustration, and the international match he missed for Chile nearly broke his heart, but in the end he couldn't complain about all the extra time spent with Eva.

She'd seen him through the months of recuperation and physical therapy with the same level-headed positivity he'd come to expect in everything she did. She cheered him up when he was depressed, encouraged him when he wanted to quit, and never stopped loving him no matter how tenuous the future of his career looked at times.

He moved into Eva's condo, where they slept on a mattress in the living room until he could climb stairs. He threw himself into his English lessons, motivated by Eva's suggestion of bedroom-related rewards. He ate well, slept a lot, and tried to make the most of his period on the sideline while setting himself up to come back stronger than ever.

Rebecca Crowley

The day the doctor cleared him to play was one of the best of his life. Today he intended to top it.

He glanced at the sideline, where Eva sat in the third row amongst some of the coaching staff. His English was good enough that she didn't need to be hanging by Roland's elbow anymore. It was just as well, because his sponsorship had grown the church drop-in center to become an independent non-profit providing services for undocumented immigrants. As its managing director, soon Eva would be too busy to accompany him to every press conference and PR event. They broke ground on new premises for the non-profit next month. This could be one of the last matches she attended as his interpreter, and would instead be watching strictly as his *polola*.

Nico sailed a nice pass to Laurent from the midline. Rio wheeled into position to receive it, but the Frenchman mis-shot, sending the ball into open territory.

Rio charged after it, exalting in the power of his legs, the burn of air in his lungs, the peripheral awareness that the opposition was falling away behind him, unable to match his speed.

He glanced up at the night sky, full to bursting with joy and gratitude. Damn, he loved soccer. Nearly as much as he loved Eva.

He was alone on the right side of the pitch, a long way from the penalty area. Three Tucson defenders bore down on him from three different directions. Deon tussled with the fourth defender, trying and failing to get clear.

He looked toward the goal. Locked eyes with the goalkeeper.

Screw it. Why not?

He swung his leg back and kicked for goal.

The ball arced toward the net. The defenders paused in their assault to watch it. The keeper threw himself up, arms stretching, hands reaching.

The brick-red Skyline flag went up, and ten thousand fans leapt to their feet.

His name echoed around the stadium, Roland punched the air, his teammates cheered, but he had only one person in mind.

He turned toward where Eva stood, her hands raised in applause, and pulled off his jersey. He'd written a message on the white T-shirt he wore beneath, and he watched Eva freeze as she read it: *¿Te casarías conmigo?*

Nico whooped in delight, and although Rio didn't hear him, the increasingly enthusiastic noise of his teammates told him Nico had translated his marriage proposal.

Eva slapped her hands over her mouth, but when she lowered them she was smiling.

"*Sí*," she called over the din of the crowd. "*Claro que sí. Te amo,* Rio."

"*Te amo,*" he shouted back, his grin so wide it practically hurt. He barely noticed when the referee approached and booked him for taking off his shirt. He burst back into action, his smile stuck fast to his face, the happiest man ever to get a yellow card.

Don't miss another great Lyrical Press release!

To Win Her Love

To win the game, they'll have to risk losing their hearts. . .

When a bizarre child custody stipulation pits popular sports blogger Gracie Gable against football superstar Jake Malone, losing the battle for her twin nieces isn't the only thing Gracie has to worry about. Forced to live for three months under the same roof as the sexy tight end, will she fall prey to his flirtatious pursuit? Or worse, will the skeletons in her closet destroy her chance for the love and family she so desperately wants?

Neglected by his parents as a boy, Jake doesn't believe in happily ever after. Yet living with Gracie and the twins might be enough to change his mind—and his womanizing ways. But when the press unearths a scandal from Gracie's past, will he lose the one woman he was ready to open his heart to?

Chapter 1

Like pure, walking sin, Jake Malone closed the distance in a deceptively lazy saunter. Gracie Gable fought the nearly overwhelming urge to take off running. Clenching her jaw, she lifted her chin. Without knowing her true identity, the various press publications flooding her blog's inbox with requests for interviews had been stymied in their attempts to track her down physically. How the hell had Jake?

And oh, God, why now?

A horrified groan rumbled deep in her chest. Having no idea what was in Pete's will, she couldn't afford to do anything to jeopardize her guardianship of the girls—like going toe-to-toe with the Manhattan Marauders' *Outlaw Tight End* right here on her brother-in-law's front lawn. She shot a worried glance down the historic farmhouse's long driveway, relieved to find it empty. With a little luck, Pete's attorney would be delayed long enough for her to deal with the famous all-pro's justified, but still overblown ego. She'd promise him anything—apologize profusely for insulting his integrity, offer him a bribe, whatever would get rid of him before Anthony Spinoza arrived.

Six foot five, with a fallen angel's face and the body of a god, Jake continued to approach. Gravel crunched beneath the heels of his boots, marking his long-legged swagger, as his thigh muscles flexed and stretched under faded blue jeans. A worn and battered leather bomber jacket rode his yard-wide shoulders. His trademark black Stetson and snakeskin boots completed the image of the Outlaw who held his own against opposing defensive lines and cast him in countless feminine fantasies. Hers included. She'd enjoyed more than her share of secret imaginings concerning the Marauders' number one tight end.

Though his nasty insults during their disastrous exchange on her blog the other day should've dealt a death blow to her foolish infatuation, the two-dimensional image she'd admired on her TV screen couldn't have prepared her for the flesh and bone temptation that was Jake Malone. Dismay crowded panic as every double X chromosome in her body quivered with giddy, XXX delight.

The X girls danced with anticipation, and the erratic thump of her heart increased with every fall of his size fifteen feet. *Down, girls. He may look like every woman's deepest sexual fantasy, but those boots are more likely to stomp us into the ground than end up under our bed.*

As angry as he must be to have taken the trouble to discover her true identity *and* find her, she could clearly imagine him grabbing her with those meat hooks he called hands and shaking her until her bones rattled.

Try it, buster. If you think the press is in a frenzy now, wait till I'm done with you.

The silent threat boosted her flagging confidence. She angled her chin a bit more defiantly. At five ten, she was used to looking most men in the eye, but despite the added height from her three-inch heels, her gaze fell even with the sharp blade of his nose. Dark stubble shadowed the solid line of his jaw and upper lip, the same blue-black as the silky locks falling below the brim of his hat to brush his collar in the shaggy hairstyle popular among the ranks of pro football these days.

Disturbed at how badly her fingers itched to shove the hat from his head and stroke the glossy strands, she curled her hands into fists, and met his gaze. Blatant curiosity sparkled in eyes as verdant green as the needles of the pine trees lining the drive at his back. A slow smile curved his cleanly cut lips.

Huh? A sneer or even a dismissive smirk she could understand, but a smile? Where was his anger? She blinked when, instead of snatching her up, and shaking her like a dirty rag, he spoke in an easy, Texas drawl.

"You don't look like any Anthony I've ever met."

"Excuse me?"

"Anthony Spinoza. I'm supposed to meet him here."

Meet Anthony Spinoza? Why would Jake be meeting with Pete's lawyer, and why pretend ignorance of her identity? Why the pretense? Her temper simmered as logic provided a nasty explanation. Jake Malone had powerful connections and was famous for his ability to strategize. How many times had she applauded his knack for finding his opponents' weaknesses and using them to his advantage? Somehow, he must have found out, not only who she was, but her reason for being here today. She wouldn't put it past the seasoned predator to play her, acting as if he didn't know who she was, then pouncing when she relaxed her guard.

Like hell!

She bared her teeth in a tight smile. "Do you have business with Mr. Spinoza?"

"Of a sort." He didn't expand on the cryptic comment, crossing his arms, and raising an inquisitive brow. "Are you his assistant?"

Oh, he was good. The question contained the perfect amount of curiosity to make it believable. "No, I'm not. I'm supposed to meet him as well."

"Oh, yeah?"

Speculation replaced curiosity in his dark green eyes. Starting at the top of her head and moving down with a slow thoroughness, his gaze traveled her body, pausing momentarily at her chest. Her nipples immediately pouted in response. She fought the urge to slap her palms over them and prayed her fitted winter coat provided the necessary camouflage. Biting her bottom lip, she attempted to calm the girls by picturing him a good foot shorter with scrawny arms and nerdy glasses perched on a bulbous nose.

The vision refused to form.

His steady inspection continued down over her slim skirt. Winged eyebrows lifted at her leather half boots, and his smile slid toward a smirk. He examined her calves beneath the sheer protection her panty hose provided before his gaze made the return trip to her face.

"I should have known."

She bristled at both the disdain in his eyes and his snide drawl. "What, exactly, should you have known?"

"Sorry, sweetheart. You're a looker, but you're a little young, even for an old hound dog like Pete Thompson."

Hound dog? The derogatory description made no sense when attached to the loving older man her sister, Sarah, had adored, but then the rest of his comment registered. The insinuation quieted the remnant whispers of feminine awareness. Indignation strangled thoughts of crushes, walking sin, *and* expediting his departure.

She matched his stance, crossing her arms. Over the years, Sarah had done her best to break Gracie of her quick temper. When her sister's efforts had failed, she'd predicted one day, the personality flaw would get Gracie into more trouble than she could handle. Today was shaping up as that day, but the possibility didn't stop her from reacting to the insult his speculation represented.

She pinned him with a narrow-eyed stare. "Pete Thompson happens to have been my sister's husband."

His dark brows shot up. "No shit?"

She cleared her throat. "No shit."

He startled as though having his words tossed back surprised him. After studying her in silence for a long moment, the legendary charm for which he was famous made an appearance. Matching dimples popped in his cheeks with his unrepentant smile. "My apologies."

Whether the apology was for his implied insult or her familial connection to Pete, she couldn't tell. Before she could ask, he stuck out a hand and doubled down on his ruse of having no clue of her identity.

"Why don't we start over? Hello, I'm Jake Malone."

She should call him out, of course, demand he tell her what he was up to, but she couldn't resist the opportunity for a little tit for tat. She unfolded her arms to place her hand in his. "Gracie Gable."

"Nice to meet you, Gracie."

Despite her supple leather gloves, the tingling warmth of his large, bare fingers reached hers. She tugged back her hand, relieved when he let go. Equilibrium shaky, she sucked in a stealthy breath, crossed her arms once more, and cocked her head to study him. She tapped a fingertip to her bottom lip in mock concentration.

"Jake Malone? Isn't there a semi-famous…um, *soccer player* or something with the same name?"

His wry grin said he clearly recognized her slight for what it was. "Famous football player, actually. I play for the Marauders."

She repaid his slow inspection with one of her own, sliding her gaze from his dark hat to the tips of his booted feet. At two hundred forty-seven hard-muscled pounds, there was a lot of territory to cover. All of it radiated the superbly conditioned perfection of a pro athlete. Her pulse picked up a notch as her gaze roamed over powerful thighs, past trim hips, and over a flat stomach to a broad chest and impossibly wide shoulders. By the time she reached the chiseled line of his jaw, she'd forgotten how to breathe. She needed every bit of concentration to offer him a smirk instead of licking her lips.

"I should have known."

As paybacks went, repeating his insult was lame, but it was the best she could manage. He surprised her by laughing a full-throated, head thrown back, rumble of male approval. His eyes twinkled with appreciation when he lowered his head and winked. Despite the disturbing fluttering in her belly, she didn't try to disguise her satisfied smile.

"Touché, Gracie Gable." Hip cocked in a seemingly relaxed pose, he glanced away to look up at the house for the first time. "So, the old man was married?"

"Pete?"

Rolling his shoulders, he tucked the fingers of both hands into the front pockets of his jeans and nodded. She frowned at the unmistakable tension in the tight line of his mouth. What was that about? Her future was at stake here, not his.

She followed his gaze. Steady and welcoming, the familiar weathered shingles and pitched roofs of Thompson Farm brought a pang of grief to her heart. As always, whenever she visited the Long Island home Sarah and Pete had shared, Gracie was reminded of the promise she'd given her sister before she died. A promise neither had expected to come due this soon.

"To my sister. She died three years ago." Even after three long years, the words left the foul bite of burnt ash on her tongue.

"I'm sorry." He turned, his eyes full of sober intensity.

The erratic whip of emotions, from panic at why he was here, to helpless feminine interest, and back to suspicion made her dizzy. Enough already. If he was going to cause a scene, she wanted their confrontation over and done with while they were still alone. "Why are you here?"

Thick lashes lowered at her bald demand, shuttering the green of his eyes. He shrugged. "Damned if I know."

Confused, she opened her mouth to demand a better answer when the distant crunch of gravel announced the arrival of two vehicles bumping down the drive. She stifled a self-disgusted groan. He'd managed to sidetrack her, and she was out of time.

Outmaneuvered by a pro...with killer dimples.

A dark sedan stopped behind Jake's SUV. A sleek yellow sports car rolled to a halt several yards away. The door swung open and a petite, redheaded woman rose from the small high-performance machine. The bold, red-woolen power suit covering her curvy frame should've clashed with her mane of rusty curls, but somehow didn't. Bright and vibrant, her steady blue gaze roamed the face of the house and surrounding property before landing on Jake. She lifted a slim hand in a flirty, fingertip wave and beamed a smile.

Gracie disliked her on sight.

A thin, older man emerged from the second vehicle. Only the pale oval of his face beneath a classic fedora relieved the steady black of his heavy overcoat, conservative business suit, and wingtips. He clutched a briefcase in one gloved hand. Crossing to the woman, he greeted her in a short exchange. They turned together and headed up the walkway.

"Lawyers." Jake grumbled at Gracie's side. "They usually have a slick, plastic look. Figures this one resembles an angel of doom."

Her head whipped around at his odd comment, but his gaze was locked on the approaching couple.

She turned and eyed the woman. "The redhead doesn't resemble any lawyer *I've* ever seen."

He chuckled and cast her a slight smile. "I'm sure she'll be happy to hear that. Her name is Victoria Price, and she isn't a lawyer. V is my publicist."

His publicist? Am I about to be double-teamed?

She braced for disaster as Anthony Spinoza and the vivacious "V" arrived.

"Mr. Malone." The black-clad lawyer greeted Jake then smiled at Gracie. "Miss Gable, I'm Anthony Spinoza. Thank you for coming."

Gracie nodded and shook his offered hand.

"I see you've met Mr. Malone. Miss Price is acting as his representative this morning."

Okay, what the hell is going on?

Obviously Jake was here for some reason other than to have it out with her over their blog spat, but what the reason was, she couldn't imagine.

"Call me V, please. Everyone does. Nice to meet you, Miss Gable."

Gracie shook the publicist's hand, noting the Texas accent similar to Jake's. "Likewise."

"It appears we're all here." Anthony lifted a hand toward the front door. "Shall we proceed?"

Gracie's gaze flew from face to face, desperate to discover why Jake Malone and his publicist would be sitting in on the reading of Pete's will. No plausible explanation presented itself.

Well, crap. I've slipped down a rabbit hole.

Meet the Author

Rebecca Crowley inherited her love of romance from her mom, who taught her to at least partially judge a book by the steaminess of its cover. She writes contemporary romance and romantic suspense with smart heroines and swoon-worthy heroes, and never tires of the happily-ever-after. Having pulled up her Kansas roots to live in New York City and London, Rebecca currently resides in Johannesburg, South Africa.

www.ingramcontent.com/pod-product-compliance
Lightning Source LLC
Chambersburg PA
CBHW020445270626
47155CB00022B/1658